03

GW00793166

L F

Stage Fright

In the light of recent experience, Paul Crook is understandably reluctant to take on another murder investigation: as he is the first to admit, his heart is not really in the private-eye business. But gang-boss Harry Sheiling is a hard man to refuse; and faced with the threat of actual bodily harm, Crook glumly accepts Harry's brief to 'nose around and flush out the murdering bastard' who killed Mary Dean.

As usual, all Crook's dismal forebodings are justified: the case turns out to be quite as messy, dangerous and life-threatening as his previous escapades. 'Nosing around' among theatre folk soon evokes the smells of old greasepaint and musty, faded programmes and—most insidious of all—the ripe whiff of blackmail.

by the same author

LITTLE RIPPER
STONEFISH
FUNNELWEB

CHARLES WEST

Stage Fright

THE CRIME CLUB
An Imprint of HarperCollins *Publishers*

First published in Great Britain in 1993
by The Crime Club, an imprint of
HarperCollins Publishers, 77–85 Fulham Palace Road,
Hammersmith, London W6 8JB

9 8 7 6 5 4 3 2 1

Charles West asserts the moral right to be identified
as the author of this work.

© Charles West 1993

A catalogue record for this book is
available from the British Library

ISBN 0 00 232316 8

Photoset in Linotron Baskerville by
Rowland Phototypesetting Ltd
Bury St Edmunds, Suffolk
Printed and bound in Great Britain by
HarperCollins Book Manufacturing, Glasgow

CHAPTER 1

The rain came soon after nightfall, exactly as the forecasters had said it would. It swept in from the ocean accompanied by a lurid and theatrical barrage of thunder and lightning, drenched the eastern suburbs and advanced across the city, sending pedestrians scurrying for cover and slowing the rush-hour traffic to a crawl.

The murderer, who had planned for this moment with some care, judged that the time was now ripe. It was impossible to eliminate risk entirely; but the darkness and the driving rain afforded the best concealment that could reasonably be expected.

Acting calmly and decisively, the killer put on a wide-brimmed hat, checked the street guide yet again, and started the car. A short drive, a quick reconnaissance, a few minutes of sweating effort, and it was done. The woman lay on the pavement, her hair trailing in the gutter, her cheap overcoat spread out under her like a fan.

The murderer got back behind the wheel and drove away. At the end of the street, the big car skidded on the wet road and its rear wing grazed against something— possibly the front of a parked van, but in the darkness and the pouring rain, it was impossible to be sure. The driver swore briefly, but after one gut-wrenching moment of panic decided it was too insignificant an incident to worry about. There were more interesting things to consider. The media coverage ought to be quite amusing, for instance; and sparring with the police would be an adventure. But the thought that wouldn't go away, wouldn't be suppressed, was the knowledge that this was just the beginning. Only one of the Hydra's heads had been struck off. The other heads were still there, just as cunning, just as dangerous, just

as greedy. They would have to be struck off, too. All of
them.

'That's the third time,' Paul said.

'What? What?' The psychiatrist took off his spectacles
and pinched the bridge of his nose. He wished he didn't
feel so tired. He wished he didn't have to cope with this
problem right now. Most of all he wished he was at home
with a glass of whisky in his hand and the bottle by his
elbow. He was just not in the right frame of mind to deal
with this dangerous young man.

'That's the third time you've apologized,' Crook said
gently. 'You're sorry you had to ask me to come here, you're
sorry that you couldn't see me immediately, and now you're
sorry about something that sounds as if it's going to be bad
news. What are you softening me up for, Mr Garland?'

The psychiatrist smiled wanly, and apologized again
before he could stop himself. 'Sorry, Paul: I was just mark-
ing time while I worked out what to say. The fact is, I want
to ask for your help, and I'm not sure how to begin.' He
wondered if it had been a mistake to use the boy's first
name: he never had much confidence in his judgement at
the fag-end of the working day. But one thing he was certain
of: he would have to go very carefully here: he could recognize the symptoms of distress when he saw them, and this
boy was under a lot of pressure. He was too cool, too controlled: that unnatural stillness was masking a lot of emotional turmoil. There was also the uncomfortable fact that
the kid was a killer. Garland wished he could think of it in
less melodramatic terms, or better still, forget it altogether;
but the knowledge kept nudging uninvited into his mind.

Crook shrugged. 'Just dive in, Mr Garland.' He felt
vaguely sorry for this sad-looking old bottler. The guy's
face was red and lumpy, and there was a yellowish tinge
to his eyes. Probably drank too much. Not surprising, if he
did nothing but talk to nutters all day long.

Garland tried to appear casual, but he couldn't conquer

his unease. As usual when he was nervous, his stomach began to rumble cavernously, and his face darkened with embarrassment. 'It's about Robyn Paget, of course,' he said. He pulled a large white handkerchief from his trouser pocket and carefully wiped his hands with it.

Crook said nothing, and the psychiatrist's apprehension increased. He was no coward, but it was hard not to be intimidated by the younger man's size and muscularity. Garland himself was quite short, and wore thick cork wedges inside his shoes, a vanity for which he secretly despised himself. It was not in his nature just to 'dive in'. It was his custom to approach every problem obliquely and cautiously, as if he was stalking some particularly dangerous animal. He pretended to study some handwritten notes on his desk. 'The account I have of the . . . incident, is that you and Miss Paget were abducted by a dangerous psychopath and both given a near-lethal injection of some drug—probably a barbituric acid derivative. For some reason—probably to do with physical size—you had no serious after-effects from the drug; whereas she suffered an anoxia which resulted in prolonged coma.' He was well into his stride now, and feeling more confident. 'Robyn's recovery has been remarkable, in the circumstances. That she should have come out of such a deep coma at all is a small miracle: a triumph for the medical staff at the hospital.'

'I know all that,' Crook said solidly. 'I was there.'

'Yes, yes, of course.' Garland was irritated by the interruption, and uncharacteristically let his irritation show. The need for a drink kept pushing its way into his mind, upsetting his concentration. 'But—' his annoyance made him brutal—'the inescapable truth is that part of her brain was destroyed in the accident.'

'I know that, too,' Crook said.

With an effort, Garland recovered his composure. 'That isn't quite as cataclysmic as it sounds. According to the consultant neurologist, prolonged physiotherapy can

restore at least ninety per cent of the lost neural and muscular response. Assuming that the patient cooperates, of
course.' Garland could see no harm in putting an optimistic
gloss on what the specialist had actually said.

Crook slumped deeper into his chair. He looked relaxed,
his eyes half closed. 'Now comes the cruncher.'

'Yes . . . There is psychological damage too. Well—you
more than anyone, must be aware of her mental and
emotional condition.'

'She's been through a lot.' Crook made a curious sideways movement with his hand, as if he was smoothing
fabric under his fingers. It was an absent-minded gesture:
he seemed quite unaware of it. 'But she's improving. She
just needs time.'

'No, Paul. Robyn needs more than just time,' Garland
said forcefully. 'Much more. She needs a great deal of help.
Professional nursing; careful psychotherapy. That's why I
asked you to come here and talk to me. I need your co-
operation.'

Crook nodded, his eyes wary. 'Tell me what to do.'

Garland became aware that he was still holding the wad-
ded-up handkerchief. He pushed it back into his pocket. 'It
won't be easy for you.'

'If it will help her, it can't be hard, Mr Garland. I love
her.'

The psychiatrist winced and looked away. It always
hurts, he thought: that naked innocence of the young—it
slips through one's middle-aged hide like a needle between
the ribs. He said, forcing himself over the first hurdle: 'I—
we—that is, the whole medical team—want you to stop
visiting Robyn for a time.' He added quickly, 'I told you
it wouldn't be easy.'

Crook stiffened momentarily, then forced himself to
relax. 'No,' he said levelly, 'that won't be easy.' He made
the absent-minded gesture with his hand again. 'Why do
you—and the whole medical team—think it necessary?'

'Because—' there was no way to soften this—'in the

present circumstances, we think your visits are actually inhibiting her recovery.'

Crook gave himself a moment to absorb this blow. A little colour began to creep back to his cheeks. 'This is her pa's idea. He's told you to warn me off.'

'No, I swear that's not true. Mr Paget likes you a lot. It took a lot of persuasion—and not just from me—before he would agree to this. He *likes* you,' Garland insisted.

'He has plenty of reason to hate me.'

'No, Paul, he doesn't hate you. He doesn't blame you for what happened. And you mustn't blame yourself. Feeling guilty won't turn the clock back; we have to face the situation as it is now. The reality is this: the shock of the attack, plus the actual physical damage to her brain, may— I emphasize, *may*—have wrought some changes in Robyn's personality.'

'What are you saying? That Robyn has become a different person?'

'No, that's stating the case too baldly. What I'm trying to say is that Robyn has suffered—is still suffering—a great deal, both physically and mentally. But to put it bluntly, her body is recovering faster than her brain. In particular, her loss of memory is causing her considerable distress.'

'But her memory is improving all the time,' Crook protested, at last showing some signs of animation. 'She didn't even know who I was at first, but it all came back to her after a few days.'

'I agree there is some improvement, but there are still wide gaps in her memory. I wonder if you can understand how terrifying that condition is, for her? How confused and frightened she gets at times?' Garland abruptly changed direction: 'Tell me, how was she, on your last few visits? How did she behave towards you?'

'She was a bit quiet,' Crook admitted.

'Did she say anything at all?'

'Look, I just said she was a bit quiet. In the circumstances, I wasn't looking for sparkling conversation.'

'So she didn't say a great deal?'

'No.'

'How did you interpret her silence?'

'I didn't "interpret" it, I just accepted it,' Crook said with dogged patience. 'Yes, OK, I see where you're heading. If she's a different person, her feelings are different, too. Her feelings for me, I mean.'

'It's more complex than that.' Garland paused, and in the silence his stomach whimpered like a lost puppy. Again he changed tack: 'It would help my understanding of her case if you would tell me something more about your relationship with Miss Paget. For instance: were you and she planning to get married?'

Crook frowned momentarily, resenting the question. 'We hadn't actually talked about it. I guess, the way things were going, the topic would have come up eventually; but the fact is, we hadn't known each other all that long.'

'But you were lovers—in the physical sense, I mean?' It seemed a ridiculous question, but for the sake of thoroughness, Garland had to ask it.

'Yes.' Crook's expression made it clear that his patience was wearing thin.

Garland fiddled with his notes again. 'Forgive me: these are not random or impertinent questions, Paul. Have you discussed marriage with her, since she recovered consciousness?'

'Of course not! I'm no genius, Mr Garland, but I'm not so crass as to put any emotional pressure on her while she's ill.'

'Are you sure?'

The sharpness of the question took Crook by surprise. He wondered if the psychiatrist was trying to goad him into some unguarded response. 'I am sure that Robyn and I never discussed marriage, sir. But that doesn't mean that the subject is permanently off the agenda.'

'I see.' Garland felt that he had come through the worst part of the minefield, but he still picked his way very carefully: 'Please don't regard me as your enemy, Paul. We both have the same objective: Robyn's welfare. Asking personal questions is a necessary part of my job.'

'You're certainly fonder of asking questions than answering them, Mr Garland,' Crook said levelly.

'Bear with me, Paul. Believe me, you are being most helpful. May I continue?'

'Sure.'

'I understand that you are a Catholic?'

'My parents were Catholics. I can't pretend to be particularly religious myself. I don't go to Mass or Confession, or anything.'

'But you had religious instruction as a child?'

'Some. My mother wasn't very strict about it, though. Is it significant?'

'The Pagets are a Protestant family. I wondered if your different religions caused either of you any anxiety?'

'I don't think either of us gave it a second thought. I don't think we even gave it a first thought.'

'Like marriage, it was never discussed?'

'No, sir. And if it had been, it wouldn't have posed a problem.'

'Because you would have given up your religion for her sake, you mean?'

'Of course. As I said, religion isn't all that important to me.'

Garland had heard this sort of assertion many times before, and knew better than to let his scepticism show. His private opinion was that superstitions absorbed in childhood endured a lifetime. 'I see,' he said again. 'Thank you for being so candid.'

'Now it's your turn to be candid.' Crook was not going to be put off any longer. 'You still haven't explained why I'm to be banned from seeing her.'

Garland shook his head tiredly. He'd been throwing hints around like confetti: why hadn't the boy worked it out for himself? A small cloud of suspicion formed in his mind. *Surely they hadn't been so irresponsible . . . ?* He shuffled quickly through his notes again, but of course they were no help. He said, buying himself time to think: 'Robyn's loss of memory is a psychological problem, not a physical one. In layman's terms, what she has done is to build a mental barrier to protect herself from memories that are too painful to contemplate. The irony is that suppressing terrors only makes them more potent and therefore more dangerous. My job is to help her to face those terrors and to overcome them: only then, I believe, will her memory be fully restored.'

'You'll have to spell it out more simply than that, sir. Are you saying that she's trying to blot out all memory of the incident in Queensland? And that because I was part of it—responsible for it—my presence distresses her?'

'No, no.' Garland covered his mouth with his hand and belched discreetly. His stomach, which had been adding a noisy counterpoint to the conversation, fell silent. 'I keep telling you, it's a complex case. She's not *trying* to blot out the episode in Queensland: she *has* blotted it out. All of it.'

'But—' in another context, Crook's bewilderment would have been comic—'she remembers *me*. She hasn't blotted me out of her mind.'

'Not completely. But her memory of you is only partial.' Garland felt an unexpected twinge of embarrassment. He picked up a pencil and fiddled with it, twitching it to and fro in his fingers. 'She remembers that you are a private detective, and that she planned to write an article about you. She remembers that you were engaged to an acquaintance of hers, although she can't remember who. She knows, both from your attitude and the reaction of the nurses, that you are fond of her. But, crucially, she does not remember that you were lovers.'

'Oh my God!' Crook's face was white with dismay. 'Why didn't anyone tell me?'

'Because no one knew. I learned it myself only today. Can you understand now why your visits are making her confused and unhappy? Angry, even?'

'I suppose so.' Crook wasn't sure that he understood anything, at that moment. 'You mean the shock of the Queensland episode has erased me from her mind almost completely? That all she remembers is our first meeting?'

'That wasn't the only shock, remember.' Garland was prodding for a reaction. When none came, his suspicions deepened, and with it his feeling of despondency. He could see that there was still work to do.

The mask of wooden impassivity settled over Crook's face again. 'OK, Mr Garland, have it your way. I'll stay away from her until you give me the all clear.'

Garland tackled this final problem at a tangent, as usual. 'You have been visiting her at weekends, I believe?'

'Yessir, I work in Sydney. Usually I bludge a lift on one of the Paget Company planes, but if that's not possible, Peter—Mr Paget—pays for my air fare.'

'I'm told that while she was unconscious you never left her side?'

'That's an exaggeration, sir. I stayed near her as much as I could, but when her father brought her home—to the hospital in Perth, I mean—I couldn't accompany her straight away. We were separated for over a fortnight.'

'Oh?'

Crook said matter-of-factly: 'I had to attend the inquest of the man I killed at Talavera.'

'Ah.' Garland wished the boy wouldn't sound so off-hand about the taking of human life. 'When was this?' He had already guessed the answer.

'About the middle of December.'

So that was that. 'Yes, I see.' *A hell of a lot more than I want to see*, Garland thought savagely. *Damn all nice, kindly, cowardly, gutless people. This just isn't fair.*

The boy was looking concerned. 'Are you OK, Mr Garland? You look bushed.'

Garland wanted to say that he bloody well wasn't OK; that he needed a bloody drink, badly. Really badly. But instead, he folded his hands over his unquiet stomach and began to talk in his most gentle and avuncular manner. It was a kindly talk, and all but the first part was about how everything had turned out for the best, if one viewed it reasonably. The great thing about being young, he observed didactically, was that time was on your side. He took quite a long time saying all this, addressing most of his remarks to the pencil he was still twiddling in his fingers, since the sight of Crook's gaunt, woebegone face upset his concentration.

Afterwards, when Crook had left, Garland felt wretched and old. He went home to his empty house and tried to drown his depression in whisky. It didn't work. It never did. What he really needed was some expert counselling.

CHAPTER 2

The barefoot man studied Crook for a long time before speaking. Then: 'Don't cry, mate,' he said.

Crook came to slowly, the images of his dream dissolving in the air like smoke. The dream left nothing behind but its unexplained sadness, as bitter as the sour after-taste of bad wine. But the sadness was as nothing compared to the swamping tide of misery that engulfed him as consciousness returned. His shirt was unbuttoned and hanging loose: he lifted the front of it to his face and wiped his eyes. The fabric felt warm against his skin and was full of the stale smell of his own sweat.

'You was dozin',' the man said. He sat down at the far end of the bench, breathing hard, throwing his head back as his chest expanded, and puffing out his cheeks as his lungs emptied. His large, raw-looking hands rested on his knees, the nails close-bitten and rimmed with oily black dirt. He was wearing jeans, a sweat shirt and a broad-brimmed brown hat which was held in place by a cord under his chin. His feet were coated with wet sand.

'Dozing?' Crook seemed to weigh the word carefully. 'Yes, I suppose I was.' He felt sick. The respite had been all too brief; now the wretchedness that dogged his waking hours came back with added spite, burning like fever.

'Bad dream?' The man was not looking at Crook now, but gazing tactfully out at the ocean.

'I can't remember.' Crook wished the man would go away.

'You was havin' a bad dream,' the man assured him. 'The booze, I expect. You look as if you've been on the grog?' It was a question: when Crook made no response, the man made it an accusation; 'You look as if you've been on the grog for days.'

'No.' Crook stood up and stretched, his joints cracking. 'Booze doesn't help. I've learned that much.'

'Help?' The man snorted. 'Are you telling *me*? Grog's a poison, did you know that? I mean, it really can kill you. Did you know that?'

'Yes.'

'Too right.' The man turned his head and looked over his shoulder at the street behind them. He seemed tense for a moment, then relaxed and stared thoughtfully at the empty beach and the slowly-changing slabs of colour on the horizon. 'Soon be sun-up,' he said. He was short, muscular, middle-aged: his face, grey in the uncertain light, was deeply pock-marked. 'Another day. Another friggin' day to get through.'

'Yes.' Crook sat down. His neck was hurting: he closed his eyes and moved his head slowly from side to side, hoping to ease the pain.

The man watched him for a few moments and then shrugged, apparently losing interest. He leaned forward and began to brush the sand from his feet. 'I used to drink,' he said, his voice muffled. 'I used to drink a lot.'

Crook didn't even try to look interested. He had his own troubles.

'It turned me into a ragin' beast,' the man said sombrely.

'It made me so's I wasn't a human bein' no more. One time, I was livin' like a pig. Sleepin' in shop doorways, beggin' in the streets.' The man straightened up. 'Are you listenin' to me?'

'Nope.'

'Well, you should. You don't know who I am, do you?'

Crook stopped moving his head about and opened his eyes. 'I'll level with you, old timer. I don't give a stuff if you're the Queen of bloody Sheba.'

'Huh.' The man was not offended. 'You think you got troubles. I tell you, son, I'd trade my troubles for yours right now and give you a thousand quid bonus on top. I'm Stan Dean. Mean anythin' to you?'

'Nope.'

'Nah, you'll of been too pissed to know what's goin' on in the real world. I'm Stan Dean, the infamous wife-killer. If you'd a' watched Mollie Muffin on TV last night, you wouldn't have any doubts about that.'

The man had managed to catch Crook's attention at last. 'Mollie Muffin accused you of murder?'

'As good as,' Dean said. 'She never says anythin' straight out, but you know damn well what she's gettin' at. She messed me over good, the bitch.'

Crook scratched at the stubble on his jaw. 'She's some ballbreaker, that one. She had a go at me last year, but I got off lightly. She didn't make me out a villain: just a prat.' His mouth twisted. 'Couldn't argue with that. So? Was she right? Did you kill your wife?'

'What kind of question is that? Am I likely to tell you, if I had?'

Crook looked steadily at the older man's profile. 'You just might. You look like a man who needs to talk to somebody. You look like a man with a load on his mind.'

'Yeah.' The man looked towards the sea again and shivered. The beach was no longer empty: the joggers were arriving in force now, and ragged files of health-seekers ran towards each other at the water's edge.

'You're sweating,' Crook said. 'You ought to rug up. You'll get a chill.'

'I'm not cold,' Stan Dean said. 'I suddenly got a spooky feeling that my whole future's already settled, know what I mean? It's like I can see my whole life laid out on a circular track like a kid's train set. Darkness to darkness; and every inch of the way laid out in advance. Even my talking to you right now—it's like I got no choice. I guess I'm crackin' up, at that.' He shivered again and folded his arms as if the cold had got to him despite his denial. 'I saw you lyin' on this bench here, and you was weepin' and makin' little mewin' noises in your sleep. And I had to stop and talk to you. I *had* to. I wanted you to know that there's people in this world worse off than you. Me, for instance.'

Crook frowned. 'You didn't really think that would make me feel any happier, did you?'

'No . . .' Dean seemed to be directing his argument to himself rather than Crook. 'I guess what it was, I was mad at you for what you were doin' to yourself. You're young, you're strong: you're a fool to let the grog get such a hold on you.'

'It wasn't the grog,' Crook said wearily. 'It's just . . . I've got something on my mind I need to think through. I tried booze: it just made me feel suicidal. So I . . . I just *walked*. Until I had to stop.'

'But why're you sleepin' rough? Can't you get a job?'

'Look, don't worry about me, OK? I'm not a dero, and I'm not on the meths.' Crook was touched by the older man's concern.

Dean stood up. 'Sure.' He took something from his hip pocket. 'To answer your question: yeah, I did kill my wife. I told 'em at the time, but they wouldn't listen. This latest thing—well I guess it's God's way of making me pay for it. As if I don't pay for it with every damn breath I take.' He paused, looking down at Crook's bowed head. 'I wonder why the hell I'm talking to you like this? I just wanted to . . .' His voice trailed away. He shifted from foot to foot, seemingly uncertain what to do next. 'Here: get yourself a meal and a shave, for God's sake.' Abruptly, he thrust a folded paper into Crook's hand and jogged away across the sand.

Crook slowly unfolded the piece of paper. It was a twenty-dollar note.

The two women drinking tea in the main office of the Agre Detective Agency on Liverpool Street could easily have been mistaken for mother and daughter. They were similar in physique: both tall, slim and strong-featured; and both had the self-confidence of women used to making their own way in a male-dominated world. They were discussing Paul Crook's disappearance.

The younger one, Elspeth Cade, said, 'Are you sure he's not still in Perth? That's where he's been for the best part of the last four months.' Her tone was neutral, but the other woman thought she detected a faint note of bitterness: perhaps because she was listening for it.

'Quite sure, Miss Elspeth.' Mrs Parsons picked up the teapot and refilled her employer's cup. 'I've been in touch with Mr Peter Paget. Mr Paul returned to Sydney in the early hours of Monday morning, on a Paget Enterprises plane. That's the last anyone has heard of him. He's not at his flat in North Ryde, and he hasn't turned up here for work.'

'Robyn Paget had a house near the University,' Elspeth said. 'Do you suppose he's gone to ground there?'

'No. Our Mr Basil has been there to investigate. All Miss Robyn's things have been moved out, and the house is being used by the Paget Company's aircrew for overnight stopovers.'

Elspeth smiled in spite of her concern. The translation of 'Bam-bam' Butcher, retired pugilist, ex-con and arguably the ugliest man in Sydney into 'Our Mr Basil' was a constant source of pleasure. 'How's Bam-bam taking it? Paul's disappearance, I mean?'

'Not well, Miss Elspeth. He's very concerned about it. Distraught would not be too strong a word. You know how he dotes on Mr Paul.'

Elspeth's smile turned wry. 'Don't we all?'

'In our different ways,' Mrs Parsons said tactfully. She knew that Elspeth Cade's feelings for Paul Crook ran a lot deeper than that young lady was prepared to admit. Elspeth was a talented and successful musician; although she had no experience of business matters at all, she had bought the near-bankrupt Agre Agency on a romantic whim, simply because Paul was one of its employees. However, if she had hoped that their business relationship would develop into something warmer than mere friendship, she had been disappointed. Crook liked her well enough, but remained obstinately indifferent to her considerable feminine charms.

Mrs Parsons returned to the subject in hand: 'His disappearance has had a catastrophic effect on our work here. The girls worship Mr Paul, and his absence upsets them dreadfully. Even worse, Mr Basil has been absent for long periods since the weekend, only showing his face here to ask if we've heard anything. He's been out for hours every day, scouring the city for news of Mr Paul. This whole situation is costing us a lot of money. I have had to refuse all the commissions that our menfolk usually undertake— repossessions, writ-serving, document delivery, and the like; and the girls are so distracted with the drama of it all that their work has become thoroughly slipshod.' Mrs Parsons sat even straighter in her chair. 'It really is a tragedy. We were doing so well. Even Mr Paul himself had almost got the hang of the computer, though the fax machine still baffles him.'

Elspeth looked rather pained. 'Forgive me, Mrs P., but you seem rather more concerned for the agency's profits than about our missing Managing Director. Is there something you haven't told me?'

'It's just that I can't think he's in any actual danger,' Mrs Parsons said. 'One thing I've observed about our Mr

Paul is that he has a two-fold response to a personal problem: he becomes hyperactive, and he seeks solitude.'

'You're saying he's gone walkabout?'

'That's what I believe, yes.'

'Do you mean in the bush? Way out in never-never land?'

'It's possible. Mr Paul has a sentimental attachment to the outback,' Mrs Parsons said judiciously. 'The only thing I feel certain of, is that when he has resolved his problems in his own way, he'll come back to us.'

'Will he?' Elspeth was unconvinced. 'He's never shown much enthusiasm for the job from the beginning.'

'Oh, his attitude has changed completely over these last four weeks. He has worked and concentrated really hard. Believe me, Miss Elspeth, he's no longer just a figurehead: he makes a genuine contribution.'

'Hm.' Elspeth made allowances for the older woman's partiality. Mrs Parsons fussed over Crook like a mother hen over its chick. 'What's his latest emotional dilemma, then? I understand that Ms Paget had made a miraculous recovery.'

'I believe she may have had some sort of relapse. Her father told me that her medical advisers have requested that Mr Paul stop visiting her for the time being.'

'No visitors? That sounds ominous. Is she dying, Mrs P.? Is that what's putting our Paul through the mincer?'

Mrs Parsons tugged a lace handkerchief from her sleeve and dabbed the corners of her eyes with it. Her face crumpled momentarily and unexpectedly. 'That was the first thought in my mind. Of course I couldn't put the question directly to Mr Paget, but I could tell he was very upset.' Her voice strengthened. 'However, that was mere speculation on my part. It is just as possible that Miss Robyn is merely suffering a temporary setback.'

'You don't really believe that, Mrs P.,' Elspeth said with characteristic bluntness. 'A temporary setback wouldn't have gutted Paul like this. He's a mug as far as women are concerned, but he's not a total idiot.'

Mrs Parsons managed a half-smile. 'He's actually quite intelligent, for a man. What's more, he's developing into a resourceful and strong-willed member of our team: a very different prospect from the raw youth who came in here eighteen months ago.'

'Not surprising, considering what he's been through.' Elspeth shuddered, remembering recent events. 'The poor young bastard's having to grow up awfully fast.' She was actually the same age as Crook, but refused to acknowledge the fact. 'Hell, I hope he's all right. I just wish I knew where he was.'

She learned where Crook was, the next day; but it didn't immediately make her a lot happier. She was about to leave for rehearsal, when Mrs Parsons phoned her from the office. 'You'll be happy to hear that Mr Paul is perfectly safe,' Mrs Parsons said. 'They say that apart from being depressed, he's suffering from nothing worse than slight malnutrition. I'm expecting to see him this afternoon.'

'Who are "they", Mrs P.? Is he in hospital? Again?' Crook's escapades had often finished up in the Emergency Ward.

'No, no. I've just heard from a Detective Mulhearn, a pleasant-sounding young man. He called me from the Bondi police station. Mr Paul has been detained there since six o'clock this morning.'

CHAPTER 3

As Mrs Parsons had said, Paul Crook's way of coping with his unhappiness was simple and instinctive: he walked until he was exhausted. On the principle that one pain is driven out by a worse one, he walked until fatigue and physical suffering blotted out the torment in his mind. It was not perhaps the most cerebral response in the world, but Crook had few intellectual pretensions. Depression clawed at him like a live and malignant thing, and he had a superstitious belief that he could loosen its grip by keeping on the move. His misery demanded action: he walked because he could think of nothing better to do.

His thoughts moved in a tight and punishing circle. He couldn't escape from the notion that it was all his fault. If only he hadn't allowed himself to become involved with Robyn in the first place; if only he hadn't encouraged her to play at detectives ... His stupidity had put her into hospital. There was no escaping the fact: it was all his fault.

In his wretchedness, he kept remembering his mother's death, seven years earlier; and he felt a nagging sense of shame that his present misery seemed worse than the grief he had felt then. It seemed unnatural and out of proportion that it should be so: his mother's death was an irrevocable loss, whereas Robyn was still alive and well cared for. There was every chance that she would recover completely.

But if Crook was no intellectual giant, he was not a complete fool either. Whatever the scale of her recovery, Robyn would never be the same again. She would be changed, a different person: the psychiatrist Garland had said as much. And that posed some unsettling questions. How changed would she be? Would the new Robyn still love him? Would she even like him? Knowing what he now knew, Crook thought it improbable. She would most likely blame him for everything, as he blamed himself. But—he tried to squeeze this treacherous thought from his mind but it kept coming back—if she was dramatically different, would *he* still love *her*?

Crook worried each question to shreds as he walked aimlessly along street after street, head down and shoulders bowed.

But one thing he pushed resolutely into the deeper recesses of his mind and tried to forget: one horror he was not yet ready to face. Perhaps he never would be.

The meeting with Stanley Dean forced Crook out of his emotional rut, at least for a time. He stared at the money that Dean had thrust into his hand, and for the first time in days felt something other than self-pity. The conversation with the old man had been bizarre enough, but his unexpected act of charity left Crook exasperated and—in spite of himself—profoundly touched. It was infuriating to be patronized by a crazy old drongo who looked as if he needed a hand-out himself; but what was worse was that the old fool obviously saw Crook not as a tragic hero but as a pathetic no-hoper.

Deflated by this thought, he was in no mood to cope with the two beefy men who rushed him from either side, looking avidly at the money in his hand. Twenty measly dollars were not worth suffering for. 'OK,' he said, holding out the note. 'I don't want a blue with you guys. Just take the money and leave me alone, will you?'

The taller of the two men angrily slapped Crook's hand aside. 'You guys make me puke, you know that?' he snapped. 'Listen, kid, you'd better sober up fast. We want some answers out of you, and we want them right now.' He waved a small wallet under Crook's nose. 'Police.'

'Wait a minute.' Strangely enough, although Crook had been resigned to being mugged, he bitterly resented being called 'kid' by someone barely older than himself. He grabbed the man's wrist and held it so that he could examine the wallet closely. 'I've never really looked at one of these before. Is this you?'

'What the hell do you think you're doing?' The detective tried to yank his hand away. 'Let go of me!'

' "Ivor B. Winpenny, Detective-Constable," ' Crook read aloud. 'Your photo doesn't do you justice, Ivor B. Winpenny. You're really a lot prettier than this.' He looked coolly up into the man's scarlet face and slowly released his grip.

Winpenny furiously massaged his wrist. 'Did you see what this guy did?' He addressed his companion but avoided meeting his eye. 'First he tries to bribe me and then he attacks me.'

'I thought you were muggers,' Crook explained with a shrug of apology. 'How was I to know it was the famous Ivor B. Winpenny bounding over the beach? If I had, I'd have been just naturally quivering with respect.'

'You're asking for it, snotnose, you know that?' Winpenny clenched his fists. 'I'm not going to be slagged off by some deadbeat bloody wino. I've a mind to hammer the shit out of you.'

Crook stood up. 'All by yourself, Ivor?' he asked meekly. 'Or are you going to whistle up another big fat nellie to help you out?' A minute ago he had been too depressed to fight; now, his blood sang at the prospect. His tiredness slid away without his even noticing it.

The other detective had stayed a few paces back, aloof from the proceedings. He had a pained and slightly defeated air, as if the human race had worn down his expectations. 'For God's sake!' he drawled contemptuously. 'We've got work to do here. Ivo, you look as if your blood-pressure's giving you a hard time. Down, boy!' His manner suggested that he had gone through this routine many times. He turned to Crook. 'Relax, kid, we're not about to roust you. We just want some information. Like, just for starters: what's your name?'

Crook was not keen to let go of his anger. 'What's yours, *kid?*'

'Jack Mulhearn,' the man said calmly. 'I'm a cop, too. You wanna see my card?'

'No. See one, you've seen 'em all.'

'OK. Let's start again. Like I said, we're not here to give you a hard time.'

'Unless we have to.' Winpenny scowled and hunched his shoulders.

Mulhearn winced, and kept his eyes on Crook. 'What's your name . . . *sir?*'

'Paul Crook.'

'Crook? No kidding? You mean, like that old comedian, Benny Crook?'

'Barney Crook. Yeah, just like him.' Crook braced himself for the usual spate of reminiscences about his father.

Predictably, Mulhearn said, 'God, he was funny. I never missed his TV show when I was a kid. Yeah, you're right, it wasn't Benny it was Barney.' His woebegone expression became almost cheerful for a moment. 'Did you ever see his Irish Tax-Inspector sketch?'

'Yes.' Only about a zillion times, Crook thought.

'Gee, they don't make comics like that any more.' Mulhearn dragged himself reluctantly back to the subject in hand. 'OK, Paul Crook. Do you . . .' He paused, then rephrased the question. 'Where do you live, Paul?'

'North Ryde. 21c, Matthias Street.'

Mulhearn covered his surprise well, but it was clear that he hadn't expected such a direct answer. 'Do you live with your parents?'

'No, it's my apartment.'

The two men looked at each other with raised eyebrows. 'Paul,' Mulhearn said, 'from the state of your clothes and the stubble on your chin, you look as if you've been on a seven-day binge. Half an hour ago you were flaked out on this bench here. Is there any particular reason why you've been sleeping rough?'

'Yeah, well, I had things on my mind. I needed to think. I've been walking around, thinking.'

Winpenny started to say something, then glanced at his partner and fell silent. Some kind of signal passed between them. Crook didn't see what it was, but he sensed an immediate change in the atmosphere. Something in what he had said excited them, made them both eager and wary, like hunters coming unexpectedly on a fresh spoor.

Mulhearn did his best to hang on to his casual style. 'OK, let's get to it: just how well do you know Stanley Dean?'

'Who?'

'Don't jerk me around, Mr Crook. Stanley Dean. You were talking to him a minute ago.'

'Oh, *him*. I don't know him at all. Never met him before. He just stopped to talk to me, that's all.'

'Not quite all. He woke you up and he gave you money. We saw him do it.'

'That's right. Twenty dollars.' Crook sat down again and leaned back on the bench. The sun was clear of the horizon by now, and he was grateful for its feeble warmth. 'I guess why he did it was, he thought I was a wino who could do with a hand-out and a few uplifting words. Crazy guy.'

'You know who he is?'

'He told me something about himself, yeah. He said Mollie Muffin practically accused him of murder, on her TV show.'

'Did you see the Mollie Muffin show last night?'

'Nope.'

'What else did Dean say? This is very important, Mr Crook: I want to hear the whole of your conversation with him, word for word.'

Crook told them, word for word. When he had finished, Mulhearn said, 'Let's get this clear: he said, "I did kill my wife." You're sure of that? Those were his exact words?'

'Yes.'

'Now, there's just one other thing I want to be certain of: you said that you'd never had any contact with Stanley Dean before today's incident, right?'

'That's what I said.'

'And that's the literal truth?'

'As literal as I can make it.'

'Fine.' Mulhearn attempted an ingratiating smile, which sat oddly on his careworn face. 'I'm sure you'll understand that we have to ask you to come with us and make a formal statement, Paul. This is very important evidence.'

'Is it? The guy's as troppo as a cut snake. A rational bloke doesn't jog around telling perfect strangers that he's murdered his wife.'

'Murderers aren't particularly rational blokes,' Mulhearn pointed out.

Crook persisted: 'But he also said, "I told them at the

time, and they wouldn't listen." Then he talked about God making him pay for it. The poor old guy's obviously not right in the head.'

'The thing is,' Mulhearn said, 'that whatever Dean's state of mind, your evidence ought to be on record.'

'Yes, OK.' Crook could hardly refuse.

'It won't take long,' Mulhearn assured him. 'And the guys at Bondi make great coffee.'

But as it turned out, they kept him at the Bondi station on one pretext or another for most of the day. Everyone there was so polite and pleasant that it was some time before Crook figured out that they seriously suspected him of being Stanley Dean's accomplice.

CHAPTER 4

The Incident Room at Toongabbie was crowded and noisy. There was a general feeling of satisfaction in the air: the Dean case was all but sewn up, and most of the men and women present looked forward to being released for more interesting duties. Domestic cases were always depressing, and usually boring.

The hubbub died down as the two senior officers entered the room. Detective-Superintendent Albert Rocco, who was the Senior Investigating Officer on the Dean case, was respected and well liked by all his staff; but the man who walked in alongside him was held in a kind of awe by all present. Detective Chief Superintendent Graham Mintlaw, Rocco's immediate superior, was well known to be a merciless, hard-nosed bastard: a slave-driver with a tongue like a rawhide whip. Mintlaw's reputation, even more than his personality, dominated the room, cowed the junior detectives into silence.

'OK, pay attention, everybody,' Rocco said unnecessarily, apparently unaware of the churchlike hush in the

room. 'As you all know, we reckon we've got enough to get
a result on this one. But the Boss here is not yet completely
persuaded that it's a copper-bottomed certainty. He's
called this meeting to give us a chance to convince him.'

'And the first thing on the agenda is that fucking
TV programme,' Mintlaw growled. His voice had a dry,
throaty quality that was unpleasant on the ear. 'How the
hell did we let that bloody woman get away with all that
shit?'

'*The Copper File* has been a very useful programme for us
in the past,' Rocco said defensively. 'The item on Mary
Dean brought us two very good leads.'

'But that stupid cow—what's her name?'

'Mollie Muffin.'

'Muffin, that's right—she practically announced to the
whole world that Stanley Dean was the murderer. Seems
to me the whole case is compromised. How's the bastard
gonna get a fair trial after that?'

'Well, sir, the programme employs a whole battery of
lawyers. They went over the script line by line. It's their
job to ensure that the programme is completely free of bias
and libel.'

'That's bollocks,' Mintlaw said angrily. 'That's typical
lawyers' drivel. Everybody knows Muffin's style by now:
she's got a thousand mannerisms, which make the actual
words she says virtually irrelevant. Nobody who saw that
item on the Dean murder was in any doubt that Mollie
Muffin had shown the cops who the murderer was.'

'I dunno whether mannerisms are evidence, sir,' Rocco
said with pained politeness. 'That's something for the
lawyers to sort out. Like I said, the programme's useful to
us: it helps us put a lot of crims behind bars. We can afford
to let Muffin have her moments of triumph now and then.'

'If you say so, Bert.' Mintlaw was still irritable. 'What's
done's done. Show me what sort of case you've got outside
of that TV crap.'

'OK.' Rocco picked up a wooden pointer and walked

over to a blackboard with a list of names scrawled on it. A row of photographs was pinned to the wall near the blackboard. 'I'll assume—'

'Don't assume anything, Bert,' Mintlaw snapped. 'Take me through the whole lot. All of it. Just in case—' he smiled tigerishly—'I've forgotten anything.' Some of the young detectives smiled nervously back at him. Mintlaw was reputed to have a memory like a computer databank.

'Fine.' Rocco cleared his throat. 'Mary Dean, aka Mary Kafko, was strangled to death on the 22nd March, probably between two and five p.m. She was last seen alive at twelve noon in Vaucluse and her body was discovered on Livia Street in Holroyd at six-thirty p.m. She had been badly beaten just before she died; and her body carried the marks and bruises of many previous beatings. There were no tights, stockings or panties on the corpse; but neither was there any evidence of sexual congress or assault. The pattern of bruising on her throat suggests that her attacker stood in front of her and strangled her with his hands. Two little bones here—' Rocco indicated his own throat—'were fractured, probably by thumb pressure. The killer's hands are strong and broad, but not necessarily huge—smaller than mine, in fact, according to the pathologist.' Rocco held up his hands for them to look at.

Mintlaw said, 'Remind me how the time of death was arrived at?'

Rocco shrugged. 'Guesswork. Balance of probabilities— contents of her stomach, onset of rigor in her face muscles, the usual medical flim-flam. It's not all that important. We're working on the assumption that the guy who killed her was the same guy that dumped her on Livia Street; and we know that she was dumped there sometime between six-five and six-thirty.'

Mintlaw nodded, remembering. 'Because of the rain.'

'Yeah. The storm got to Holroyd at six-five.'

'And the pavement under the body was wet.' Mintlaw applauded ironically. 'Great. That's the stuff that impresses a jury. Now, Bert, quit hogging the limelight. Let me hear from your young lions.'

'I was just about to suggest it,' Rocco said stiffly. 'Tuttle, take the floor.'

Detective-Sergeant Tuttle coloured slightly, but spoke up sturdily enough. 'Me and DC Parks checked out the movements of the deceased on the day of the murder, sir. We found witnesses who saw her leave her home in Richmond at approximately seven-thirty a.m., and she was seen getting on the seven forty-six train at East Richmond station. We don't know exactly what time she arrived for work at the Arrigo Hall in Vaucluse, but several people attested to the fact that she was there from about nine-thirty onwards. She left at about twelve noon, and walked off in the direction of the New South Head Road. From that moment, sir, she effectively disappeared. We haven't found a soul who admits to having seen her between that time and six-thirty, when her body was found.' Tuttle paused, seeing that Mintlaw was about to ask another question.

'Tell me more about this Arrigo Hall,' Mintlaw said. 'Is it some kind of church, or what?'

'I think it was originally built as a Chapel or Meeting House, sir, but it's now owned by the Arrigo Choral Society, who use it as a rehearsal room. Mary Dean had a part-time job as assistant to the Secretary of the Society; and part of her duties entailed keeping that Hall clean and tidy.'

'Thank you, Sergeant,' Mintlaw said. 'Sorry to interrupt. You were saying that Mary just disappeared after she left work?'

'Yessir. But you didn't interrupt, sir. That's it. Our investigation drew a blank. We just haven't found anyone who saw her from midday onwards.'

Mintlaw said, gently for him, 'No, I reckon you've got something else on your mind, Sergeant. Let's hear it.'

Tuttle shifted in his seat. 'Well, we concluded—that is, DC Parks and me concluded—that it would be damn near

impossible for the deceased to have been abducted anywhere in that part of Vaucluse, particularly in the middle
of the day, without somebody seeing it happen. In fact, we
covered that journey from Vaucluse to Richmond over and
over again; and we reckoned there was no way she could
have been snatched without *somebody* noticing something.'

'So you don't think she was snatched, in fact?'

'No, sir. She either went with somebody of her own free
will; or she went straight home, with nobody paying any
particular attention to her. That was our opinion, anyway,'
Tuttle added cautiously.

'Uh-huh.' Mintlaw looked sideways at Rocco. 'What else
are you doing?'

'We're putting up pictures of Mary at all the stations
along that line,' Rocco said. 'That may jog someone's
memory.'

'Right. Who's next?'

Rocco got to his feet and looked around, wagging a finger
as if he was taking a tally. 'How about you, Mabel?' he
said, pointing. 'Wanna say your piece?'

The policewoman took her time answering. She was certain that she detected condescension in the use of her first
name, and her pained expression said that it was just the
kind of chauvinistic bullshit she'd learned to expect. 'My
brief,' she said coldly, 'was to collate all the facts on the
murdered woman, build up a character profile.'

'Look for skeletons in the cupboard, eh?' Mintlaw said
genially. 'Did you find any?'

'Not really. No form anyway, according to Central
Records. To be honest, our main source of information
about the woman was Stanley Dean himself. He told us
that her age was forty-eight or thereabouts; that she was
an orphan, adopted by a couple called Barrett, who lived
in St Kilda; and that the Barretts died when Mary was
fifteen. Her first job was in a clothing factory in Melbourne;
she stayed with that for nine years, until the firm went bust.
Then she took a number of jobs—shop assistant, waitress,

barmaid—and finally married a conjuror, a stage illusionist
called Kafko. She took part in his act. They called themselves the Kurius Kafkos. They were together for about
twelve years; then Kafko died in an accident. Mary quit
the stage, but stayed with show business—she got a job as
a Wardrobe Mistress on one of the big K. P. Lachlan shows.
She worked on and off for the Lachlan Organization for
the next seven years, doing different jobs—dresser, cleaner,
even some clerical work. Then she met Stanley Dean and
moved in with him. She took Dean's name, though she
never married him.'

'How did she and Stanley meet?' Mintlaw asked. 'He's
not a theatre bloke, surely?'

'No, sir, he's a car mechanic. It seems they met in a pub.
Or so Stanley thinks: he's a bit vague about it. He's a
reformed alcoholic, and his memory's unreliable where his
binges are concerned. Anyway, according to him, their
relationship was OK; but the neighbours tell a different
story. Lots of noisy quarrels, and frequently sounds of
actual physical violence. The local police and the Social
Services were alerted, but Mary flatly denied that there
was any problem: told 'em to mind their own business.
And that's about it, sir. She got the part-time job at the
Arrigo Hall about six months ago: one of her mates from
the Lachlan Organization recommended her.'

'Good.' Mintlaw was striving for exactly the right tone
of voice: neither off-hand nor patronizing. 'What's your
name, by the way?' It was a minor rebuke to the Superintendent.

The policewoman recognized the olive branch, but her
expression remained unforgiving. 'Tyler, sir.'

'OK, Tyler. Good report. Concise. Just one comment:
when I asked you if there were any skeletons in Mary's
closet, you said "not really". Now, I reckon the Tyler style
is to say no if she means no.' Mintlaw waited poker-faced
for the male chuckles to subside. 'What does "not really"
mean?'

'It means there's no hard evidence, sir. Nothing usable in court. But I picked up some scuttlebut which could be significant, if it were true.'

'Go on.'

'I talked to a couple of women who had worked with Mary at that clothing factory in Melbourne. They both told me the same story, though they admitted they couldn't vouch for the truth of it. They said there was a persistent rumour that Mary was actually a part-time prostitute, specializing in really rough trade.' She fixed Mintlaw with a hard and penetrating stare.

Mintlaw scratched his chin. 'OK, I'll buy it. Why would that be significant?'

For a moment, Policewoman Tyler allowed a glimmer of enthusiasm to show. 'It ties in with a detail in the autopsy report, sir. Not only was the dead woman wearing no underclothing, but her—' Tyler lowered her head and coughed—'her vagina was smeared with a well-known brand of lubricating jelly. *Liberally* smeared, according to the lab report.'

There was an uproar of bawdy comment, which Mintlaw impatiently waved down. 'You're suggesting that Mary had prepared herself for sex, is that it?'

'Well, sir, some middle-aged women have problems . . .' Somehow, WD Tyler managed to make it clear that she was not speaking from personal experience.

'Yes, yes.' Mintlaw scowled until the boisterous element in the room fell silent again. 'Could there be any reason other than sex for using this jelly? Does it have any actual medical properties?'

'I don't know, sir. You'd have to ask a doctor.'

'I'll do that.' Mintlaw nodded appreciatively. 'Good point, Tyler. If Mary got herself all ready for sex at midday, some fifty kilometres from home, it suggests she was planning to cheat on her husband. That would certainly give Stanley a motive for murder.'

'With respect, sir,' WD Tyler said, 'that wasn't quite the

point I was trying to make. It occurred to me that Mary might have taken up prostitution again.'

'I see. "Rough trade," I think you said. Your idea is that she could have been beaten up and killed by a client?'

'Yes, sir. But that,' WD Tyler said without emphasis, 'is just speculation.'

'*We've* speculated about that, too,' Rocco said. So far, we haven't found a shred of evidence to support that idea.' He was irritated, but trying not to show it. The Chief had twice encouraged junior officers to air their personal theories about this case. That sort of indulgence only led to anarchy, in Rocco's opinion. 'The fact is, there's only ever been one guy in the frame for this killing, and that's the husband, Stanley Dean. So far, we've just talked about the victim; now let's take a look at the suspect. First of all, Stanley *does* have a record. He did time in a Young Offenders' Centre for stealing a car, and he did a stretch at Parramatta for robbery with violence. He's been charged with serious assault no less than eight times. He's a violent man. Secondly, we know that he and Mary quarrelled, and often came to blows. Thirdly—and this is a direct result of the Mollie Muffin programme—we have two witnesses who saw him driving a car along Livia Street at six-fifteen on the night of the murder.'

'Wait a minute, Bert.' Mintlaw held up a hand. 'I don't want to nitpick, but that isn't exactly the deposition I read. The witnesses identified the guy's *hat*.'

Rocco nodded impatiently. 'Yeah, sure. But it's not as if it's any old hat. *I've* never seen another one like it, anyway. It's a great, wide-brimmed thing, tied on with a thong, like an old woman's bonnet. Dean wears it to cover an ugly scar on his scalp.'

'Well, OK,' Mintlaw said. 'It's a corroborative detail, but it's a long way from being proof. You know as well as I do that some hotshit lawyer is going to produce an identical hat in court, and make us all look like king-size prawns.

Anyway, Dean's got an alibi: he says he was with one Ashley Stuker, a retired miner, all afternoon.'

'With respect, Graham, that alibi is a bloody joke. Stuker's eighty years old: a flakey old ratbag with birdshit for brains. He doesn't remember anything accurately: he just repeats the last thing he's been told. Nobody's going to take him seriously as a witness. Particularly—' Rocco had saved the best for the last—'since we've got a confession.'

For a moment Mintlaw was slack-jawed with surprise. 'Dean's coughed his guts? So that's why you're all looking so bloody smug. When did this happen?'

'This morning. We've been keeping twenty-four-hour surveillance on our Stanley, and this morning it paid off. Stanley went for a jog on the beach at first light, got in conversation with a young no-hoper who'd been sleeping rough, and would you believe, coughed up the whole thing. "I killed my wife," he said. Straight out: no ifs or buts. Detectives Winpenny and Mulhearn interviewed the witness immediately after his conservation with Dean; and that's what he said. *And*,' Rocco said heavily, 'the witness had definitely not seen *The Copper File* programme, so there's no question of prejudice.'

'But you called this witness a no-hoper. Is he reliable? What sort of no-hoper? Wino? Derelict?'

'Just a guy down on his luck. He'd been on the grog, but Mulhearn says he was stone sober *and* coherent when he talked to him. Cleaned up, he'd be impressive in court, Mulhearn says.'

Mintlaw surveyed the rows of grinning faces in front of him. They were expecting to be congratulated; but he'd be damned if he'd give them that satisfaction just yet. 'It sounds too good to be true.'

'There's more, sir,' chortled one of the young detectives. 'This witness—the guy on the beach—he's actually a private dick.'

Mintlaw looked up quickly, and stared hard at the man. He was suddenly very still.

A chorus of voices wanted to tell him the best bit. 'And
. . . the guy's name—'

'Crook.' Mintlaw's voice was harsh and his mouth bitter.
'Paul Crook.'

It was Rocco's turn to be astonished. 'That's right. Hey!'
Something stirred in his memory. 'Wasn't that the kid
who . . . ?'

'Yeah.' Mintlaw did a strange thing. He covered his face
with his hands and uttered a long, whistling sigh. 'That
young sod brings nothing but trouble,' he muttered. 'Death
follows him around like his bloody shadow.'

CHAPTER 5

'Bam-bam' Butcher shambled into Crook's office with the
solemn air of a man on a difficult and delicate mission.
'Brought yer a cuppa tea an' a curran' bun,' he said
sombrely.

Crook scowled at him over the top of his computer ter-
minal. 'I don't want a bloody bun,' he snarled. 'And why
can't you remember to knock on the bloody door?'

Bam-bam sighed and leaned his substantial belly against
the edge of Crook's desk. I din' knock,' he explained with
pained dignity, 'because I din' like to disturb your friggin'
concentration. Such as it is,' he added obscurely. 'Eat yer
bun. I got somethin' to tell yer.'

'I told you, I don't want the damn thing.'

'Suit yerself.' Bam-bam crammed the bun into his own
mouth and munched noisily but without obvious enthusiasm, revealing an incredible number of large, horse-like
teeth. 'They finally nicked Stan Dean for toppin' his old
lady,' he said indistinctly. 'They've shoved him in the
remand clink at Rosehill.'

'Oh?'

'I knew you'ld be interested. He wants you to go an' see him.'

'Me? Why?'

Bam-bam sucked his teeth and rolled his eyes at the ceiling. 'I 'spect he wants to thank you in person for droppin' him in the fertilizer after connin' him out of twenty bucks.'

'I didn't con him out of anything. He shoved the money into my hand. And all I told the cops was what he had said to me. No more and no less. Look—' he sounded apologetic in spite of himself—'Dean's a prawnhead. And a deeply troubled man. He needed to confess to somebody: he just happened to pick on me.'

'Be that as it may,' Bam-bam said heavily. He wiped a fat thumb across his mouth. 'Be that as it may,' he said again, enjoying the sound of the phrase, 'he wants to see yer. He sent me word.'

'How?'

'On the grapevine.' Bam-bam tried to illustrate the workings of the grapevine by fluttering his fingers incomprehensibly. 'He knows I work for you. Everybody knows I work for you,' he added with conscious pride.

'Well, I don't want to see him,' Crook said dismissively. He turned back to his computer screen and tapped at the keyboard as if he knew what he was doing.

Bam-bam refused to take the hint. 'Yes, you do,' he said doggedly. 'You owe him something. It ain't just the twenty bucks: it's what it stands for. Why d'yer suppose he gave you that money?'

'Because he's nuts.' Crook saw the shock and reproach on the old pug's face, and recanted immediately. 'Yes, OK, I know what you want me to say. The guy felt sorry for me,' he said quietly.

'Yeah. He tried to help yer 'cause you were down on your luck. An' you took his charity an' then shopped him. That's what they're sayin', anyhow.'

Crook was beginning to see daylight. 'You're not worried

about Stanley Dean at all, you old fraud. You're afraid you might be losing face among your street cronies.'

'Bloody hell!' Bam-bam's face was a mask of injury and indignation. 'Don't the word *honour* mean nothin' to you?'

Now that Crook was on top of the situation he could afford to be magnanimous. 'Yes, all right: if it'll improve your standing with your hardnosed mates, I'll go and see the bloke as soon as I've got the time.'

'Ta.' Bam-bam sucked his thumb and then examined it closely, as if he thought it might have changed colour. 'I fixed it for this arvo.'

'You *what?*' Crook was at first bewildered and then furious. 'What do you mean, you fixed it? Listen, you punch-drunk old ratbag, we're supposed to be running a business here. I've got work to do.'

'Yeah, well, that's another thing.' Bam-bam rapped the top of Crook's workstation with his knuckles. 'This friggin' TV thing just ain't your bag. You'll have to give it up.' He held up a magisterial hand. 'Now wait a minute. Answer me this: you've always worked in the open air, right? Right. That's where you belong—out there on the street, where the action is.'

'What do you think I am, a bloody postman? And what the hell—are *you* trying to tell *me* what to do?' Crook thought of adding 'How dare you?' but the words had a kind of middle-aged, theatrical ring that he didn't think he could carry off.

Bam-bam clicked his teeth and swung his massive head to and fro. 'Hold on: there's no need to do your lolly. You 'n' me gotta talk.' He levered himself away from the desk, tiptoed grotesquely to the office door and closed it. 'This ain't woman's work. So I guess it's down to me.'

'What the hell are you talking about? What's down to you?'

'Somebody's gotta tell yer.' Bam-bam rolled his shoulders and rocked belligerently from side to side. 'You're stuffing this Agency down the gurgler. You've gotta start pullin' your weight.'

Crook considered this wickedly unjust. 'I *am* pulling my weight,' he said indignantly. 'I've been working harder these last few weeks than I ever have in my life.'

'You've been puttin' in the hours,' Bam-bam conceded. 'But that *thing*—' he pointed at Crook's workstation—'that bloody machine's got you on the ropes. If you don't chuck in the towel soon, the whole flamin' business is goin' down for the count.'

'Who says so?' Crook tried to sound indignant, but his voice was already tinged with self-doubt. 'I got the hang of the system ages ago.'

'Boss—' Bam-bam explained as tactfully he knew how— 'it ain't a job you can do with your mind in neutral. You're makin' too many mistakes.'

'Mistakes? What do you mean, mistakes?'

'Look, this is our bread-an'-butter, according to Mrs P.: we get info out of the computer and flog it to our customers, right?'

'We supply financial information to selected clients, yes,' Crook said loftily. 'We have access to over four hundred databases.'

Bam-bam shrugged off the attempted put-down. 'Yeah, well, the point is that the gen we supply has gotta be spot-on, right? I mean, when you're makin' out a report, if you bung a coupla noughts in the wrong places, that report becomes just so much pelican shit.'

'I haven't done that!' But Crook's protest lacked conviction, even in his own ears.

'You bloody have, mate. And worse. And that ain't all. Your spellin' ain't up to the mark, either.'

'Spelling?' This was too much. 'These are financial reports, not literary bloody essays.'

'All I mean is, you're careless with the keys. If a bloke's a waiter, it ain't fair to bung him down as a "waster". You pegged one guy as a "Central Cheating Engineer"; and one of our richest clients got a mention as a "successful bonker".' Bam-bam's expression said that this was hurting him more than it was his employer. 'Mrs P. and the girls are havin' to re-do over half your work, Boss. It's costin' us time an' money. And it's takin' the heart out of everybody.'

Crook's shoulders sagged. 'Why didn't anyone tell me this before?'

'You're the *boss*,' Bam-bam said simply. He stopped fidgeting from foot to foot and sat down in one of the clients' armchairs. He looked tired, as if the argument had taken a lot out of him. 'Anyway, everybody's makin' excuses for you. You can't be expected to concentrate, after what you've been through, meanin' Miss Robyn's accident an' all: that's what they say. The women out there—' he jerked a thumb in the direction of the outer office—'they can't talk about it without bawlin' their eyes out. You're young, tragic, romantic—which of that lot's gonna front up to you and say you're a total fuckwit?'

'So it's down to you?'

Bam-bam looked glum. 'They'd kill me if they knew I'd told you. But I can't afford to see this company go belly up. This job means a lot to me.'

'Belly-up? Things aren't as bad as all that.' Trust the old ham to go right over the top, Crook thought.

Bam-bam swivelled his chair sideways and stared at the grimy office window. 'It's the *respect*,' he muttered. 'That's what a proper job gives you. I never had no respect before, ever.'

'Sure you did,' Crook said. 'They respected you in the ring. You had a crackerjack boxing career. You were a title contender.'

'I was a mug. Everybody knew that, including my so-called manager. Nobody respects a mug, even if he's a winner, and I wasn't a winner. Fifteen years of cuts and bruises, and for what? Sod all, that's what. An' after my crackerjack career, what do I end up as? A head-banger for a greasy loan-shark. I tell you, mate, when I met you I had less self-respect than a jacked-up pimp.'

Crook had never known Bam-bam so low-spirited. 'That's old history. You've got respect now, and a job. We couldn't do without you.' He crossed his fingers.

'Yeah.' Bam-bam frowned horribly, as he always did when he was in deadly earnest. 'You know what Mrs P. says? Every day, when I take her a cuppa, and maybe one of her fav'rite sugar buns, she says, "Mr Basil," she says, "you are ab-so-lute-ly indispensiable."'

'She's right.'

'I'd kill for that woman,' Bam-bam said seriously. 'She's got a brain *that* big—' he held his massive hands about a metre apart—'and yet she can find the time *every day* to say something nice to a mug like me.'

'She wouldn't say it if she didn't mean it,' Crook said.

'Too right. An' when somebody with a brain *that* big—' Bam-bam once again indicated the size of Mrs P.'s brain— 'says that you're indis-fuckin'-pensiable, you'd better believe it.' He rested his hands across his belly and nodded several times, pleased with his debating skills, then he heaved himself to his feet. 'Well, OK,' he said. 'Time we got movin'. Get yer coat and do up yer tie. I don't want 'em thinkin' yer a slob.'

'What?' Crook had a sinking feeling that he had somehow been outmanœuvred. 'I'm not going anywhere!'

'Rosehill,' Bam-bam said firmly. 'I fixed it. You owe that unhappy sod twenty bucks' worth of your time.'

'I don't owe him anything! And I don't need you to tell me what to do.' But try as he might, Crook couldn't summon up the necessary outrage at having his authority challenged so flagrantly. It just didn't seem to matter. Nothing really mattered, when you got down to it.

'Listen, son—Boss, I mean,' Bam-bam said urgently, 'you don't belong behind a desk. As a paper-pusher, you're a total bloody mollydooker. You're embarrassin' the womenfolk by doin' their work, pertickly as you're doin' it

badly. You oughta be out there—' he gestured extravagantly towards the window—'walkin' the stingy streets,
like a proper detective.'

Crook reached for his coat. '*Stingy* streets?'

'Yeah. I dunno who made that up, but he knew his stuff.
That's what city streets are, all right.' In the outer office,
he paused by Mrs Parson's desk. 'Me an' the boss are goin'
to see a bloke,' he announced. 'On business.'

'Oh, *good*.' Mrs P. was just a shade too hearty in her
approval, Crook thought. 'I do hope you're going to revive
the Private Client Division, Mr Paul. Having all one's eggs
in one basket is such a gamble.' Her assistants, Mandy,
Jane and Lilian (Crook knew their names, but could never
match them with the faces) chirped their agreement with
such enthusiasm that his worst fears were confirmed. They
too wanted him out there on the stingy streets, so they
could get on with their work unhindered.

In the ancient lift that juddered them unconvincingly
to street level, Bam-bam offered consoling words: 'They
worship you, them kids back there. They think you're
second cousin to Godawmighty.'

'They know I'm a mug.' Crook was in no mood to be
comforted. '"A total fuckwit", in your memorable phrase.'

'That don't make no difference. Nice sheilas've always
got a soft spot for a mug,' Bam-bam said complacently.

CHAPTER 6

'Fifteen minutes,' the guard said. 'No physical contact, and
nothing may be passed to or from the prisoner. If anything
at all crosses the barrier—' he pointed to the foot-high
metal partition that bisected the wide table—'an alarm will
be triggered and there'll be hell to pay. Remember that.'
He sat down on a chair by the door and watched them
with an expression of bored indifference. There was no pre-

tence that this was going to be a private interview: the room was so small that the guard had to overhear everything that was said, whether he wanted to or not.

Stanley Dean was wearing new headgear: a blue denim cap with a jutting, spade-like brim. His eyes were bright and he seemed full of nervous energy. It was hard to recognize him as the melancholy individual who had accosted Crook at the beach.

'I got a message that you wanted to talk to me,' Crook said.

Dean nodded vigorously. 'Yeah. First off, I want you to know that I don't hold it against you, you talking to the cops about me. You din' have no choice. You're a PI, aren't you?'

Crook couldn't seriously think of himself as a private investigator. He gave his usual evasive answer: 'I work for a Detective Agency, yes.'

'The minute I heard that, I knew what I had to do. It took a weight off my mind, I can tell you. It's like a miracle.'

'A miracle?' Crook's spirits sagged. He should never have agreed to come here. The guy was obviously several cards short of a full deck. 'Mr Dean, I—'

'No, no, let me talk, let me have my say. It's not you that's the miracle: it's Fate.' He was trembling with excitement. 'Listen, there's a lot I've got to say. First off, I didn't kill Mary.'

'You said you killed your wife.'

'Yes, yes, I know I said that. That just slipped out: I didn't know at the time what made me say it. But I know now. Fate. I din' have no choice. Look, time's slippin' by. There's something I gotta show you.'

He slowly peeled off his cap. His grey hair was cropped short, and on the right side of his head it was as thick and smooth as cat's fur. But his scalp on the other side was a mess: a lumpy patchwork of scars covered with mottled, brittle-looking skin. Isolated tufts of hair sprouted randomly between the deep pits and furrows, as forlorn as

44   STAGE FRIGHT

weeds on waste land. High up on his left temple was a
puckered, circular dimple, like a bullet-wound. 'Car accident,' Dean said, tapping his forehead. 'Took a dozen
operations to keep me alive, and I still can't figure out
why the hell they bothered.' He pulled on his cap. 'Do you
ever get the feeling that God's got you on a string, like a
puppet? That it doesn't matter what you think or feel or
strive for, because everything's already mapped out?
You've just got to walk the path that's laid out for you?'

'You said pretty much the same thing down at the beach,'
Crook said.

Dean grinned, bobbing his head. 'You dodged the question. It don't matter: I *know* you understand.' He suddenly
shivered and folded his arms, just as he had done at the
beach. 'I was drunk,' he said, confident that Crook would
follow his train of thought. 'I drove like a crazy man. Skidded on a bend and rolled the car over. I passed out, but
they managed to cut me free. Janet died while I was still
unconscious.'

'Janet?'

'My wife.'

'Your first wife?'

'My *wife*. Mary borrowed my name, but she was never
my married wife.'

'So you were just playing games,' Crook said disgustedly.
'You knew that the cops had you under surveillance, and
it was a racing cert they'd question me after that cosy con-
fab down at the beach. So you sent them a message through
me: that you'd killed your wife. Only now you say that
Mary wasn't your wife. What exactly are you up to, Mr
Dean?'

Dean hung his head, avoiding Crook's eye. 'You make
it sound like it was deliberate, like I was *using* you. But it
wasn't like that. I swear to you that I didn't know what I
was going to say until the words were out of my mouth.' His
exuberance seemed to have deserted him: his face, though
partially hidden from Crook's view by his peaked cap, was

taut with some inner pain. 'I was drunk,' he said again. 'I murdered my wife and my unborn kid, and I was never punished for it. I was never even charged with anything. You wanna know why? Because some clown lost the result of my blood test.'

Dean sat silent for a moment, breathing deeply. When he raised his head, he looked calm and determined, as if he had passed through some sort of crisis. He said quietly, 'What I'm telling you is that I didn't kill Mary. They're trying to say I did it out of jealousy, but I wasn't jealous. I didn't love the poor cow enough to be jealous. I loved her, but I didn't love her *enough*, do you understand? Anyway—' he swallowed hard, trying to get his voice under control—'think of this: if I didn't kill her, somebody else did. And he's still out there. I want him found. I owe her that much.'

'Five minutes,' the guard called out, tapping his wrist-watch with his fingernail. He tilted his chair and leaned backwards against the wall, yawning hugely.

Crook looked at the prisoner in some dismay. He was struggling with an all-too-familiar sensation of being carried out of his depth by unexpected currents. 'What are you saying? Are you trying to hire me? Is that why you wanted to see me? Are you trying to hire me to find your wife's killer?'

'Nah. Anyway, she wasn't my wife. Also, you're a prosecution witness: my lawyer says I mustn't offer you money.' Inexplicably, Dean had shaken off his melancholy, and was all animation again. 'No, I needed to tell you about Mary. They're saying bad things about her, and that isn't fair. She wasn't a loose woman.' He spoke more quickly, anxious to finish before his time ran out. 'She wasn't killed because of sex. You'll have to look for some other reason.'

'Mr Dean, I don't plan to look for anything. I have no excuse—no *reason*—to meddle in this case.'

Dean almost smiled. 'Don't worry about it, OK? Whatever will be, will be. It's Fate.'

'Time's up,' the guard said.

Dean stood up and offered to shake hands, then remembered the barrier just in time. He made a thumbs-up sign instead. 'Thanks for comin', son. If you find anythin', let me know, will you?'

'Sure.' No harm in humouring the poor sod, Crook thought.

'That's it,' the guard said. 'Come along, Stan.'

'You can't alter the future, any more than the past,' Dean said sombrely. 'I don't reckon it would have changed anything, even if I could've given Mary what she needed.'

'Look, you can't order these things.' Crook's sympathy was born of his own experience. 'Love just *happens*. You can't force yourself to love somebody.'

Dean's cheerfulness evaporated again. 'You've got a lot to learn, son,' he said sadly. 'She didn't just want to be loved. She wanted to be hurt.'

It was symptomatic of Crook's listless frame of mind that he had allowed himself to be driven to the Rosehill remand prison in Bam-bam's car. It was not an experience he would willingly have submitted to, in normal circumstances. Being chauffeured by Bam-bam in Bam-bam's ancient Cadillac was only for the recklessly heroic or the totally mad.

Actually, the car and its owner were remarkably well matched. Both were ugly, over-large and battle-scarred; and both tended to eccentric movement under stress. Whenever its brakes were applied, the Cadillac's front end would dip violently, as if sniffing the road, and when its nose eventually came up, the car would settle into a bad-tempered rocking motion, like a boat pitching in a heavy swell. But unpleasant as this sensation was, it was not as alarming, in Crook's opinion, as the sinister medley of noises that accompanied their progress. The rattles and squeaks were bad enough, but far worse were the muffled, strangely human-sounding moans that came from somewhere deep in the car's vitals. From time to time the engine issued a loose protest like the wanton clattering of pan lids.

'That's new,' Crook said nervously. 'I've never heard that noise before.'

Bam-bam crouched over the wheel. 'It goes away,' he said airily. 'It don't last.'

'What is it?'

'I dunno. The old girl's not as young as she was. But there's still a lot of power under this bonnet.' This had to be construed as blind faith, since Bam-bam was no speed-ster; on the rare occasions when he whipped the hearse-like vehicle up to 40 kilometres an hour, he tended to whoop with the sheer white-knuckled excitement of it all. As the car was left-hand drive, and Crook was on the vulnerable, outer side, the sedate speed suited him just fine.

Crook realized, soon after they left the prison, that Bam-bam was taking a roundabout route. 'Why not use the freeway?' he asked. 'City-bound traffic won't be heavy at this time.'

Bam-bam didn't answer immediately. He pouted with concentration as he pulled out to pass a double-parked van. When he spoke, it was not a direct answer: 'I been on the blower while you were inside. How did you get on with Stan?'

'I reckon he's more than a shingle short. I still don't know why he wanted to see me.'

'What did you talk about?'

'Fate, mainly.'

'What about his wife?'

'If you mean Mary, she wasn't his wife. He said he didn't kill her.'

'Yeah.' Bam-bam nodded judiciously, as if Crook had confirmed something.

'You still haven't said why we're going home this way,' Crook pointed out.

'We ain't goin' home yet. We gotta go see a man.'

'What man? Why?'

'Harry Sheiling. He'll tell you why.'

The name meant nothing to Crook, and Bam-bam was too busy looking at road signs to explain further. He braked nervously and eased the Cadillac into the parking area of a big supermarket. 'Harry often meets people here,' he said as they slowly toured the massed ranks of parked cars. 'His missus wanders round in there for hours. She's a very careful shopper.' At last he found a space big enough for his car. 'Let's go find him.'

'Find him? In this lot?' Crook looked out in dismay at the shining acres of chrome and steel.

'He'll be easy to spot,' Bam-bam said confidently. He stood on tiptoe and looked around, craning his head from side to side. 'Over there.'

Bam-bam's confidence was not misplaced. Harry Sheiling's car was indeed easy to pick out. It was an old Rolls-Royce Phantom, conspicuous not merely on account of its size and style, but also by reason of a large, pennant-shaped sign mounted on its roof. The sign was bright red in colour, and featured the letters HS in gilt, bracketing an unlikely-looking coat of arms.

'I see your friend's the modest, self-effacing type,' Crook said.

'He ain't my friend,' Bam-bam said coldly. 'He's just a guy.'

A man got out of the driving seat of the Rolls and raised a hand in greeting. He was short, moon-faced and button-eyed; and he wore a black uniform which tapered from extravagantly wide shoulders to narrow, pigeon-toed feet. 'That's "Piney" Woods, Harry's minder,' Bam-bam informed Crook in a hoarse undertone. 'Ex-wrestler. Can't punch worth pussy, but in his prime his bear-hug would break your back.'

'Hi, Bam-bam,' Woods said languidly. 'This your guv'nor?' He eyed Crook, and in particular Crook's clothes, with an expression of mingled contempt and disbelief.

'Yeah.' Bam-bam's growl was a warning.

'Harry's waitin'.' Woods led the way, moving with smooth, dainty steps, like a dancer. He rapped on the rear door before opening it. 'That private dick's here, Harry, OK?' He stepped back and made a theatrical bow. 'In you go, kid.'

'Now just a minute!' Bam-bam was furious. 'Just one goddam minute!' He elbowed Crook out of the way and advanced on Woods, his massive beer-gut quivering with indignation. 'This is my boss you're talking to, shitface. Show some friggin' respect, or you'll be spittin' teeth all over your friggin' fancy jacket.'

'What—?' Woods was clearly nonplussed. 'What the hell—?'

'My boss don't get called "kid" by no ponced-up toe-rag like Piney Woods,' Bam-bam said grimly. 'He gets called "sir", understand?'

The man in the car crackled his newspaper irritably. 'Piney, you're a prawnhead,' he drawled. 'Apologize to the young gent.'

'Apologize?' Woods seemed to have difficulty in understanding what was going on. He pondered the problem for a long moment, looking confused and unhappy. 'OK, if you say so, Harry.' He looked at Crook and moved his huge shoulders slowly up and down. 'Sorry, kid—*sir*, I mean.'

'Now piss off and take that other clapped-out bruiser with you,' Harry Sheiling said. 'See if you can track down Mrs Ess. If she ain't starin' at the cornflakes like a hypnotized rabbit, she'll be in a trance at the deli counter. Tell her if she ain't out here by midnight, I'm gonna drive the pumpkin home without her.'

Piney's smooth brow wrinkled. 'You mean, tell her don't bother to buy no pumpkin? You already bought the pumpkin, right?'

Sheiling winced. 'Just deliver the message, Piney.'

'Yeah, but—' Woods was determined to prove himself useful—'midnight? Harry, the store closes at nine o'clock.'

'Just keep a sharp look-out as you go, Piney,' Sheiling

said tiredly. 'If you see any brains lyin' around, they're prolly yours.' The hand he extended to Crook glittered with diamond rings. 'I'm Harry Sheiling. 'Scuse the hired help. Piney's a thicko, but he's loyal. I always say, you can buy brains, but loyalty's a pearl beyond price, eh?'

Harry Sheiling didn't look like the kind of man who would erect a vulgar advertisement on the roof of his car. A casual observer might easily take him for a banker or a successful barrister. His face, with its high-bridged nose and narrow jaw, had a fastidious look; while his pinstripe suit and handmade English shoes were in carefully conservative taste. But some details didn't match the image. His voice had a dockyard twang, and his hands, notwithstanding the fancy jewellery, were knobbly and arthritic from past hard labour. In particular, there was a coldness behind the pale blue eyes that warned Crook that there was something devious and predatory under the civilized veneer.

'Mr Sheiling,' Crook said, 'I just wonder if my own hired help is on your payroll, too? First he virtually blackmails me into visiting Stanley Dean in Rosehill gaol; then he pressgangs me into this meeting. I'd dearly like to know what the hell's going on?'

'I wanted to talk to you.' Sheiling fidgeted under Crook's scrutiny. He took a pair of sunglasses from his pocket and put them on. 'Bam-bam's a reasonable guy. He knows I always repay a favour.'

'You could have saved yourself a lot of time and trouble just by picking up the phone,' Crook pointed out.

'I wanted to look you over as well. So you're Paul Crook?' He clicked his tongue. 'I always say, never judge a book by its cover. You don't look anything like what I'd imagined. So you're the guy that shot Benny Cantelo's hand off and put Sam Sati out of business. Pardon my frankness, but lookin' at you, it's hard to believe.'

'I didn't shoot his hand off. The gun he had was defective: it exploded when he tried to use it.'

'I'm only telling it the way I heard it. Don't apologize, son. Any bloke who stomps a bug like Spaghetti Sam gets a big round of applause from my corner. I also heard you killed a guy up in Dubbo.'

'He was trying to kill me.'

'Yeah, well, I agree with the take-out ploy, myself. A stiff in time saves mine, as the saying goes. Well anyway, what did you make of Stan Dean?'

'Dean?' Crook was slow to adjust to the sudden switch. 'I dunno. It's like he's got a cog loose somewhere. One minute he's talking sense, and the next he's away with the birds.'

'Do you reckon he iced that woman he was shacked up with?'

'I just don't know. He says not. What's your interest in Dean, Mr Sheiling?'

'We go back a ways. He used to work for me on and off, but he got too fond of the grog to be reliable. Anyway, I owe him a favour, and now he's all set to collect it.' Sheiling's thin lips stretched in a humourless smile. 'You're the favour he's asked for.'

'Me?'

'You. Stan's got some kind of hang-up about you. He reckons you're the only guy in the world who can find out who did the job on his lady.'

'The police think Dean did it.'

'No way.'

'What makes you so sure?'

'Because—' Sheiling hesitated, as if choosing his answer from several alternatives—'Stan's not a strangler. He's a knuckle artist, a thumper. And then only when he's on the grog. Sober, he's as peaceable as a lamb. Listen, son, I *know* Stan Dean. I know he didn't choke that slag. Let me tell you something. That Mary Thingo was a whatsname.'

'A whatsname?'

'Yeah. You know what I mean.' He clicked his fingers. 'Can't think of the word for the minute. Anyway, Stan met

Mary in a pub, right? Stan was pissed. And when Stan gets pissed, he gets violent. The story goes that she went home with him that night, and he beat the living shit out of her. And she liked it. She moved in permanently with him the very next day. You hear what I'm saying? She *liked* it. She enjoyed being knocked about. She was a whatsit.'

'A masochist?'

'That's the word. That's the exact word.'

'Have you said all this to the police?'

'Aw, come on!' Sheiling banged his fists on his knees in disgust. 'I'm dealing with *you*, not the cops. *You're* the guy Stan wants, and you're the guy he's gonna get. Look, I'm a busy man: let's tie this up right now. Here's the deal: I give you two grand cash money right now, and you go out and find the guy who did this thing. It can't be too hard, for Chrissakes. It's pretty damned obvious what happened. The slut was playing her kinky little games with some pervert, and things just got out of hand. You nose around: you'll flush the bastard out, no sweat.'

Crook said, 'Mr Sheiling, I'll level with you. I'm no great shakes as a detective. I've no training or anything. I just drifted into this job by accident, sort of. You could save money and get better results by talking to the police.'

Sheiling clicked his tongue some more. 'Negative attitude. You disappoint me, young feller. There's something wrong with your hearing, too. I distinctly said no cops. What's the matter? Don't you want the job?'

'Yes.' Curiously, Crook *did* want the job, quite badly. He was surprised at the strength of his own feeling. 'I just didn't want to take it under false pretences.'

'*I* didn't pick you, son, Stan did. I'm doing this as a favour to him.' He took a thick envelope from an inside pocket and handed it to Crook. 'Here's the doin's. So go get 'im, Tiger.'

Crook hesitated. 'It's customary to have a written contract, Mr Sheiling. That way it's easier for me to look after your interests.'

'How do you mean?'

'If you're my official client, I can legally refuse to answer any questions about you or your concerns. I don't even have to reveal your name unless a court orders me to.'

Harry Sheiling uttered a long, whistling sigh. After a moment's contemplation, he lifted a hinged segment of his padded armrest and pressed a button on the console beneath. A panel in the partition behind the driver's seat slid open. 'Wanna cold beer?' he said. He uncapped two stubbies without waiting for an answer and handed one to Crook. 'The way I see it is, we already got a contract. You've taken the job: I've put up the money. What's more, I've given you the crackle up front, 'cause I trust you. I trust you to do a good job for Stan's sake. I trust you not to make a monkey out of me, or blab my name or my business to anybody at all, whether they've got a friggin' court order or not. I trust you implacably. You've taken my money, mate: that makes a contract, in my book. I trust you to look after my interests well, because if you don't I shall send hard, unpleasant men to torch your office and break both your fuckin' legs. I don't see any need for crappy bits of paper. Do you?'

Crook ran a finger round the rim of his collar. 'Since you put it that way,' he said warmly, 'I guess not.'

'That's positive thinking,' Sheiling said. 'I appreciate that. Drink your beer.'

CHAPTER 7

The Arrigo Hall looked as if it had seen good times and bad in its century of existence. Now, was one of the good times. The building was neat and cared-for; its brickwork—dark blue to waist level and cinnamon-yellow above—was clean; and the stone arches above the main door and the tall windows had been sympathetically restored. However, past brutalities had left indelible marks. The roof, once steeply pitched, was now flat, leaving gable ends pointing uselessly at the sky; and the drainpipes and guttering had been ruthlessly modernized. A brass plate in the centre of the massive door announced that this was the registered office of the Arrigo Choral Society.

Crook pushed the door open and entered a room so dimly lit that at first he could see nothing but vague shadows. The heavy door swung to behind him, cutting off all outside sounds; the sudden deathly silence was startling and slightly unnerving. The only illumination came from a small window high in the opposite wall: by its light Crook could make out that he was in a square, box-like foyer with several doors, all closed. No lights showed under any of the doors; and the oppressive silence suggested that no one was about. Crook cleared his throat self-consciously and called 'Anyone there?' with no expectation of a reply.

Almost immediately the door to his right opened, flooding the room with light; and a voice demanded sharply, 'Are you from the Agency?' It was a woman's voice, deep and authoritative.

'The Agency?' Crook repeated stupidly. He blinked and held up his hand to shield his eyes from the sudden glare. The woman was a featureless silhouette against the light. 'I didn't know I was expected. Did Mrs Parsons phone you?' It was typical of Mrs P. to try to smooth his path, Crook thought.

'I phoned *them*,' the woman said crisply. 'Come along.' She preceded Crook through double doors marked *Members Only* into a large, high-ceilinged room. The contrast with the gloom of the foyer could not have been greater: this room glittered with light and colour. The parquet floor shone; there were bright tapestries on the whitewashed walls. Tall windows sparkled on either side; and framing the windows, loose-weaved curtains hung from ceiling to floor. There was a stack of folding chairs in one corner; and at the far end of the hall a young man stood near a grand piano, sorting papers.

'I must say,' the woman commented, 'that I wasn't expecting them to send a *man*. But times change. I suppose you young people take whatever job you can get, nowadays.' She was a short, sturdy woman: in her early sixties, as far as Crook could judge. Her white hair was tightly permed; and her pleated skirt, tailored jacket and floppy bow tie gave her an oddly stagy look, at once girlish and old-fashioned. 'Right,' she said, making a gesture which encompassed the hall and everything in it. 'This is it.' She paused, as if expecting a reaction. 'What's your name, by the way?'

'Crook. Paul Crook.'

'Right, Paul. I'm Mrs Want, and the gentleman down there by the piano is Mr Trimmer.' She lowered her voice. 'Please remember *at all times* that your task here is to assist *me*, and not to run errands for Mr Trimmer, however persuasive or importunate he may be.'

'I'm sorry, Mrs Want,' Crook said, 'but I'm afraid we're at cross-purposes. I'm from the Agre Detective Agency.'

'The what Agency?' Mrs Want stepped backwards and adopted a stately pose of horror and disbelief, one hand pressed against her bowtie. 'Are you some kind of policeman?'

'Not exactly.' Crook swallowed hard. 'I'm a private investigator. I'm making inquiries about the circumstances of Mary Dean's murder.'

Mrs Want bridled. 'To what end? We—that is, the permanent staff here and all our membership—have suffered exhaustive questioning by the police about that unfortunate creature. I understand, moreover, that they have in fact charged someone with the crime. What purpose can be served by your pestering us further?'

'My client believes that they may have charged the wrong man,' Crook said evenly. 'We simply want to be sure that justice is properly served.'

'Fiddlesticks!' To Crook's confusion and dismay, Mrs Want snapped her fingers under his nose. 'You simply want an excuse to pry into other people's business. You shall not do it here, young man: not while I am in charge. Leave!' In her grandest manner, Mrs Want pointed to the double doors, in case Crook had forgotten where they were. 'Leave immediately!'

Crook was not going to make any headway against such determined opposition. He left. At the doors, he looked back, curious to see if she was still pointing the way. She was. Her chin was held high; and she looked for all the world as if she was expecting a round of applause.

The man caught up with Crook at the corner of the street and touched him on the sleeve. 'You mustn't judge Dottie Want too harshly. She always does her Edith Evans imitation when she's nervous. She's terrified of losing her job.'

Closer to, the man didn't look as young as Crook had thought, by a good ten years. 'Mr Trimmer?' He mentally congratulated himself on remembering the name.

'Call me Ian. Can we talk? I usually take coffee at Cafferty's at this hour of the morning. Would you care to join me?'

'Sure.' Crook wondered whether Trimmer had suggested Cafferty's because it was chic and expensive, or because it was a discreet distance away from the Arrigo Hall. 'Just what do you want to talk about, Ian?'

'The murder, of course. I was intrigued to hear you say that the police might have charged the wrong man. That is really rather a terrifying thought. If true, it means that the real murderer is still at large, and could strike again.'

He was inviting confidences, but Crook refused the hint. He suspected that this source of information would dry up once Trimmer's curiosity was satisfied. 'Why should my visit make Mrs Want nervous?'

'Dorothy's fairly neurotic at the best of times. This Mary

Dean business has shattered her completely. She believes the members are blaming her.'

'Blaming her? For the murder?'

Trimmer laughed explosively. 'No, no. For the *fuss*. Police and reporters swarming all over the place, asking questions, taking down names and addresses, checking *alibis*, for God's sake! These people—the members—are very tall poppies indeed, my friend. They do not like to be interrogated by elements of the lower classes. Arrigo is called a Choral Society, but in fact it's one of the most exclusive clubs in Sydney.'

'But however important they are, these people can't expect to be spared the inconvenience of a murder inquiry,' Crook said. 'Surely they don't blame Mrs Want for that?'

'Dottie feels responsible for Mary Dean being at Arrigo at all. She wangled the job for her. They were old cronies from way back.' Trimmer suddenly stopped in mid-stride and rapped his forehead with his fingertips. 'Excuse me, I've just remembered something I neglected to do.' He took a small notebook and pencil from his hip pocket. 'If I don't make a note of it, I'll forget it again.'

Crook now had his first chance to look at Ian Trimmer properly. He saw a tall, spare man with a round, soft-looking face and dark wavy hair. The eyes were the most striking feature: large and brown and fringed with incredibly long lashes. Cow's eyes, Crook thought maliciously: the kind of eyes that women go soony over. The clothes were what had deceived Crook about his age. At first glance, the baggy sweater, wrinkled slacks and scuffed trainers would not have been out of place on a teenage student; except that the average student would have been hard pressed to afford them. It might look casual, but it was all expensive, designer-label gear.

Trimmer put the notebook away. 'Sorry about that. I'm cursed with a thoroughly disorganized mind. I have to write notes to myself all the time.'

It occurred to Crook that writing notes to oneself was

the sign of an organized mind, but he offered no comment.
Trimmer set off at a rapid pace, as if to make up for lost
time, and Crook fell in beside him. 'Tell me something
about this Music Society, Ian,' he suggested. 'What do *you*
do, for instance?'

'I,' Trimmer said, with a touch of archness, 'am an assistant to the Musical Director. Not, you will note, *the* Assistant Musical Director. The distinction is quite important,
in an outfit like Arrigo. *The* Assistant MD would be a somebody. *An* assistant MD is a dogsbody.'

'But what do you do?'

'I *assist*, dear boy. I play the piano for rehearsals, I am
the répétiteur for the soloists, I coach the non-readers in
their parts, I share the job of librarian with Dottie; and I
am general nursemaid to our distinguished conductor, Wolf
Kirche. That is to say, I mark up the orchestral and vocal
scores in letters large enough for him to read; and on the
numerous occasions when he is too drunk to stand up on
his own, I take him home and put him to bed.'

They had reached Cafferty's, and Crook could ask no
further questions until Trimmer had attended to the important business of ordering coffee for them both and a substantial slab of cheesecake for himself. 'I know I can't resist
it,' he admitted with child-like frankness, 'so I don't even
try.' It was clear from his welcome at Cafferty's that he
was a regular and valued customer, which answered one
of Crook's questions: Trimmer's motive in bringing him
here was not so much discretion as greed.

He was glad that he could look directly into Trimmer's
face when he asked his next question: 'What really made
you decide to talk to me, Ian? Is something about the case
bothering you? Do you think something's been covered up?'

'Oh no!' It was impossible to tell from Trimmer's goggle-
eyed expression whether he was horrified or amused. In his
way, he was just as theatrical in style as Mrs Want. 'It's
just that—well, golly, after *The Copper File* programme on
TV, I assumed that the whole thing had been wrapped up.

I mean, that woman practically *said* that the husband had done it. I couldn't see them making an accusation like that on TV without bags of proof. But then you come along and say that the husband could be innocent, for gosh sakes! I have to admit, I'm agog with curiosity. I mean, if not the husband, then who, for gosh sakes? Has some new evidence turned up?'

'Nothing that I'm allowed to discuss as yet,' Crook replied deceitfully. 'Did you know Mary Dean well?'

'Oh, you know how it is when you work with people but don't mix socially. You know them and you don't, in a manner of speaking. I mean, I knew that her husband beat her up occasionally: everybody knew that. Also, I knew that she'd worked in the theatre years ago,—that's where she met Dorothy Want. Actually, she reminded me that our paths had crossed back in '87, when we were both working on a show for the Lachlan Organization; but since I was the musical director, and she was a dresser or some-thing, it's not surprising that I didn't remember her.'

'What was the name of the show?'

'Oh gosh, I can't remember. *The Golden* something, I think. I could look it up if it's important.'

Crook nodded his thanks. 'I need to talk to somebody who knew Mary Dean really well. At the moment she's just a name, as far as I am concerned: I know hardly anything about her. I don't even know what she looked like.'

'Small, mousey woman. Little doll-like features.' Trim-mer tilted his head back and frowned at the ceiling, as if striving for photographic recall. 'Dowdy,' he said finally. 'Dull.'

'My client thinks that if we could get to understand the woman, we might begin to understand why she was murdered.'

'Mm.' Trimmer chased the last crumbs of cheesecake round his plate with his fork. 'You know, that's not as far-fetched as it sounds, now I think about it. Mary had a sort of manner—how can I describe it?—that *invited* cruelty. She would look at you as if she was frightened of you, and visibly flinch if you stepped close. And yet you knew that she wasn't afraid of you at all: quite the reverse. It was a sexual invitation: it was her way of flirting.'

This was a variation on a theme Crook had heard before. 'Did she flirt with everybody? Or anyone in particular?'

Trimmer held up his hands in protest. 'No, no, I'm expressing myself badly. Forget flirting—I was just being fanciful and Freudian when I said that. There was something in her personality: a kind of dog-like cringe, that seemed to expect pain. It almost made one want to inflict pain, out of exasperation. But if you're asking was she involved with anyone at Arrigo, the answer is no, definitely not. The police checked and double-checked everybody— the whole membership, even including people who couldn't possibly have done it.' He looked pointedly at his watch and signalled to the waiter for the bill.

Crook said, 'You mentioned that Mrs Want was an old friend of Mary Dean's. I guess she's the one I really ought to talk to. Do you have any influence with her?'

'Oh, I doubt you'd get anywhere with Dottie, not after that scene this morning. There are few things on earth more stubborn than a stupid and frightened old woman.' The malice in the words contrasted sharply with Trimmer's pleasantly bland expression. He heaved himself to his feet, paused, then rapped himself on the forehead, exactly reproducing the gesture he had used earlier. '*The Golden Governess*,' he said. 'That was it. That was the name of the show. It did well in Melbourne but fizzed out here in Sydney. The local critics generally rubbish a show that Melbourne has approved. It's a tribal tradition.'

'*The Golden Governess*,' Crook repeated. 'That could be useful. Thanks.' He wasn't going to get much more out of Trimmer, but he could try. 'Don't you miss the theatrical life? I couldn't tell whether you were being serious when you described your job at Arrigo, but you sounded pretty disenchanted.'

'Oh, it's all *right*,' Trimmer said carelessly. 'It's well paid, and there are perks. I get free accommodation—a small apartment next to the Chapel—and plenty of free time to teach privately, which is what I really enjoy. In fact—' the smooth, round face looked insufferably smug—'I was with a pupil—and a rather grand personage at that—the afternoon Mary was murdered. I probably had the most *distinguished* alibi of the lot.'

They parted company outside the restaurant. 'I'd love to know how you get on.' Trimmer clasped Crook's hand warmly. 'Do keep in touch.'

'I'll do that,' Crook promised. He waited until Trimmer was out of sight, then hunted vainly through his pockets for a piece of paper. Finally he wrote on the back of his cheque-book:

1. *The Golden Governess*
2. Ian Trimmer
3. Dorothy Want

He regarded the list with a certain pride. It felt like a solid achievement: a proper morning's work. Absent-mindedly, he doodled question-marks around Ian Trimmer's name. The guy had been helpful enough—compared with Mrs Want, anyway—but had he also been manipulative? Had he told Crook only the things he wanted him to know? Had he left anything out? And if so, what? And why?

Crook grinned mirthlessly. He was getting to be as suspicious as a proper detective. He put the list away, and then took it out and studied it again. Thoughtfully, he added another item:

4. Buy notebook

CHAPTER 8

'I niver saw the piece meself,' Barney Crook said heartily. 'But I know somebody who would've. I'll give him a ring.'

'Pa, I wish you wouldn't shout.' Crook rubbed his ear and held the receiver at a distance. His father tended to address the telephone as if he was playing to a capacity house.

Barney snorted indignantly. 'I was using the far-speak machine before you were born,' he bellowed implacably. 'Anyway, I've niver been one of your modern mumblers. Are you at your office?'

'Yes.'

'Wait there while I call you back.'

Mrs Parsons brought in some papers as soon as Crook put the phone down. 'Here's all the data we have on Harry Sheiling, Mr Paul,' she said. 'Frankly, it doesn't amount to much. He's obviously a very rich man, but since all his companies are privately owned, it's impossible to say exactly how rich. He owns at least seven interlocking companies, all of them in the automobile business. The largest, in terms of people employed, is HS Fleet Services, which supplies company cars on a rental basis to small and medium-sized firms. The other companies are mainly ancillary—garages, repair shops, car dealerships.'

'Anything dodgy about his operation, Mrs P.?'

She considered carefully before answering. 'It's impossible to tell from this data, Mr Paul. Generally speaking, the motor trade is known to offer opportunities for sharp practice. Do you have any grounds for suspicion?'

'Mrs P., the man talked like a gangster. Very convincingly. He damn near scared me to death.'

Mrs Parsons allowed herself one of her rare smiles. The thought of her Mr Paul being afraid of anything or anyone was quite amusing. 'Well, if there *is* anything untoward, I'm sure Mr Basil will ferret it out. He has invaluable contacts in the underworld.'

'You sent Bam-bam out to investigate Harry Sheiling?'

'No, Mr Paul. Mr Basil indicated that he had received his instructions from you.'

'What!' Crook was both exasperated and alarmed. 'I hope the old fool knows what he's doing. Harry Sheiling's got the social instincts of a man-eating shark.'

'Oh, Mr Basil can take care of himself,' Mrs Parsons said confidently. 'There's a keen intellect within that muscular frame.'

Crook was momentarily speechless. This image of Bam-bam was so far removed from his own that he was stumped for an adequate response. Fortunately at that moment the phone rang.

It was Barney, sounding pleased with himself. 'I've found your man for ye,' he boomed triumphantly. 'Name's Bobby Cooper. He played the father in *The Golden Governess*. Gossipy old queen. If there was any scandal in that company, you can be sure that Bobby will have clocked it.'

'Good work, Pa,' Crook said warmly. 'Give me his phone number and I'll contact him right away.'

'I've already done that, boy. He'll see you tonight. But you'd better get over here beforehand, so's I can brief you. You'll not get anywhere at all with Bobby unless you're properly rehearsed.'

Crook's spirits sank again. 'Pa, are you trying to tell me that this Cooper guy is some kind of nutcase?'

'Not at all. He's just a nervy and insecure old woman, is all. He needs handling right: flattering, you know. I'll put you in the picture. Anyway—' Barney's voice throbbed with pathos—'I haven't seen much of you, these last months.'

This was true enough. In his preoccupation with Robyn, Crook had neglected everything and everyone. He swept the papers from his desk into an empty drawer. 'I'll get over there right away.'

'Good lad. It'll be fine to see ye.' In a tone so casual that Crook knew it was no afterthought, Barney added, 'Call in at the deli on the way, will you? I've not a thing to eat in the house.'

The briefing had been as thorough as Barney could make it, but there hadn't been time to cover everything. The outside of Bobby Cooper's house offered no surprises: it was just as pretty as Crook had expected it to be, with honeysuckle round the windows and plump-buttocked ala-baster Cupids simpering on either side of the front door. But nothing Barney had said had adequately prepared Crook for his first sight of Bobby himself. Crook had been warned about the lipstick, the rouge, the plucked eyebrows and the innumerable ropes of pearls; but what he could not have foreseen was that his host would be dressed from head to foot as Mary, Queen of Scots.

It was not a particularly becoming costume for a fat little man with several chins, but he wore it with pride and panache. 'You must be young Paul,' he said throatily. 'Come in, dear.' He left just enough room for Crook to slip past him, then slammed the door shut and secured it with an impressive number of bolts and chains. 'This way, lovey.' His skirts rustled as he preceded Crook through a hallway lined with theatrical posters. 'Come and meet Roger.'

The room they entered was so crammed with furniture and bric-à-brac that Crook froze in the doorway, afraid to move lest he should demolish something. Every available surface was covered with small, fragile objects. A spindly sideboard bore up bravely under the weight of a whole army of china figurines, all facing one way, and so tightly packed together that they looked like some miniature politi-cal rally. Tables, shelves and cabinets sported tiny tea-sets, snuff boxes, thimbles, vases, bowls and a whole menagerie of glass animals. A pair of ballgowns, in blue silk and silver lamé, were pinned like butterflies to opposite walls, and around them hung a haphazard miscellany of paintings, photographs, plates, fans, masks and horse-brasses. An imitation log fire flickered in the fireplace, and above the overcrowded mantelpiece a brass blunderbuss was bracketed by a pair of duelling sabres.

Bobby Cooper observed Crook's expression with satisfaction. 'I *know*, dear. Everybody feels the same when they first set eyes on our little shrine. It's—'

He paused, and Crook recognized his first cue. 'Aladdin's Cave,' he murmured reverentially, blessing Barney's forethought.

Bobby was delighted. 'Everyone says that, dear. I suppose it's true, but we like to think of it as our personal little museum.'

It was not the royal 'we', Crook realized. Standing in front of the fireplace was an immensely tall man in a kind of military uniform. It was no ordinary uniform. In wide-eyed wonder, Crook took in the skin-tight pink riding breeches, the patent leather knee boots and the high-collared cutaway jacket in red satin. The jacket had wide, gold-faced lapels and epaulettes like overhanging balconies. The man's pill-box hat almost touched the ceiling, and was prettily adorned with a double row of sequins. Under the hat was a round, very red face and an enormous black moustache. Crook bit hard on his lower lip and willed away the hysteria fluttering in his stomach.

'This is Roger,' Bobby Cooper said majestically. 'Roger, let me introduce young Paul, Barney Crook's boy.'

Roger clicked his heels and made a creaky salute. 'I'll tell you something,' he said, winking broadly. 'The tickler comes off.' He slowly peeled the moustache from his upper lip and stuck it on his forehead.

Bobby squealed with laughter. 'Stop it, Roger! You'll give me a pain.' He took Crook by the wrist and led him to a high-backed armchair. 'He just slays me when he does that,' he confided hoarsely. 'He's so witty, he's positively dangerous to be with.'

Crook slid his notebook from his pocket. If his father's assessment was right, it was time to play his opening gambit, and to play it without a hint of subtlety. He arranged his face into a mask of artlessness and spoke the lines Barney had made him rehearse: 'Mr Cooper, I hope you won't think I'm taking advantage of your open-hearted welcome if I ask for your autograph?' He still thought it was way over the top, but Barney had a habit of being right about such matters.

'Oh my dear!' Bobby went pink with pleasure. He glanced quickly at Roger, then briefly covered his eyes with his hand. 'You can't possibly remember an old stick like me. You're far too young.'

Crook was growing rather pink himself. He tried to ease his conscience by sticking to the literal truth: 'I've heard so much about you from my pa. He said that when he was courting my mother, he took her to all your shows. He told me that your performance in *The Rose Rosella* was quite legendary.' Barney had actually said 'unbelievable', but Crook accidentally substituted one ambiguous word for another.

'Legendary?' Bobby's lip trembled and he fumbled shakily with his pearls. 'Excuse me just one moment.' He lifted his skirts and fled, threading his way nimbly through the close-packed furniture. Outside the door he made a sound like an old-fashioned motor horn. He was blowing his nose.

Roger wrapped the moustache round his fingers like a hairy Band-aid. 'He's blubbing,' he observed sombrely. 'Bobby's blubbing. It's the memories, you see. He used to be so . . .' He moved both arms in wide circles, as if he was doing the breast stroke. The word eluded him and he abandoned the chase. 'That show—*Rosie*—that was umpteen years ago. Before you were born. You couldn't have seen it.'

'No.' Crook was still embarrassed. 'My father told me about it.'

'*I* saw it,' Roger said. 'I saw that show fifty-seven times. I didn't know Bobby then.' The moustache dropped from his fingers and he stooped arthritically to pick it up. After a moment's contemplation, he draped it round the shoulders of a china shepherdess. 'But that was when I fell in love with him,' he said simply. 'Been in love ever since.' His long face drooped. 'I hope you haven't come here to laugh at him.'

'No. I've come to ask his help.'

'I don't want him hurt,' Roger said. '*I* don't mind being laughed at: I've never been anybody. But he was—*is*—one of the greats.'

Bobby bustled back, smelling of fresh powder and eau-de-Cologne. He held out a rather dog-eared photograph. 'There! Will that do?'

The face that grinned confidently out of the studio portrait was of a young man of about Crook's own age. But the slicked-down hair, the wide-spread shirt collar and the neatly folded cravat all spoke of fashions long forgotten: Crook guessed that the photograph must be all of forty years old. Yet although the face was not particularly handsome, it was easy to see why Bobby Cooper had been such a favourite. Barney had said, 'He had the priceless gift of being able to look cheeky and wistful at the same time. Audiences loved him.'

Across the young actor's shirt front, the old actor had written, *To My Friend Paul, with Love and Hugs, Bobby*.

Crook was feeling decidedly shabby by this time, but luckily Bobby mistook his discomfiture for shyness. He brushed aside Crook's shamefaced thanks. 'It's nothing, dear, really. I signed it out in the kitchen because the light's so much better there.'

Roger snorted. 'Vain old tart,' he said without malice. 'You just didn't want him to see you with your specs on. Vain old tart.'

'Silly old faggot,' Bobby said affectionately. They both laughed, the familiar exchange warmed by a thousand repetitions. Bobby said, 'I'd like you to have this, too.' He handed Crook a picture postcard.

If the photograph had been in colour, Crook might have recognized its subject immediately. As it was, he had to read the lettering at the bottom of the card before the penny dropped. 'It's—'

'Yes!' Bobby chortled. 'It was his finest hour.'

The postcard showed a picture of Roger dressed in exactly the same uniform he was now wearing. The caption at the foot of the picture read 'Roger de Lannion as Lord Cardie in *Oh! Flo!*'

'Thirty-seven years ago,' Bobby breathed. 'He was magnificent. And he can still get into the same costume!' He cocked his head sideways and looked into Crook's face, studying his reaction.

Crook at last realized he had been given another cue. Hastily he said, 'I wonder if Mr de Lannion—?'

'Call him Rog, dear. And call me Bobby. There's nothing grand about us, not these days.' He carried the card over to Roger. 'The nice young man wants your autograph too, Pooh-face.'

'Feller's got taste,' Roger said gruffly. He held the postcard against the wall and made some jagged and illegible marks on it.

Bobby clapped his hands. 'Now we can all sit down and talk. How about a little drinkie?'

Roger stroked his upper lip and leered horribly. 'Madeira, m'dear?'

Bobby shrieked. 'Stop it, Roger, you'll give me a pain! How can we talk seriously when you're playing the giddy ass? Now take off your buskins and do your Ganymede, there's a sweetie.'

Roger pulled off his boots and put on carpet slippers. When he straightened up, he was a good nine inches shorter than before. 'Golly, it's warmer down here,' he said. Tucking his boots under his arm, he tiptoed from the room.

Bobby sat down on a pretty Victorian sofa. 'You probably think we're quite mad. We always dress up for visitors. People's lives are so dull, nowadays; Rog and I like to redress the balance with a smidgin of fun and colour. And love,' he added, his eyes misting a little under his pencilled brows. 'Have you ever been in love, young Paul?'

Crook had a sudden vivid memory of Robyn, unconscious on her hospital bed. 'Yes,' he said. And then with more emphasis, 'Oh yes.'

'Fun is the key to making it last,' Bobby said. 'Laughter is the key. Make her laugh, and she'll love you for ever. Now, your dad said you wanted to ask me something about *The Golden Governess?*'

'There was a woman employed on that show—as a dresser, I think. I want to find out all about her and if possible talk to someone who knew her well.'

'A dresser? What was her name?'

'Her first name was Mary. I don't know what her second name was at that time.'

'Hm.' Bobby pushed his headdress to a rakish angle and scratched at his forehead. 'Let me think who was in that show. There was George and Randolph and Laura—that's it! Laura's dresser was a Mary something.'

'Kafko,' Roger said from the doorway. He carried in a tray with three small glasses. 'Mary Kafko. The Conjuror's Widow.' He made it sound like the title of a play.

'That's right!' Bobby exclaimed in wonder. 'Now, how did you come to remember that? You weren't in that show.' He looked at Roger with some dismay. '*Were* you?'

Roger glanced heavenward and shook his head. 'I was your dresser, you stupid old tart.' He set the tray down and handed a glass to Crook.

'Of course you were, dear.' Bobby picked up his glass and sipped delicately. 'Of *course* you were.' He made haste to explain to Crook: 'We like to stay together, when we can. I would have been *his* dresser, if it had been t'other way about.'

'Only it never was,' Roger observed drily. He sat down with some effort, supporting his weight with both hands on the arms of his chair.

'Mary Kafko.' Bobby squeezed his eyes shut, striving for some visual memory. 'May one ask why you're interested in her?'

'I've been hired to find out something about her past,' Crook said.

'Why is her past so interesting? Has she suddenly become famous?'

'In a way. She was murdered a few days ago.'

'Huh!' Roger glared fiercely at the fireplace. His head shook. 'Can't say I'm surprised.'

Bobby leaned over and touched his hand. 'Why not, dear? What have you remembered?'

'The woman was destined for a bad end,' Roger said disgustedly. 'She was a thief.'

'A thief?' Crook was not finding it easy to build up a consistent picture of the late Mary Dean. Everyone he spoke to had a different view of her.

'Rog, you're just saying that to be nasty,' Bobby said reproachfully. 'Just because you didn't like the woman.'

'She was a thief,' Roger repeated. 'And a wanton strumpet.'

'She was nothing of the kind, dear. All that hoo-hah about things being stolen—it was all a false alarm, don't you remember? Everything that had gone missing turned up again. It was either a case of people being careless, or—' Bobby faltered under Roger's scornful gaze—'somebody was playing a silly prank.'

'Silly prank!' Roger was grandly contemptuous. 'Malicious mischief, more likely. You know what it's like backstage when there's a thief about.'

Bobby shuddered. 'It's a truly dreadful atmosphere, dear,' he explained to Crook. 'Everybody suspects everybody else. But anyway, there was no thief, because nothing was stolen. Nobody lost anything.'

'Laura did.'

'So she said. But it couldn't have been anything terribly valuable, because she flatly refused to bring the police into it. She actually only mentioned it once.'

Crook steered them back to the subject of Mary Dean. 'You suggested that she was promiscuous as well as a thief,' he said to Roger. 'What made you say that?'

Bobby giggled and bit his lip. 'Tell him, dear.'

Roger's face went a deeper shade of red. 'Because that's what she was,' he said angrily. 'A wanton strumpet.'

'You can't leave it like that.' Bobby rocked with silent laughter. 'Tell him all, dear.'

'Huh!' Roger snorted again, then half-smiled in spite of himself. 'Shut your silly fat face, you old tart.'

'She propositioned him,' Bobby cackled. 'She offered him the freedom of her sweaty little body.'

'It was the *words* she used,' Roger said stiffly. 'Disgusting. The things she asked me to do to her! Well, anyway, I soon put a flea in her ear. I am not that kind of person, I told her.'

'She wanted to be knocked about,' Bobby said bluntly. 'That's what lit her pathetic little flame. She would turn up for work with bruises on her face, black eyes, cut lips, the lot. The rumour was that she shacked up with one fellow—a security guard—who damn near killed her. Roger's right: it isn't really surprising when a woman like that comes to a violent end.'

This, at any rate, was a point of view that Crook had heard before. 'Is there anything else you can tell me about her?'

Both men shook their heads. 'Apart from her nasty little fetish, she wasn't really very interesting,' Bobby said.

'What about the show's musical director, Ian Trimmer? Was he interesting?'

Roger and Bobby glanced at each other, eyebrows raised. 'You first, dear,' Bobby said.

Roger said flatly, 'No, he wasn't interesting. He was a stuck-up little twerp.'

'A baby-snatcher,' Bobby added primly. 'Thirty years old, if he was a day, and having it off with a seventeen-year-old chorus girl. Wait a minute, I'll tell you who she was.' He took a theatre programme from the folder on his knee. 'Here we are—Amy Truelove. Her name was for real, believe it or not.'

Crook scribbled the name in his notebook. 'I'd like to borrow that programme and have it photocopied, if I may?'

'Of course, dear. But only if you promise to bring it back in person, and tell us all the gossip.'

'The Laura you mentioned—' Crook consulted the programme—'that would be Laura Farrant?'

'That's right, dear. The so-called star of the show.'

'Any idea where she could be contacted?'

'You could check the Yellow Pages,' Roger drawled. 'Look under S for Slut.'

'Ignore him, dear.' Bobby made a *moue* of apology to Crook. 'He's just a naughty old puss. La Farrant lives in Melbourne: she had a house in Toorak, I think. Rumour has it that she's being kept by "Hog" Wheeler.' He clearly expected Crook to recognize the name.

'Is he in the theatre, too?' Crook asked.

Bobby laughed. 'God knows, dear. I wouldn't bet against it. He's in more things than you could shake a stick at. Made a fortune in the nickel boom of the 'seventies and he's gone on making money ever since.'

'Not a nice man,' Roger said.

Bobby agreed. 'Not a nice man at all.'

Crook was still leafing through the programme. A name leapt up from the mass of credits near the end. 'I see that Dorothy Want was the Wardrobe Mistress.'

'Oh, do you know her, dear?'

'We've met. Briefly.' Crook was trying to remember

whether Ian Trimmer had mentioned her in connection
with this show. 'She was rather grand, in a theatrical way.'

'That would be Dorothy,' Roger said. 'A weird lady.
Good at her job, though. She'd been a leading light in the
am-drams in her youth, and she never got over it.'

'Was she friendly with Mary Dean—Kafko, as she was
then?'

Roger pursed his lips. 'Yes, she was. But I'll tell you a
funny thing. Although Dorothy was a good fifteen years
older than Mary, she seemed to defer to her. They seemed
almost like mother and daughter, but a mother and daughter who had switched roles, if you see what I mean..' He was
suddenly embarrassed by this flight of fancy, and squirmed
uneasily in his chair. 'That's what I thought, anyway,' he
muttered.

'That's very helpful,' Crook said mendaciously. He
judged that he had garnered as much information as he
was likely to get, and prepared to leave. Bobby escorted
him to the door. 'You can see why I'm devoted to Rog,' he
said. 'He's so witty. Oscar Wilde, eat your heart out, that's
what I always say. Remember what I told you, young
Barney's boy: you make your love laugh, and you'll keep
her for ever.'

'I'll bear that in mind, Bobby.' Crook had a sharp, stab-
bing memory of Robyn's smile. 'Thank you.'

'You look sad, dear,' Bobby said worriedly. 'Don't be
sad. Come and give old Bobby a hug.'

Crook gave him a hug.

CHAPTER 9

Chief Inspector Joseph Ricordi, as elegantly dressed as
ever, strolled into the Agre Agency offices early the following morning. He was a slim, solemn, darkly handsome
young man who prided himself on his level-headedness and

sang-froid. He was in fact a good and conscientious cop, although he had a number of prejudices in common with his fellow officers. In particular, like most of his colleagues, he took the view that your average private investigator was a distinct pain in the ass. What's more, personal observation had convinced him that private investigator Paul Crook was immature, inexperienced and as thick as two short planks. However, against his better judgement, he quite liked the kid.

Ricordi had not visited the Agre Agency for some time, and he was impressed by the general air of industry and efficiency. He noted that another desk had been squeezed into the outer office, and that there were now three attractive young women working at the computer terminals. The recession didn't seem to be hitting the private-eye business.

Crook's spirits were not cheered by the sight of his visitor. He always felt dim and mediocre in Ricordi's presence. The guy was so dapper, so self-possessed; and worst of all, so goddam handsome. Robyn had liked him a lot.

'Trouble, Joe?' That was another thing: Ricordi and trouble were closely associated in Crook's mind.

'No.' Ricordi, who did everything gracefully, reinforced the denial with a graceful gesture of the hand. 'This isn't official. I was just passing, and I thought I'd drop by.'

He sat down in one of the armchairs facing the desk. 'I was just wondering—have you had any recent news about Rob . . . about Miss Paget?'

'Not recent, no,' Crook said carefully. 'You heard that she came out of the coma OK?'

'Yes, I heard that. I sent her a card. Got a thank-you note from her pa. He said that the accident had left her a bit shook up, but she was going to be just fine. He needn't have taken the trouble to reply: it was only a card.' Ricordi was silent for a moment, eyeing Crook's face. 'How is she, really?'

'She's . . .' Crook wished he knew the answer. 'The prognosis is quite good,' he said bleakly. 'The medical team say she's improving all the time.'

'That's good, that's really good news.' Ricordi's expression stayed as serious as ever. 'I hear she's seeing a shrink?'

Shock thickened Crook's voice. 'Who told you that?'

'It's true, then?'

'There is some—' Crook struggled to remember Garland's exact phrase—'psychological damage, yes. Nothing too serious.' He moved his hand sideways across his desk as if he was smoothing fabric with his fingers. 'Who told you about it?'

'I have friends in Perth,' Ricordi said evasively. 'Actually, they rang last night to tell me that she's no longer in that hospital, and the authorities won't say where she's been moved to, or why. I was worried in case . . . I mean, I was just curious to know whether she's OK?'

'As far as I know, she is.'

'Does that mean you don't know for sure?'

Crook hated to admit it. 'Yes.'

'But on the other hand—' Ricordi was determined to be optimistic—'if there had been any serious problem I'm sure you would have been the first to hear about it. She told me last year that you and she were very close; "an item", is the way she put it.'

Crook didn't try to answer. Suddenly all the old heartsickness was back, as searingly painful as ever. He was tempted to confide in this man. It would be a relief to unburden his heart, to talk about Robyn to someone who knew and admired her; but Crook couldn't bring himself to do it. There were some things that couldn't be said, couldn't yet be faced.

With deliberate tact, Ricordi moved smoothly to another topic. 'I hear you're interested in the Mary Dean case. Mind telling me why?'

'Somebody's paying me to look into it.' Crook's face was

pale and hostile. He smoothed the imaginary fabric again. 'Is that a problem for you guys?'

'I couldn't say. It's not a problem for me personally, because I'm not on that case, thank God. It's turning into a regular dog's breakfast.'

'In what way?'

'I ought not to tell you but I will, since you're in the family, so to speak.' Ricordi half smiled. 'On the side of the angels, I mean. The fact is, there's a bit of friction building up among the top brass. Do you remember Graham Mintlaw? You met him a couple of times, I know.'

'I'm not likely to forget him. That guy is a human steam-roller.'

'He speaks very well of you, too. Anyway, Mintlaw is unhappy with the way the case has been handled. The Investigating Officer, one Albert Rocco, aka Bert Thicko to his associates, was in a hurry to bring in a result inside the budget. Mintlaw thinks the collar was over-hasty.'

Crook was out of his depth again. 'What does "inside the budget" mean?'

'Policing is paid for out of public funds,' Ricordi explained patiently. 'It's not a bottomless purse. If a single investigation costs too much, then things get out of balance and other services start to suffer. The politicians get restless. A quick result saves taxpayer's money and is very popular with our political masters.'

'Does that mean—' Crook wanted to be sure he'd got it right—'that if an investigation costs too much, it gets called off?'

'Of course not!' But Ricordi's indignation was only skin deep. 'An investigation is never abandoned. Not really. But if it gets stalled, if there are no new developments, it's just plain inefficient to leave squads of trained people hanging around twiddling their thumbs.'

'So you shove the case into the files and wait for something to turn up?'

Ricordi didn't deny it. 'Only a brutally cynical person would put it that way,' he said smoothly.

Crook abandoned the digression. 'Are you telling me that Mintlaw believes that Stanley Dean is innocent?'

'Not at all. What he thinks is that Rocco shouldn't have made the pinch until the evidence was absolutely water-tight. Right now, the only evidence that isn't circumstantial—the only thing they can actually *prove*—is that Dean lied about his alibi. He claimed he spent the day with an old guy called Ashley Stuker, but according to the local Health Visitor, who called on Ashley that arvo, Dean certainly wasn't anywhere around. Who are you working for, by the way?'

'You know I can't tell you that,' Crook said primly.

'Meaning your client wants to keep his name out of it. That's interesting. I wonder why?'

'I thought you said the Dean case was no concern of yours?'

'Just trying to help out.' Ricordi's expression remained unreadable. 'If I were in your shoes, though, I'd be asking myself why anybody other than Stanley himself would be concerned about Stanley's innocence. However, that's your business. I was telling you why Graham Mintlaw is not best pleased with the evidence in the Dean affair. Mintlaw hates loose ends; and this case is full of them. For instance, there's the problem of the dog.'

'What dog?'

'Good question. According to our lab experts, it's one of those little wire-haired terriers. Now, the Deans didn't own a dog; and none of their neighbours has a terrier. So why was the left side of Mary's coat smothered in dog hairs?'

Crook thought at first that Ricordi was going to answer his own question, but then saw that he was expected to contribute. 'If the hairs were as localized as you say, she must have been lying—or had fallen—on some surface where the dog had been. A carpet or rug, maybe.' He saw that more was expected of him. ' "Smothered in hairs"

possibly suggests a confined space. The floor of a van, perhaps. Or the back seat of a car.'

'A car, yes, that's quite possible. Now the evidence about
the car is really interesting.' He waited blandly for Crook
to pick up the cue.

Crook sighed. 'Tell me about the car.'

'OK. Three witnesses have come forward to say that
someone answering Stanley Dean's description was driving
a white car in Holroyd on the night of the murder. One
witness swears that the car was a Mercedes. Dean's own
car is a green Holden. Inference?'

'If it was Dean, it wasn't his car.'

'Excellent. And?'

'Again, *if* it was Dean, he must have stolen the Merc.'

Ricordi frowned judiciously. 'Not necessarily. You can't
rule out the possibility that he merely borrowed it. However, that wasn't the deduction I was looking for.'

Crook gave it some thought. 'If the white Merc was the
murder car,' he said slowly, 'then its owner probably also
owns a wire-haired terrier.'

'Isn't this fun?' Ricordi said drily. 'But you're quite right
to enter the caveat. *Was* the Mercedes the murder vehicle?
Which brings us to the next piece of evidence: on the night
of the murder, a carelessly-driven white car clipped the
offside wing of a van parked on Livia Street, Holroyd. They
know it was a white car because they found specks of white
paint in the scratches on the van. The lab technicians
believe that, given time, they can reveal what make of car
the paint came from.' Again, Ricordi waited placidly for
Crook's response.

He's acting, Crook thought: he's having fun, playing the
part of a kindly professor leading a worthy but dull-witted
student. And yet there had to be more to it than that.
Ricordi wasn't the kind of man to waste time on simple
game-playing: he had to have some serious objective in
view. Crook wished he knew what it was. He said, accepting

his allotted role: 'I suppose they've checked all the car body repair shops?'

'First thing they thought of. No luck. No Mercedes, that is. Of course, until they get confirmation from the lab, they can't be sure that the car that clipped the van *was* a Mercedes. And even if it was, that doesn't prove that it was the murder vehicle. Naturally, they called for a computer print-out of all white Mercedes cars registered in the State; but they don't have a wire-haired terrier list to cross-reference it with. As I said, and no pun intended, it's a dog's breakfast of a case. I'm just glad it's nothing to do with me.'

After Ricordi had left, Crook sat for a while wondering what the conversation had really been about. He had the feeling that there was a hidden agenda, some coded warning behind the detective's words. But he was damned if he could figure out what it might be.

CHAPTER 10

Crook liked Melbourne. He liked the trees, the trams, the straight roads, the manicured parks, the quiet river. It was flat, unchallenging, pedal-cycle country, but he didn't mind that, nor the all-embracing atmosphere of genteel self-satisfaction. It all made a pleasant change. After Sydney, the place seemed as soothing as a sanatorium.

He had been doubtful about the value of this trip; and in fact wouldn't have undertaken it if Mrs Parsons hadn't insisted: 'We cannot reach that actress person on the telephone, Mr Paul.' Her own call to Laura Farrant's theatrical agent had been singularly unproductive, and she was still smarting from the rebuff. 'And therefore I think you must try to speak to her in person. It's not a very promising lead, but it's the only one we have.' Her eagerness to get him out of the office and "into the field", as she put it, and the speed with which she organized his travel and hotel arrangements had only confirmed his worst suspicions. His own staff felt they could only operate efficiently with him out of the way.

Incautiously, and with the uneasy conviction that he was not going to enjoy the answer, Crook had asked where Bam-bam was.

'Mr Basil is still out in the field, pursuing his investigations.' Mrs Parsons had positively glowed with enthusiasm. 'He telephoned while you were in conference with that nice policeman. He apolgized for his absence from the office, and explained that he was on a stake-out.'

'A what?'

'It's a form of covert surveillance, Mr Paul.'

'I know what it is.' Crook tried to blot from his mind the alarming vision of Bam-bam spying from cover. With that face and that physique, the old warrior had about as much chance of being covert as a gorilla at a garden-party. Also, the prospect of what the old fool might be up to didn't bear thinking about. All in all, Crook was not sorry to be escaping to Melbourne.

The plane journey was short, but the enforced idleness gave him ample time to worry about the news—or rather lack of news—about Robyn Paget. As Ricordi had said, the Perth hospital was giving out no information; and he had encountered frustrating and uncharacteristic stone-walling from the staff at Paget Enterprises' head office. He had tried Peter Paget's private number, but got no response at all: it seemed that even the answering service had been disconnected.

The more he agonized over the situation, the more his anxieties became tinged with anger. He chafed at the unfairness of it—Paget, Garland, the surgeons and doctors—they were all making him suffer unnecessarily. Someone should have told him *something* about what was going on. Even Robyn herself—if she was fit enough to be moved, surely she could have scribbled him a note? He had been on this see-saw of hope and despair for more than six months: somebody owed him a little consideration. He caught himself thinking: *If she had died in that flood, I might have come to terms with my grief by now*; and the thought filled him with guilt and self-disgust. Even more horrible was the fact that the thought refused to go away.

His emotional trauma seemed to be inducing hallucinations. As he was waiting at the Avis counter to collect the car that Mrs Parsons had booked for him, he could have sworn he saw Elizabeth Holland, his ex-fiancée. It was only a fleeting glimpse: then she passed through the automatic doors and out of sight. He was badly shaken: what could Elizabeth be doing here, fifteen hundred miles from home? Not that it was any concern of his, but . . . He pulled himself together. He must have been mistaken. The girl was a mirage, cast up by his troubled mind. There must be thousands of women with long blonde hair.

And yet the image of Elizabeth stayed obstinately in his mind: he could still see the arrogant tilt of her head, her swaying walk, and that truly magnificent, incredibly perfect bust. Was it just the product of his fevered imagination? He became aware that people were looking at him oddly, and he turned back to the counter.

He was dismayed to find that his hands were shaking. This, he told himself, was a warning of what prolonged depression could do to a guy: he was seeing things that weren't there; he was talking to himself. He was in serious danger of coming completely unglued.

Breathing deeply and trying to relax, he sat in the rental Toyota and studied the street map that Avis had thoughtfully provided. The knowledge that he had a job to do steadied him a little; but it was a setback to find that one of the addresses Mrs Parsons had written down for him was on Elizabeth Street. It was a meaningless coincidence; yet he was alarmed at how jumpy and neurotic he was becoming: seeing omens and portents in the most commonplace things. What did it matter where Laura Farrant's agent had his office? Thank God there wasn't a Robyn Street in the city centre. After a few minutes he began to feel calmer. He drove to the downtown motel that Mrs Parsons had booked him into, dropped off his luggage, parked his car and walked the few blocks to Elizabeth Street in warm afternoon sunshine.

The building that housed the Swan Theatrical Agency was older than the office blocks that dwarfed it, but just as charmless. Its neighbours were big and brutal: it was merely squat and shabby. But it was home to dozens of businesses, all haphazardly listed in the dingy foyer: accountants, financial advisers, computer specialists, designers, importers, prospectors and a rabble of companies with mysterious titles like Sissink and Palikin, whose functions could only be guessed at. There were theatrical agents, Press agents, travel agents and a wigmaker. There was also—Crook acknowledged the sign with a fraternal salute—a detective agency. Somehow the place wouldn't have been complete without one. He noticed with interest that the lift was the same make as the one in his own office building, back in Sydney. He took the stairs.

The Swan Agency was on the third floor, between the Hoopla Novelties Co. and Durmaglo Cosmetics Ltd. The sign on the door said 'Ring & Enter', but this instruction was countermanded by a handwritten note pinned underneath: 'Bell doant work. Knock.' Crook knocked and entered.

The room he found himself in was conspicuously lacking in showbiz glamour and razzmatazz. In fact it was drab, cheerless and quiet as a church. A line of empty chairs stood against the wall on his right, facing a tacky-looking desk helpfully labelled RECEPTION. At the desk, and behind piles of what looked like textbooks, sat a young woman with a truly impressive quantity of hair. It hung straight down from a crooked centre parting to within a handsbreadth of her waist: a thick, glossy curtain which concealed all but a thin sliver of her face. Outsize tinted spectacles poked through the curtain like a birdwatcher's binoculars through a bush.

The young woman became aware of Crook's presence slowly and reluctantly, as if he had roused her from a deep sleep. She raised her head from her book and Crook caught a glimpse of a pointed chin and a firm, well-shaped mouth. 'Mm?' It was a small sound, but she managed to convey a wealth of disinterest with it.

Crook wasn't sure whether her manner was intended to be insulting or sexually provocative, and was annoyed to find himself responding on both counts. He put his hands in his pockets and surveyed the dingy room with a critical eye. 'It ain't exactly boom time in the entertainment industry, huh?'

The girl sat up straighter and gently caressed her hair with both hands. 'Crudely put,' she commented, 'but I expected no better. You are not, I take it, seeking representation?'

'Do you mean, am I looking for a job? No, I have a job.'

'How fortunate for you,' the girl said drily. 'Surprising, too. Now, before I actually expire from curiosity, perhaps you would care to state your business?'

'I want to talk to Mickey Swan.'

'Generally, or on some particular subject?'

'It's about one of his clients. My office called you earlier today.'

The intercom on her desk crackled into life, startling them both. 'Goddie,' it said hoarsely, 'is that the detective?'

The girl had to move several books out of the way before she could operate the machine. 'Damn it, you know I hate being called Goddie,' she snapped, making the switch from apathy to anger with a speed that made Crook blink. 'There's a man out here wants to see you.'

'I know that, Cass. I can hear every frigging word that's said out there.'

'Then why are we using this stupid machine?'

'Because I paid good money for it. Just tell me if it's the detective or not?'

'Improbable, I should say.' She lowered her spectacles a fraction and played peek-a-boo with Crook over the frames. 'Are you the detective?'

Crook nodded. '*A* detective, anyhow.'

'Good God.' She pressed the switch again. 'He says yes.'

'I heard. Send him in.'

Crook's first thought on meeting Mickey Swan was that the agent and his receptionist were conspiring in some bizarre double act. For where the girl had a superabundance of hair, Swan had none at all. He was bald as an egg. His head was a shiny pink ball, ornamented with little red ears, large, wet-looking eyes, a putty nose and a mouth like a puncture. He regarded Crook with gloomy resignation, as a debtor might look at a bailiff. 'Jeeze, they get younger every day,' he muttered, closing his eyes briefly. 'What's your name, son?'

'Crook.'

'Crook? That's not a name, it's an affliction.' The man looked a shade more cheerful. 'I can't call you Crook. What'll I call you?'

'Paul.'

'Fine. I'm Mickey. Now, Paul, I'm glad you dropped by. I want to meet this problem head-on, and I want to deal with it in a real civilized way, understand?'

'Not quite, Mr Swan. What problem is that?'

'Call me Mickey. Shit, we're old friends, we've known each other thirty seconds already.' The man suddenly yawned, stretched, then slapped himself noisily on the top of his head with the flat of his hand. He seemed to find the action invigorating: he did it several times with alternate hands. 'You're the guy that rang up this morning about Laura Farrant, right?

'My secretary called you, yes.'

'Yeah, well, I guessed you wouldn't take no for an answer. Which is good, because it gives us a chance to straighten things out, face to face. Do you want to tell me who's hired you to do this thing?'

'Mr Swan, I think we're at cross purposes here. All I want to do is to ask Miss Farrant a few questions.'

'That's good.' Swan nodded slyly and winked. 'I liked the way you dodged that question. If you'd told me who your client was, I'd have known not to trust you. Now I know I can. Now we can talk straight. Have you seen Laura's performance in *Grail Abbey* yet?'

'No, sir.'

'Don't miss it. It's elevating. It's a performance that turns soap opera into a spiritual experience, know what I mean? But more important, the show is already well into the ratings. D'you know what *that* means?'

'No, sir. Are you telling me I can't talk to Laura Farrant because she's a TV star?'

Mickey Swan slapped the top of his head again. 'Christ, kid, do I have to spell out the facts of life for you? Basically, we're talking about money, here. Big money. Now understand this—the guys who control serious money always—*always*—protect their investments. *Grail Abbey* is a big investment, and it's about to pay off. That means the series—and its stars—are going to be protected.'

'But—'

'Please.' Swan waved down Crook's attempt to interrupt. 'Just suppose you get what you want. Suppose you get a handle on this . . . this *incident* in Laura's past? We both know what I'm talking about. What is your client going to do with the information, huh? We're not talking about any crime here, so you gotta look out for the libel laws. And anyway, the mainstream Press won't touch the story because all the majors have got stakes in *Grail Abbey* and in the company that produces it. They'll not only squash the story, they'll squash any backstreet rag that tries to run it.' He massaged the top of his head with his fingertips, as if all the slapping had made it tender. 'Wait, wait, let me finish. There's just one more thing you ought to bear in mind: Laura is currently very close to a local tycoon, one Hogarth Wheeler. You upset Laura, you make an enemy of Wheeler; and he is a guy that carries a grudge beyond the limits of reasonable behaviour.'

'Mr Swan,' Crook said, 'you've just wasted a lot of breath barking up the wrong tree. All I want to do is to ask Miss Farrant a couple of questions about Mary Kafko.'

'Laura don't know any Mary Kafko. Who she?'

'She was Miss Farrant's dresser about five years ago, in a show called *The Golden Governess*.'

'A *dresser*? What did she do, knock off a lorryload of sequins?'

'No, sir, she got herself murdered.' As briefly as possible, Crook outlined his interest in the late Mary Dean. Mickey Swan listened intently, leaning his elbows on the desk and cupping his chin in his hands. He looked, Crook thought, rather like a pink acorn.'

Swan pondered for some time before answering. 'Now, Paul, you pose me a dilemma there.' He made two words of it for greater emphasis. 'Yessir, a real Dial Emma. I wanna help you, but I gotta protect my client, know what I mean?' He drummed with his fingers on the desk, then reverted to his primary source of inspiration by slapping himself on the head. 'First off, will you give me your solemn word that you're not digging into Laura's past, looking for dirt? Not that I'm saying there's any dirt to look for, understand?'

'Mr Swan, I promise you I'm no threat to Miss Farrant's career. All I want to know is anything she can tell me about Mary Kafko: her friends, relations, background—anything at all.'

'Fine, fine.' Swan looked relieved. 'Tell you what I'll do: I'll call her right now, and put those very questions to her. How's that suit you?'

'I'd rather talk to her face to face, if that's possible.'

'It ain't,' Swan said flatly. 'Leastways, not through me. She'd dump me hard on my little round ass if I even suggested it. Be sensible, young Paul: this is the best offer you're likely to get.'

'I guess you're right,' Crook conceded. It was, after all, better than nothing. 'It's good of you to take the trouble.'

But his gratitude was premature. After a long phone call, larded with 'darlings' and a sickening amount of baby-talk, Mickey Swan put down the receiver and shook his head sympathetically. 'She don't remember,' he told Crook. 'She remembers the show OK, and she knows she must have had a dresser, but beyond that, nothing. No recollections at all. She did say that whoever it was must have been efficient, because otherwise she *would* have remembered. Knowing Laura, that's gotta be true.'

'Oh.' Crook hadn't expected much, but a complete blank was a disappointment. 'Well, thanks, anyway.'

'Hey, wait a minute, I got an idea.' Swan did a little more head-slapping, presumably to indicate where the idea came from. 'That was a Lachlan show, right? You ought to talk to Bonnie Lachlan. She's twice as old as God, but where the family business is concerned, she's sharp as a tack. And they say she's got a memory like a filing cabinet.'

'That could be very helpful.' Crook wrote down the name. 'Where can I contact her?'

'That could be a problem. She's a recluse, sort of. I can't introduce you to her myself, 'cause she loathes agents, even loveable ones like me. But I can maybe fix it. I got contacts. Where can I reach you?'

'I'm at the Aquarius motel, on Exhibition Street.'

'Oh?' Swan made little popping sounds which Crook eventually identified as laughter. 'Is that the one near Bird-shit House?'

'I couldn't say. I don't know where Birdshit House is.'

The girl called from the outer office: 'No, it's down the other end. I know where it is.'

'Sure you do, Goddie,' Swan said loudly. His buttonhole mouth puckered with amusement, and he cocked his head for the inevitable reaction.

'Stop calling me Goddie, you pig-faced, hairless rat!' the girl yelled furiously.

Mickey Swan spluttered some more, and wiped his eyes with the back of his hand. He beckoned Crook to lean closer. 'Our Lady Godiva's an expert on all kindsa shit,' he whispered, winking broadly.

When Crook was half way back to the motel, the sky darkened abruptly and a fine, chilly rain began to fall. He walked quickly, taking what shelter he could; but he was uncomfortably damp and cold by the time he got to his room. He accepted the discomfort with unsurprised resignation: it was that sort of day.

He had not allowed himself to think about Robyn for hours; now he was hungry for news. He dialled his home number and bleeped his answerphone but heard only a baffling series of clicks and buzzes. That meant either that there were no messages, or—more likely—that he hadn't set the bloody machine properly. One day he would really master those damned instructions. He rang down to the front desk and was told that nothing new had arrived for him in the few minutes since he had collected his key.

His depression increased remorselessly as he stripped off his wet clothes and stepped into the shower. The warmth and the stinging spray brought some ease to his body but not to his spirit. He was tormented by unanswered, unanswerable questions. What the hell was he doing here? What the hell was he doing with his life? He couldn't think why he had committed himself to this so-called investigation. He wasn't interested in it. He was only interested in Robyn. Where was she? What had happened to her? Why had no one contacted him? Why had no one told him what was going on?

He felt too miserable and lethargic to get dressed. He stretched out on the bed and grimly fought the waves of self-pity that threatened to engulf him. This is it, he thought wryly: this is the authentic loneliness of the private eye,

waging his solitary battle against oppression and injustice
on the mean streets. Only, the image doesn't fit. I'm no
private eye, I'm a hayseed from Goolibah Gully. A fraud,
in fact. I don't give a stuff about righting wrongs or de-
fending the weak, or any of that shit. Anyway, where are
the mean streets in Melbourne? 'Cosy streets' doesn't have
the same inspirational ring, somehow. He yawned hugely.
Unhappiness was really exhausting. Without meaning to,
he drifted into sleep.

He came to with a jolt, his nerves screaming a warning.
Moving by instinct, he rolled off the bed, landed on all
fours and scuttled across the room before getting to his feet.
He felt sure that someone had come into the room. Heart
pounding, he checked the bathroom, the clothes closet and
under the bed before he could convince himself otherwise.
There was no one.

Dizziness made him stagger. He was naked; his hands
and feet were icy cold, though his face was dripping with
sweat. The taste of fear was still sour in his throat. 'There's
nobody here,' he said aloud, reassuring himself. Yet something had disturbed him: some small sound. He looked
round for the source of it.

He saw it as soon as his head cleared: someone had
pushed a note under his door.

Not a note, in fact, but a piece of pasteboard. A gilt-edged
visiting card, somewhat larger than average, with bold lettering:

CASSANDRA TASSE
RESEARCHER

Underneath, in much smaller type, was an address in East
Melbourne.

The writing on the back of the card was cramped but
scrupulously neat. It was also quite succinct. 'You need
me!' it said.

CHAPTER 11

She was sitting in the motel lobby, reading a book and studiously ignoring the attempts of a few adventurous males to attract her attention. Her face as usual was almost completely masked by her hair and spectacles; but her legs, clad in a miniskirt that was barely more than a pelmet, were very much in evidence. They were very shapely legs, Crook couldn't help noticing. He was almost sure that she had registered his approach, although her attitude—and those huge glasses—gave nothing away. 'Miss Tasse?' Crook asked cautiously.

She played peek-a-boo with him over her glasses for the second time that day. It looked like a favourite ploy of hers. 'Mr Crook,' she murmured. 'How delightful. Should we take a turn *en plein air*? I have spent twenty minutes being leered at by mindless yahoos, and I yearn for the healing touch of the great outdoors. You and I have matters to discuss.'

'Yes, but—' Crook felt bound to point out—'it's raining. Quite hard.'

'No, I assure you. It's dry and warm. The wind has moved to the north-west, and the evening is positively balmy.'

She was right. Less than two hours ago, it had felt like winter; now it was a sultry summer evening. 'Let us,' Cassandra Tasse said decisively, 'stroll this way.'

Crook was tired of city streets, even these genteel ones. 'There's a park in that direction,' he suggested.

'My car is in this direction. I dislike walking without some fixed objective.'

'I thought we were taking a stroll because you had things to discuss?'

'Indeed. But if our discussion proves fruitless, I do not wish to stroll further than I have to.'

After a pause, Crook said, 'I bet you do that a lot.'

'Do what?'

'Talk to people as if they were idiots.'

Cassandra thought about it. 'Not idiots, exactly. I suppose I do talk to Australian men as if they were children. With some justification, I believe. Any adult who says "Chrissie" when he means "Christmas", and "mozzie" for "mosquito", is hard to take seriously. And then there is their devastating wit.' She pointed to an office block further down the street. 'That, by the way, is Birdshit House. Its official name is Nauro House. Nauro is a small island whose principal export is phosphate. Hence the nickname. You take my point, I hope?'

'You've just proved mine,' Crook said mildly. 'Anyhow, before I actually expire from curiosity, are you going to state your business? Your card said that I need you. Tell me why?'

'Fundamentally, because you don't know very much,' Cassandra said calmly, 'and I know lots. You don't know, for instance, where or how to look for information, and I do.'

Crook was unimpressed. 'This is your spare-time job, I take it?'

'No, it's my profession. I'm a researcher. I do temporary secretarial work also, partly for the money and partly because it enables me to pry into business matters that are none of my business.' She had set out walking quite briskly; now, inexplicably, she slowed her pace to a gentle saunter. 'As a researcher, I charge twenty dollars an hour plus out-of-pocket expenses, with a discount for really interesting commissions. My first proposal, Mr Crook, is that you employ me forthwith. You really do need me, I assure you.' A gust of wind distracted her, and she halted to adjust her hair, studying her reflection in a shop window.

'Employ you to do what?'

'For a start, prepare a dossier on Mary Kafko. I can find out more about her in twenty-four hours than you could discover in a week.'

'Ah. Anything else?'

'Probably. You would have to brief me as we go along.' She produced a set of car keys and twirled them round her finger. 'End of stroll. This is my car.'

Crook nodded, unsurprised. 'Wouldn't you know it'd be a Volkswagen?'

'That sounds like a convoluted attempt to be sarcastic. Are you going to employ me or not?'

Crook temporized. 'You said that was your first proposal. Let me hear the others.'

She confronted him squarely, looking up into his face. 'You look to me like a lonely and troubled man. I think you have things on your mind that you need to offload. I, on the other hand, am a good listener and wise beyond my years. If I have a fault, it is that I thoroughly enjoy being gluttonous at someone else's expense. I think you should take me out to dinner.' She paused, examining his expression. 'As a quid pro quo, I can tell you what it is in Laura Farrant's past that her agent is so anxious to conceal.'

Crook almost refused, just for the satisfaction of denting her ego. But unfortunately he knew she was right. About him, anyway. He *was* lonely. Even the society of this self-possessed and self-opinionated young woman was preferable to being abandoned to his own maudlin company. Also, she had managed to arouse his curiosity. It was just possible that she could be useful. 'OK,' he said with more enthusiasm than he had intended, 'it's a deal.' One thing he was resolute about, however: there was no way he was going to confide any of his private troubles to that flinty and sardonic bosom. No way.

He was maliciously pleased to discover that she was a nervous and erratic driver, given to extreme caution and maddeningly slow decisions. Before they set off, she

announced that their destination was a restaurant in South
Yarra. She then ignored Crook completely and conducted
a muttered but audible monologue for her own benefit:
'Mirrors, indicator, clutch—no, wait!—*handbrake*, clutch,
yes, well done, Cassandra!' She tended to congratulate herself a lot, particularly when she had performed some taxing
manoeuvre like turning a corner. At one point she said
'Whoopee!', which Crook understood to be a celebration
on achieving third gear. Finally she parked in a side street,
not more than half a metre from the kerb, and sighed with
evident satisfaction. She put her head back and shook the
hair clear from her face.

'Well done, Cassandra,' Crook said, without sarcasm.

She blushed, but accepted the compliment with good
grace. 'I love to drive,' she said superfluously. 'Thank you
for not screaming. Most men would have.'

She evidently liked just sitting in her car too, since she
made no move to get out. 'Laura Farrant.' She introduced
the subject as if she was about to lecture on it. 'I'd better
tell you about her before we go in. I wouldn't want to be
overheard, and the tables in César's are extravagantly close
together. You said that you hadn't seen this new television
series *Grail Abbey* yet?'

'No.'

'Count your blessings. It's a sticky soap opera that makes
Neighbours look like *Oedipus Rex*. It's crammed with eccentric, lovable characters so sweet they make you want to
throw up. Laura Farrant plays Sister Felicity, a nun who
prays a lot, rescues dingo puppies from drowning, and has
the occasional naughty thought. The public laps it up, and
the tabloids have all but canonized her. The show is already
at the top of the ratings; and that, as Micky Swan said,
means big bucks.'

'Big bucks that would be at risk if some scandal in
Laura's private life were exposed?' Crook asked.

'Millions of people identify so closely with the characters
in these soaps that they can't believe they're not real. Yes,

the series would be at risk if Sister Felicity was seen to have feet of clay.'

'This is where we get to the juicy part, huh?'

'The sad part. At least, in my opinion. Laura had a baby about seven years ago. She was married at that time to a man called Roy Farrant, an architect. Less than a year after her son was born, she abandoned both husband and baby, and resumed her stage career.'

'Is that it?' Crook had been expecting something much more lurid. 'A domestic break-up seven years ago? It doesn't sound like much of a scandal to me.'

'There's more. The sad part. Laura's baby was born handicapped—a Down's Syndrome child. Laura couldn't cope—didn't even try to cope. She simply ran away. It's said that she couldn't even bear to look at her own baby. According to Mickey Swan—who is actually a nicer fellow than he seems—she hasn't laid eyes on the child since.'

Crook winced as if stabbed by a sudden stomach-cramp. His hand made a curious sideways movement in the air, seeming to smooth some imaginary material. 'The poor little bastard,' he said quietly.

Cassandra recognized Crook's response as yet another indication of his emotional disquiet. The poor guy's soul was really weighed down: that unconscious self-calming movement of the hand was a dead giveaway. He would feel better when he unburdened himself; but that would only happen when he was good and ready. She would be around when that time came: she was sure of it. She said neutrally, as if she hadn't noticed his reaction, 'You understand now why the TV tycoons want it hushed up? Sister Felicity's disillusioned fans would turn on her like avenging Furies. They would tear her—and the show—to pieces.'

Crook sat silent for a while; but whether he was considering what she had told him, or was lost in his own predicament, she couldn't tell. Finally he stirred and said, 'Is that it?'

'Yes. Be grateful. You would have taken ages to find that out on your own.'

He grunted irritably. 'Maybe, but it's all irrelevant. I'm not interested in Laura Farrant, but her ex-dresser.'

She smiled infuriatingly. 'Just give me the brief. I'll dig up the facts. Trust me.'

He grunted again, trying to keep his irritation going, but something in this woman relaxed and amused him. 'Let's go eat.'

In the restaurant, she concentrated her considerable talents on getting him to talk in detail about the Mary Dean case. He was evasive about the circumstances of his first meeting with Stanley Dean, but she didn't press him on that. There was something about his relationship with Dean that he found difficult to express: it occurred to her that perhaps he didn't fully understand it himself.

She let him talk without interruption, prompting him with the occasional question when he showed signs of flagging. He was impressed by the fact that she took no notes, and awed by her effortless recall of detail.

He was also dumbly grateful, not just for her company but also for her tact. He wasn't blind to the diplomatic way she was handling him: there was something very soothing about her coolly impersonal approach. Also, for a formidably intellectual sheila, she was surprisingly easy to talk to. Quite nice to look at, too, in an arty-farty sort of way. Pity about those bloody glasses, though.

One baffling thing about her—and even more irritating than those monster spectacles—was the way she toyed with her food. Considering how she had twisted his arm to get him to invite her here, not to mention the astronomical prices on the menu, she might show a bit more enthusiasm for the grub. She was pushing her over-priced salad around her plate with as little respect as if it had come in a plastic carton from the deli. But—count your blessings, Paul—she was not drinking. He could face the drive back to the motel with some composure, if not actual eagerness. On the other hand, it would have been interesting to see if booze had any impact at all on that serene self-control.

Cassandra tilted her head to one side and looked past Crook. 'We're in luck,' she announced in an undertone, sounding almost smug. 'Here she comes.'

'Who?' Crook turned his head instinctively. He noticed several other people turning round at the same time.

'Laura Farrant,' Cassandra said. 'And the man with her is Hogarth Wheeler.'

It had simply never occurred to Crook that Laura Farrant would be beautiful. He knew that she was an actress, of course; but that was a label that his prejudices automatically translated as "phoney". Actresses wore padded bras, false eyelashes and inch-thick make-up. They were egotistical, immoral and boring. He wasn't sure how he had come by these opinions—he didn't know any actresses, so he must have read about them somewhere—but he was quite sure his opinions were right.

However, Laura Farrant didn't fit any of his preconceptions. She was slim, and demurely dressed in a high-collared gown with a minuscule lace ruff. Her make-up was subtle, emphasizing high cheekbones and dramatically large dark eyes. She was not pretty in any conventional sense, but she had a style about her that eclipsed mere prettiness.

But what made Crook's pulse race, what struck him dumb with wonder and dismay, was that she reminded him irresistibly of Robyn Paget. This woman was at least twenty years older, but there was the same dark hair, the same poise, the same magnetic quality. He stared as if hypnotized, unable to tear his eyes away, as she crossed the room.

Then, thankfully, he began to note the differences. Her complexion was whiter than Robyn's, her chin less firm. Robyn, the non-actress, had the more mobile, more expressive face; she could never have maintained Laura's still, sculptured expression for so long. He realized that in fact there were more differences than similarities; yet he was still shaken when he turned back to the table.

'I hope,' Cassandra said, deliberately cutting across his mood, 'that I look even half as good as that at her age.'

Crook still didn't trust himself to speak. His hands were trembling, and he steadied them on the table top. After a moment his right hand moved across the cloth, smoothing it flat.

Cassandra observed him in silence. Perhaps this ploy hadn't been such a good idea after all. Her trouble was that she enjoyed being devious, liked playing games, liked stirring things up to see what would happen. But she had obviously underestimated both the seriousness of the boy's problem and his capacity for suffering. It was significant, too, that she was thinking of him as a "boy". That was a mistake, albeit an understandable one. Despite that naïve and vulnerable air, Paul Crook was no child. He was definitely an adult; and—unless her usually reliable sexual antennæ were playing her false—just as definitely a virile one. Hurriedly she called her mind to order: she didn't usually allow her thoughts to skitter about like this. She was suddenly ashamed of her own cunning. 'I think we can go now,' she said in a low voice. 'I brought you here on the off-chance that she would come in. This is supposed to be her favourite restaurant.'

'I see.' Crook's voice was not perfectly steady. 'Thank you.'

'I thought you might be interested to see her in person.'

Crook raised his head and looked at Laura Farrant again. 'She's recognized you,' he observed. 'She's pointing you out to her friend.'

'Oh?' Cassandra turned and acknowledged Laura's friendly wave with a flutter of her fingers. Just as I had planned it, she thought. Clever Cassandra. Damn, damn, *damn*.

Laura's companion was a square-jawed, grey-haired man in a white dinner jacket. He was big and fleshy, like an athlete gone to seed, with a pot belly that not even his expensively-tailored clothes could conceal. While the two women waved at each other, he fixed Crook with an expressionless, unblinking stare, like a cat weighing up an intruder on its territory. He kept it up long enough for the stare to register as a threat before turning away.

Crook was puzzled. 'I wonder what—' he began, then stopped abruptly as if some sixth sense had warned him of impending disaster. He gasped and sprang to his feet the moment he felt the touch on his shoulder.

'Polly!'

The breach caught in Crook's throat and his first attempt to speak produced only a hoarse croak.

'Elizabeth!' He felt sick with disappointment; and then angry. It was unfair of her, it was wickedly cruel of her to sneak up behind him like that. Particularly since she . . . 'You're wearing Robyn's perfume!' Absurdly, he made it an accusation.

Elizabeth absent-mindedly picked a thread from his lapel. 'It's not a Paget exclusive, my dear: it's in the shops. Anyone can buy it. If they can afford it.'

Crook's anger dissolved into embarrassment. He had made a fool of himself. When he had been engaged to Elizabeth he had found it necessary to apologize to her at least once a day; now, like a dog trained to automatic response, he resumed the habit. 'I'm sorry: you took me by surprise.' With a kind of resigned despair, he realized that his whole life would be booby-trapped with memories of Robyn. The familiar dull ache settled under his heart. With an effort he found some small-talk. 'So it was you I saw at the airport!'

'Did you, dear? I didn't see you. I must say, I was quite staggered to see you in here. Hardly your scene, I would have thought. This is the really "in" place to eat just now, I'm told. Famous people come here. That's Laura Farrant over there, by the way, the actress. Oh—' her manner became so elaborately casual that it was clear she was boasting—'this is my friend, Gary Fordson.'

The smartly-dressed young man standing at her elbow cranked his clean-cut features into an unconvincing smile. 'Glad to know you, er, *Polly*,' he said. His bone-crushing handshake belied his words.

Distractedly, Crook made the necessary introductions. He regretted young Fordson's obvious hostility, but he couldn't think of a tactful way to let him know that it was unnecessary. Elizabeth had the knack of keeping her admirers on tenterhooks, as Crook well knew. He himself had hung round her with the same bewildered, jealous look that Fordson was now displaying.

Meanwhile, Elizabeth was taking the measure of the opposition. 'Cassandra,' she drawled, making a musical phrase of it. 'What a charming name. And how intelligent of your parents to choose it for you. An unusual name is such a social advantage: such a useful way of breaking the ice at parties. It can make even the dullest person the centre of attention. Not that you're the least bit dull, my dear; anyone can see that. I just *love* your hair. So *brave* of you not to attempt to do anything with it.'

'Thank you,' Cassandra said humbly. 'You have really made my day. It is so heartwarming for someone of my age to hear such generous praise from a really mature person. May I say that I really admire your dress, Mrs Holland? It is truly ravishing.'

'*Miss* Holland.' Elizabeth's smile became rather thin. 'I'm so pleased you like the frock. One has to admit that French fashion still has a certain *chic*.'

'*Sans doute*.' Cassandra smiled with a sweetly ingenuous air. 'But it's the colour I admire particularly. It's so *bold*. And there's so much of it. It would be wasted on a less generous figure.'

'Too right,' Fordson said with perfectly mistimed gallantry. 'I can't abide skinny women.' He glared hard at Cassandra in case she had missed the point.

Elizabeth rewarded her ally with a honey-sweet glance that would have flayed the hide from a more sensitive creature, and moved smoothly to an easier target. 'I must say, I was really astonished to see you here, Polly,' she told Crook in a confidential undertone. 'Here in Melbourne, I mean. I would have wagered anything that . . . Oh golly!' Her gaze flicked back and forth between Crook and Cassandra. She lowered her voice even further. 'I hope I'm not being indiscreet?'

Crook was shocked. 'Miss Tasse and I are just . . . She's doing some research for me.'

'Research?' Effortlessly, Elizabeth made the word sound suggestive. 'Golly, it must be terribly important. I wouldn't have thought anything would have kept you away from Perth just now. Unless—' she raised her hand to her mouth in dismay—'unless things have changed between you and Robyn?'

'Changed? No. Elizabeth, what's all this about Perth? Have you heard something about Robyn?'

'It isn't what I've heard my dear, it's what I've seen.' Elizabeth at last began to enjoy herself. It was satisfactory to have hit a raw nerve with her very first thrust. She had heard the rumours back in Perth, of course: that the Paget bitch had gone completely doolally and that Crook had been banished from her company in case she turned violent; but she hadn't had a chance to verify the rumours. Until now. 'But surely—' her expression was all maternal concern—'surely you've heard from her?'

'I knew she was out of hospital,' Crook said guardedly, 'but I haven't been able to . . . Are you telling me you've seen her? Where? How is she?'

'I saw her shopping in Hay Street, only yesterday. I didn't get to speak to her, because she was obviously in a hurry and so was I. But Polly, she has never looked better. New clothes, new shoes, new hair-do. It was a joy to see her looking so well.' Elizabeth's baby-blue eyes widened. 'Did they really not tell you about it, my dear? I felt sure you would be the first to know. You and she were so close.'

Crook's lips felt stiff. 'I've . . . been away from home. I

expect they've been trying to reach me.' They ought to have been, he thought miserably. *She* ought to have been.

Elizabeth gave a little shiver. 'Isn't it *weird* that I should be the one to bring you the good news? That our paths should cross at just this moment in time? It's almost as if Fate was trying to tell us something.' She didn't attempt to explain just what Fate was trying to say. She kissed Crook lightly on the cheek and made her exit with her head held high and her fantastic bosom heaving. She registered the appreciative glances she was getting from the men in the room; but that pleasure was nothing to the savage joy she felt at her triumph. She had thought only to inflict a little embarrassment on Crook in front of his new floozy; but the way it had turned out had been simply wonderful. She had left him looking as pathetic as a whipped cur. It wasn't revenge: merely justice. But, by Golly, it was sweet.

CHAPTER 12

Mrs Parsons put the call through to the Aquarius Motel within minutes of arriving at the Sydney office. 'Mr Paul?' She hardly recognized his voice. 'I know you're busy, but I need to know if there is any likelihood of your returning to Sydney today or tomorrow?'

'No, Mrs P.' Crook massaged the back of his neck: there was a knot of pain there that seemed to be spreading right up into his head. 'I have to go to Perth today, as soon as I can get a flight. It's not to do with the case—' to hell with the case, he thought—'it's personal.'

'Perth? There is a letter for you from Perth in this morning's mail, Mr Paul. It is marked *Urgent* and *Strictly Personal*.'

'Open it,' Crook said crisply. 'Read it to me.'

'Mr Paul, it does say *Strictly Personal*.'

'Mrs P., if that letter is urgent, it may require immediate action. Read it, please.'

It pleased her to hear the note of command in his voice. The boy could be really masterful when he chose to be. 'Of course, Mr Paul.'

He heard the brief rustle of paper. 'It's from Mr Garland,' she said. She began to read in a brisk unemotional voice: ' "Dear Mr Crook: I promised at our meeting in March to keep you informed about Miss Paget's condition. I am delighted to be able to tell you that her progress has been excellent, due in part to your generous cooperation. The prognosis is looking good, particularly in regard to her physical condition. This has improved so much that she is no longer a clinical in-patient at the hospital. However, she does not yet have the full use of her right hand; and for this reason Mr Paget has decided to move her to a specialist clinic in California, which has an impressive success rate in these cases. I'm sure he will be writing to advise you of this development himself.

' "Her physical improvement has of course had a beneficial effect psychologically. With some anxieties removed, her natural courage is reasserting itself, and as a result her memory is improving day by day. In particular, she is slowly reassembling in her mind the details of her relationship with you. While this is good news in itself, there is a downside to it: the more she remembers, the more bitter she feels about what has happened. I am sure this is only a temporary phase: she is too well-balanced mentally to be permanently soured by the experience. But for now, she is in the grip of a blind, unfocused anger, which tends to fly off in every direction, like the sparks from a Catherine wheel. This is not, in my opinion, an unhealthy development: I should be far more worried if she were sunk in apathy.

' "It is perhaps fortunate that her trip to America will keep you apart a little longer. I suspect it will be easier for both of you to renew your acquaintance through correspondence than face to face. Think of this as a new beginning. Write to her; but do not be surprised or distracted if, initially, she directs her anger at you: it is part of a necessary, cathartic process. Be patient; her rage will burn itself out in due course. My personal opinion, for what it is worth, is that she still cares for you as much as ever. Yours sincerely, John R. Garland." Oh, Mr Paul!' Mrs Parsons sounded breathless. 'It's good news, isn't it?'

'Very good news, Mrs P.' Considering everything, Crook's voice was remarkably steady.

'"She still cares for you a great deal." That's what he says; isn't that wonderful? May I tell the girls?'

'Of course.'

'Shall you be going to Perth now, Mr Paul?'

'No, it won't be necessary. I'll do as Garland suggests. I'll write first.' Crook was already composing the letter in his mind.

'All's well that ends well,' Mrs Parsons said sentimentally. 'Oh, sir!'

After she had rung off, Crook remembered that he had meant to ask her about Bam-bam. He still felt apprehensive about what the old pug was up to: but his apprehension was only a very small cloud in an otherwise clear blue sky.

'The first thing I have to do,' Cassandra Tasse said without preamble, 'is to apologize.' She sounded as if she had been rehearsing this remark for some time. She put her briefcase on a chair and undid the clasp of the hooded cloak she was wearing.

Crook put the latest draft of his letter aside. 'You're all rugged-up,' he observed, surprised.

'It's like winter out there.' Cassandra dabbed at her nose with a handkerchief the size of a small towel. 'Bloody Melbourne weather.' It was the first time he had heard her swear.

'Apologize for what?'

'Oh—' She sucked air noisily through clenched teeth, a

mannerism Crook later came to recognize as self-rebuke—
'I knew Laura Farrant was going to be in that restaurant
last night. I'd planned to impress you by stage-managing
an introduction. I was showing off.'

'Hey, I'm impressed anyway,' Crook said magnani-
mously. Nothing was going to darken his mood today: particularly not anything as unimportant as this. 'These things
don't always work out.'

'It was an imbecile thing to do.' Cassandra shook her
head. 'Everyone close to Laura is paranoid about this scandal in her past, about people prying. By now, Wheeler will
know that you're a private detective. I was just plain stupid
not to have thought it out beforehand.'

'But Mickey Swan knows I'm *not* prying into Laura's
past. He'll have reassured this Wheeler guy.'

'I hope so.' Cassandra was still unhappy. 'Wheeler has
a bad reputation. The way he looked at you last night gave
me the shivers.'

'Me too,' Crook said cheerfully.

She was irritated by his facetiousness: he didn't seem
able to take her seriously at all today. Yesterday he'd been
as gloomy as Hamlet with the toothache; but right now
he looked as if he'd just won the State Lotto. That smile
transformed him, dammit. She fished some sheets of paper
from her case. 'The brief was easy, because of the unusual
name—Kafko—and the show-business connections. Dimitri Alexander Kafko married Mary Barrett at the Albert
Street Registry Office on August 21st, 1969. The wedding
was written up in the *Melbourne Weekly Gazette*, mainly
because Kafko had been performing locally, at the old Sullivan Theatre. I photocopied the item for you. As you'll
see, it's full of biographical details: Mary was the adopted
daughter of George and Emily Barrett of St Kilda, who
died in a road accident in 'fifty-eight. She left school as
soon as she could, and went to work at Dixon's, the garment
factory, where she stayed until it went bust in 'sixty-eight.
Many of her co-workers from Dixon's attended her wed-

ding, and are mentioned here by name. I have been able to trace one of them—a Mrs Ada Buck. She's in a retirement home in West Footscray.' Cassandra handed over her notes and the press cutting. 'May I ask a question?'

Crook grinned in spite of himself. 'Miss Tasse, I cannot conceive of any force in nature that is going to stop you asking questions.'

'Thank you.' She was genuinely flattered. 'Do you really believe Stanley Dean is innocent?'

'Yes,' Crook answered without hesitation. 'Yes, I do.'

'Why?'

'I don't know.' It was a feeble answer, but the truth would have sounded even more feeble. 'He told me he didn't do it, and I believed him.' Crook glanced idly at the newspaper article, surprised at how long it was.

Cassandra persisted: 'But what exactly did you expect to learn from Laura Farrant?'

'She was the only lead I had,' Crook said defensively. 'The instruction from my client was to find out as much as possible about Mary Dean in the hope—'

'In the hope that you might turn something up. Wow!' Cassandra was distinctly unimpressed. 'The Micawber School of Detection. Do you tackle all your cases like this?'

'No. I mean, all cases are different. To be honest—' Crook knew that she would work this out anyway—'I don't take cases on; they sort of adopt me. I got into this line of work by accident, and I seem to have gotten stuck with it.'

Cassandra regarded him for a long moment, inscrutable behind her tinted glasses. 'Another question?'

'If you must.'

With a gesture almost of resignation, she took off her spectacles. 'Why are you so afraid of women?'

'Afraid?' Crook was taken aback, both by the question and by his first proper sight of Cassandra's face. On the instant, she had turned from aggressive bluestocking to wistful orphan. Her huge, doe-like eyes dominated her narrow face: she peered short-sightedly out of her thicket of hair like an anxious waif peeking between drawn curtains. 'Afraid?' he repeated. 'That's pitching it a bit strong, surely? I plead guilty to being wary: a woman's a dangerous and unpredictable creature. A guy who pretends to understand the sheilas has got roos in his top paddock.'

She bit her lip. 'You're just using okker slang to be provoking. But you know very well what I'm talking about: that tubby blonde. She practically flayed you alive last night.'

'Elizabeth's not fat,' Crook protested, ancient loyalties automatically rekindled. 'Not really.'

'Fat or not, she certainly made mincemeat of you,' Cassandra said. 'Why does she hate you so much?'

'It really is none of your business, you know.' It was a token protest only: Crook knew that nothing could stem the tide of this girl's relentless curiosity.

Cassandra smiled gently. 'Tell me anyway.'

'I was engaged to her for a time. I used a shabby trick to get out of the engagement: I can't blame her for feeling aggrieved.' Crook spoke abstractedly: he was working out what was so fascinating about Cassandra's face. Her right eye was slightly larger than her left. It dawned on him that in spite of this—or perhaps because of it—she was a very attractive woman.

'She's obviously a bad picker,' Cassandra said rudely. 'First you, and then that oaf she was with last night. Gary Fordson is about as crass and chauvinistic as they come. His father is a big wheel—senior partner in a merchant bank—but Gary is so sublimely stupid that not even papa's influence can get him a job. He's what the tabloids call a playboy: which translated means thick, lazy and puerile.'

'That's Elizabeth's concern, not mine,' Crook commented severely. 'Anyway, I didn't commission you to research into my private life.'

Cassandra replaced her spectacles. 'That's just silly. If you and that bow-fronted baggage act out scenes of pure melodrama under my nose I'm bound to get curious.'

There was no point in arguing; the girl was an incurable stickybeak and that's all there was to it. Crook still had the press cutting in his hand. Something in the text had been signalling for his attention for some time: at last he looked at it properly, 'Dorothy What?'

'Hm?'

'According to this, one of the guests at Mary's wedding was a Mrs Dorothy What. Do you suppose that's a misprint for Dorothy Want? She's—'

'Yes, I remember who she is.' Cassandra was vexed at not having noticed it herself. 'The Arrigo secretary. It could be her: in fact, I'll wager it is. Let's go find out.'

On the road to Footscray, Cassandra stopped at a confectioner's shop and bought a huge box of chocolates, which she dropped in Crook's lap. 'A bribe,' she said enigmatically. She offered no further explanation until, with her usual orgy of self-congratulation, she halted the Volkswagen outside the Heatherly Retirement Home. 'If you want information, the efficient way is simply to ask for it,' she told Crook pedantically, 'but there are fall-back methods. You carry the chocolates, and let me do the talking.'

She talked quickly, confidently and at great length: first to a plump woman who wore a large badge with ASST SUPER on it; and then to a young girl in a nurse's uniform who led them to the Residents' Lounge and introduced them to Ada Buck. For some reason that eluded Crook, the girl-nurse seemed to believe that he was Ada's grandson; but when he offered to correct this impression, Cassandra silenced him with a sharp dig in the small of the back. He was being given another lesson in the techniques of information-gathering.

Ada Buck was small and ancient, with a wrinkled, simian face that looked as if it had been moulded from old cracked leather. Her reaction to being introduced to a grandson she had never heard of was wary rather than surprised, as if she thought it might be some practical joke. But her face lit up with pleasure and childlike greed when Crook proffered the box of chocolates. Swiftly, she pulled the thin shawl from her shoulders and wrapped the box in it. 'Thass for me,' she whispered, clutching the parcel to her scrawny bosom. 'Not for them greedy buggers. Gonna gollop 'em all meself.' She glanced slyly round to see if she had been observed, then settled her gaze on Cassandra. 'Whaddyer want?'

Cassandra took off her spectacles and pushed her hair away from her face, letting it fall down her back. 'We want to chat to you about the old days, Ada. About the time you worked at Dixon's.'

'That dump.' Ada cradled her parcel, rocking it like a baby. 'Bloody sweatshop. If Buck had been even half a man, I wouldn't have had to work my arse off in that hole. Twenty bloody years! Don't talk to me about bloody Dixon's.'

'Do you remember a girl called Mary Kafko?' Crook asked.

'Mary Barrett, she was then,' Cassandra put in.

Ada Buck darted one malevolent glance at him, then raised her hand to her temple, blocking his face from her sight. She shifted her body to exclude him further, and addressed herself solely to Cassandra. 'Don't talk to me about Mary bloody Barrett,' she hissed. 'She was a slut. She used to go with wharfies and Council workers: garbos. She'd let 'em knock her about for a coupla bob. She killed her ma and pa, as good as.'

'How?' Cassandra leaned forward encouragingly.

But Ada's spite was temporarily exhausted. 'Don't talk to me about bloody Mary Barrett.'

'Was there . . .' Crook choked off the question: Ada stiffened at the sound of his voice and turned her face even further away from him.

Cassandra moved in smoothly: 'Was Dorothy Want working at Dixon's in your time, Ada?'

'Huh!' The little monkey-face grimaced in disgust. 'Don't talk to me about Mrs Dorothy-hoity-toity-bloody-Want! Finished up in clink, din' she, for all her snooty ways? Serve her glad, thass what I say.'

'What are you telling me, Ada? That Dorothy Want went to prison?'

'More than once, missy. Thievin'. She'd got away with it for years. I reckon the Barrett bitch was in it with her, but they never pinned nothin' on her. But I seen how close they was. I seen Dot givin' her money. Bad as each other, I reckon, though Dot wasn't keen on the blokes, like Mary was. Thass prolly why she done her old man in.'

'Now, come on, Ada!' Cassandra chided playfully. 'You're pulling my leg, aren't you?'

'Don't talk to me,' Ada growled. 'Mrs Dottie-bloody-Want done her old man in. Gassed 'im. Got away with it an' all, lucky cow. I'd a' follered suit with my old fool, only we was all electric.'

For once, Cassandra seemed lost for words. She put on her glasses and looked to Crook for a prompt. She saw in his expression what she was thinking herself: that Ada Buck was clean off her trolley. They couldn't believe a word she'd told them.

Ada's little button eyes gleamed as if she had read their thoughts. 'Wanted to chat about the old days, eh? Don't talk to *me*. You're huntin' that murdering cow Dottie Want, I know.' Slowly, flirtatiously, she lowered her hand and gazed up into Crook's face. 'Don't say much, do you, bigfella? Bet you're more of a doer, eh? All right for some, eh, missy?' She cackled and jabbed a thin forefinger at Cassandra's chest. 'I'll wager half a crown he's got balls like coconuts, you lucky cow. Eh? Eh?'

Cassandra said rather breathlessly, 'We must be going now, Ada. Thank you for talking to us.'

'Hey, bigfella—' Ada rolled her eyes wildly—'giss a kiss before you go.'

Her cheek felt dry and powdery under his lips. Typical,

he thought, as he straightened up: my love-life's shot all to hell, but I'm going over really big with middle-aged blokes in drag and crazy old women. I bet Philip Marlowe never had this problem.

CHAPTER 13

Writing to Robyn turned out to be a lot harder than he had imagined it would be. He wasted half the morning on it, and abandoned his fifth attempt with some relief when Mrs Parsons phoned. She told him that Peter Paget's office had faxed through the address of the American clinic. 'There's a personal message, too: he says he'll be in touch again as soon as the prognosis is known; and if the treatment promises to be lengthy, he'll arrange transport and accommodation, so that you can visit her there.'

'That's good news, Mrs P. Thank you.'

But Mrs Parsons had, in her opinion, even better news. 'Our Mr Basil reported in yesterday, Mr Paul. He told me that his investigations are proceeding satisfactorily. Working in the field suits him, sir. He looked positively buoyant.'

'What did he say?'

'He's very keen to report to you in person, Mr Paul; but I understand that he has collected enough evidence to get Stanley Dean "off the hook", in his words. That was our brief, was it not?'

'It certainly was, Mrs P. Ask him to contact me here, will you? If he really has cracked the problem, I needn't waste any more time on it.'

'Yes, sir.' Mrs Parsons sounded very smug. 'I'll tell him as soon as he reports in.'

The phone rang again almost immediately. 'Listen, shamus,' the voice said brusquely, 'I hope for both our sakes you're a bloody good actor.'

'Why, Mr Swan?' Crook asked. 'Are you offering me a job?'

'Not bloody likely. I've fixed it for you to see Bonnie Lachlan. This arvo at Sullivan Place, just round the corner from your motel. Four o'clock. Tea-time. Only don't go expectin' no Lapsang Souchong, if you catch my drift.'

'Your drift just drifted right past me, Mr Swan. What's all this about being an actor?'

'Well—' Mickey Swan lowered his voice confidentially—'Ma Lachlan ain't exactly no spring chicken. She sometimes gets hold of the wrong end of the stick, know what I mean? Anyway, there's a little misunderstanding over that name of yours: she's got it into her head that you're related to a guy she once knew—a broken-down old Irish comic called Barney Crook. He used to have his own TV show, 'way back when; but he hasn't been heard of for this last zillion years. Anyway, Crook was just his stage name. The thing is, Bonnie's only agreed to see you because she thinks you're kin to this Barney guy; so when you go, you've gotta be prepared to act the part. How's your Irish accent?'

'Sure, an' it's just dandy, Mr Swan.'

'Christ, you'll have to do better than that,' Swan said rudely. 'Don't forget it's my reputation on the line here. My artistes are all top-drawer.'

'No sweat.' For once Crook was able to speak with complete confidence. 'I'll do you proud, Mr Swan.'

'You'd better. Hey, there's something else.' There was a pause, punctuated by the sound of Mickey Swan slapping himself on the head. 'You was seen in César's the other night, dining with our own Lady Godiva, who don't work for me no more. That wasn't a smart move, son. Hog Wheeler was spittin' blood when he learned you was a private dick. I'll level with you, boy: he scared me shitless. He's a closet psycho, know what I mean? Just stay away from Laura Farrant, will you? For all our sakes.'

'Sure. Don't worry about it. OK? With luck, I'll be going back to Sydney tomorrow.'

'I'll tell you something,' Mickey Swan said frankly. 'I'll be glad to see you go. I dunno why, but you give me the shakes.'

That morning Crook finally managed to finish a letter to Robyn. It was a wooden, uninspired effort; the long weary months of her illness and convalescence had taken their toll of his self-confidence, and it was getting harder and harder to recall the way they had been before the accident. Her psychiatrist had hinted that her personality was altered; Crook felt that his own was changed too, in subtle ways. He couldn't shake off the notion that he was writing to a stranger.

And the worst was, that the thing that most needed to be discussed couldn't be said, couldn't even be referred to. Not in a letter.

Cassandra Tasse sensed immediately that his mood had changed again. Yesterday, euphoria: today, another fit of the glums. Manic-depressive, she thought philosophically: probably goes with the job. She herself was effervescent with news. 'Dorothy Want *did* go to gaol!' she said. 'It took me ages to get the details, but our Ada was telling the truth. Dorothy was first arrested and charged with theft in 1970. She got probation that time; but over the next seven years she spent a total of eighteen months inside. Eventually someone mentioned the word "kleptomania", and she got some psychiatric treatment. It might be a coincidence, but she hasn't been in trouble since. Now, about her husband—' Cassandra flipped over several pages of her notebook—'Thomas Want died in his bath, asphyxiated by the fumes from a gas water-heater. It was an accident: he had draped his towel over the heater—probably to dry it—and blocked the exhaust pipe.'

'A genuine accident?' Crook asked.

'No one suggested otherwise at the time, whatever Ada

Buck says now. He had no apparent motive for suicide, and no one had a motive to get rid of him, least of all Dorothy. She was left penniless and in debt.'

'When did this happen?'

'In 'sixty-eight.' She consulted her notes, and looked cross with herself. 'No, in 'sixty-seven.'

'And three years later she was in trouble for thieving,' Crook observed. 'I wonder if there's a connection?'

'Do you mean, was her kleptomania a coded cry for help? You'd have to ask a psychiatrist that one.' Cassandra clearly despised such claptrap. 'Now, about Mary's foster-parents, the Barretts. Ada said that Mary had killed them, remember? Typical Ada-venom. What happened was that Mary ran away from home when she was fifteen. She'd done it a couple of times before, but not got very far. This time she fell in with a mob of bikies, and it was three days before she was spotted, up near Bendigo. The Barretts piled into their car and headed for the hills. Old car—bald tyres—wet road—too much speed.' Cassandra, the expert driver, shrugged resignedly. 'They skidded into a tree and were dead before anyone reached them. I suppose you could say that Mary's actions resulted in their deaths, but you could hardly hold her responsible.'

Crook agreed. 'Well, it's all interesting stuff, but I can't see that it's related to Mary Dean's murder.'

'No. Unless—' Cassandra offered her theory with un-characteristic diffidence—'unless Mary had been black-mailing Dorothy for the past thirty years.'

'Blackmail? What put that idea into your head?'

'It would explain several things that are hard to under-stand otherwise. Theirs was a strange relationship, on the face of it. Dorothy was fourteen years older than Mary, yet deferred to her—"like a daughter", someone said. Their interests were quite different: Mary was a man-chaser, while Dorothy was into amateur theatricals. But the con-sistent picture over the years is of Dorothy giving to Mary. She gave money when they were working at Dixon's, according to Ada Buck; she got her a job at Lachlan's when Mary's husband died; she wangled her another job—at the Arrigo Hall, after Lachlan's went bust.'

'But all that can be explained in terms of simple friend-ship,' Crook protested. 'There doesn't have to be a sinister motive.'

'Look, if Dorothy's employers didn't know about her criminal past, she was a prime target for blackmail, don't you see?' Cassandra had been airing her theory with more and more vehemence; now she reined in her enthusiasm and offered sweet reason: 'OK, it's far-fetched, but it's poss-ible. You came here looking for a motive for murder: look-ing for someone who might have a reason to hate Mary Dean. Dorothy Want could just fit that bill.'

'Maybe.' But Crook, having met the lady, just couldn't picture her as a murderess. 'Tell you what: let's find out if she owns a wire-haired terrier.'

Cassandra's chin lifted: she suspected raillery. 'A what?'

'They're those little yappy dogs,' Crook explained infuri-atingly.

'I know what they are, you fool. You've never mentioned wire-haired terriers before.' Her tone made it an in-dictment.

'To be honest,' Crook said with perfect truth, 'I've only just remembered it.' His refusal to explain further rendered her speechless with fury, a state of affairs Crook accepted with total equanimity.

Sullivan Place, according to the marble lozenge set in the wall by its main entrance, stood on the site of the old Sulli-van Theatre, demolished in 1984. Crook had never known the old Sullivan Theatre, but he couldn't help thinking that the citizens of Melbourne had been short-changed. Most theatres, however tatty, have some style, some touch of character: Sullivan Place looked as if it had been put together from prefabricated units by bored assembly-line workers. It called itself a multi-functional building, which suggested that the committee of architects who had cobbled its design together hadn't been able to agree what its function was to be. There were shops in the foyer, a restaurant in the basement, offices on the first five floors and apartments on the floors above. Crook noted without surprise that the apartments were listed on the Directory as 'residential units'. Bonnie Lachlan's residential unit occupied the whole of the penthouse floor.

Crook rode up to her private foyer in her private elevator, a diabolical device that shot him skyward like a rogue space rocket, leaving his stomach marooned on the ground floor.

Perhaps it was that his mind was already influenced by theatrical associations, but his first impression on being ushered into Bonnie Lachlan's presence was that he had strayed on to the set of an Edwardian drawing-room comedy. Everything in the room, including its mistress, was old but superbly elegant. Everything was perfect and perfectly arranged, as on a stage at the beginning of a play; and—the very atmosphere of the room encouraged such fancies—everything seemed to be waiting for something to happen.

Bonnie Lachlan stood in her famous and favourite pose, one hand touching her pearl necklace and the other resting lightly on the Chinese shawl artlessly draped over the boudoir grand piano. As Bonnie Clare, she had been the brightest star in the theatrical firmament some 60 years ago: the actress the newspapers had called 'the most beautiful woman under the Southern Cross'. She still looked magnificent, and she knew it: tall, straight-backed, and with a complexion a child might envy. Crook suspected that the superbly-styled hair was a wig, and that the shapeliness of her figure owed much to judicious padding; but she was nevertheless a marvel: poised, confident, graceful as a ballerina. On the wall to her left was a stunning portrait of a young girl by Max Meldrum.

'Come in, boy—Paul, isn't it? Sit over here where I can look at you.' Her voice was a slight disappointment: very clipped and British, firmly pronouncing 'at' as 'et'. She studied him critically as he lowered himself on to a frail-looking settee. 'So you're Barney Crook's son?'

'Yes, ma'am.'

'Mm.' She continued to examine him from head to foot, taking her time. 'You don't look like your father,' she said finally.

'No, ma'am,' Crook agreed gravely. 'God has been merciful in many ways.'

'Ha!' It was a cross between a laugh and a bark. 'What was your mother's name?'

'Eleanor.'

'Right.' She said it as if she was awarding a mark. 'Actually, I hardly knew your father, but your mother was a friend, a real friend. A dear, sweet child. How is she? I haven't heard from her in months.'

'She died five years ago,' Crook said.

'Oh? Yes. Yes, I believe I knew that. I had heard it, I'm sure, but I forgot. One does forget.' She had grown tired of standing: she moved grandly to a throne-like armchair set strategically with its back to the light. She creaked quite loudly as she moved: more evidence that her magnificent posture was strongly and artificially underpinned. 'I'm sorry,' she said vaguely. It was not clear whether she was regretting her own forgetfulness or her friend's death. 'Your mother once saved my bacon, did you know that?'

'No, ma'am.'

'She lent me money when I needed it. Lent me money when nobody else would, and that's when one needs it, by God!' Her voice crackled with passion. 'Kept the wolves out of the pantry for a while. Kept the pigs out of the Lachlan trough for a few years. Your mother was a saint.'

'Yes.' Crook had heard that obituary before, from many people. 'Thank you,' he added inadequately.

Without warning and without fuss, Bonnie Lachlan began to cry. She did it as she did everything, with style and dignity; not snivelling but turning her head aside and letting the tears flow, mourning unself-consciously for her lost friend. Afterwards she mopped her eyes in a business-like way and blew her nose.

Crook had been studying the Meldrum painting. 'That's a beautiful portrait of you, Mrs Lachlan.' It was a small gamble, well worth taking.

She smiled tiredly, and leaned her head against the chair-back. 'Was that a lucky guess, young Paul? Confess it, that girl looks nothing like the raddled old has-been you see before you.'

'It must be you,' Crook said simply. 'No one else ever had that panache.' He was amazed at himself: he had hardly ever flirted with anyone, and certainly no one this old.

'Ha!' It was a genuine laugh this time. 'You've got some Irish in you, my lad, that's for sure. I shall give you some cake.'

Crook wondered if this could be interpreted as a reward or as a sign that she accepted and trusted him. Perhaps she always had cake at this time of day. Anyway, it seemed that no response was called for. He was going to have cake whether he wanted it or not.

She rang a small handbell and a pert-looking maid in a dangerously short dress appeared as if she had been waiting in the wings for her cue. 'Cake,' Bonnie said laconically, 'and the Madeira.'

She served both with a generous hand. The slab of cake the maid brought to him resembled the keystone of a Gothic arch; and the brimming glass that held the Madeira looked, to Crook's apprehensive eye, to have the capacity of a small bucket.

Bonnie herself nibbled a few crumbs of cake and sipped from a thimble-sized glass. She smiled with what looked like genuine happiness. 'Cake and Madeira wine were my husband's especial weakness. Alasdair and I used to share this moment most afternoons.' Crook realized that he had been given an Alasdair-sized portion of the daily treat. He struggled manfully to do justice to it. Bonnie went on: 'I understand that you are interested in theatre history, Paul?'

'Not exactly.' Crook swallowed hastily. 'I'm just making inquiries about a couple of people who worked for the Lachlan Organization in the 1980s.'

'If it's that recent, I must know them personally. Alasdair died in '76, and I ran the business from then until the end.'

'Then I wonder if you remember a Mary Kafko? She worked as a dresser on one of your shows—*The Golden Governess.*'

'Of course I remember her—and not just as a dresser. I remember them both: The Kurius Kafkos. We employed them right here.'

'In Melbourne?'

'Right here.' She pointed at the floor. 'In the old Sullivan. We ran a six-week season of Variety here every other year. It was old-fashioned even then, but we could turn a profit on a short season. The Kurius Kafkos weren't brilliant, but they weren't expensive, either. They filled a spot.' Bonnie executed a slow, perfect double-take. '*Mary Kafko?* With all the fabulous artists we employed over the years, you pick out a mouse like Mary Kafko?'

'Yes.'

She looked baffled. 'You mentioned two people. Is the other one in the same category of dullness?'

'You might think so. Dorothy Want.'

Bonnie nodded sadly. 'Of course. The odd couple. Friends with really only one thing in common. They were both born losers.'

'One of them lost out completely,' Crook said quietly. 'Mary Kafko was murdered, not long ago.'

'So that's it.' Bonnie showed no surprise. 'I suppose it had to be something like that. What are you, a policeman?'

'No. A private investigator.'

'Are you really Eleanor Gainford's son?'

'Yes, ma'am. But she was Eleanor Crook when I knew her.'

She smiled. 'You sounded just like Eleanor when you said that. Well, I believe you. I have a weakness for handsome young men with Valentino eyes. So, what do you want to know?'

'Anything you can tell me about those two women. For instance, what made you say they were born losers?'

'Perhaps that was an extravagant way of putting it.' She bowed her head in thought. 'It just seemed to me that life never gave them a fair go. Mary had a dreadful childhood: orphaned; possibly abused by her adoptive parents—at least, she ran away from them several times; a dismal nine years in a notorious sweatshop, followed by an even more gruesome twelve years married to Dimitri Kafko, a gloomy, paranoid, sadistic pig. When Kafko died, I thought her life might improve; but obviously it didn't.' Bonnie twirled her empty glass in her fingers, gazed at it regretfully, then put it down. 'Dorothy Want was another of life's unfortunates. She had made a success as an amateur actress, and desperately wanted to turn professional. Her husband was sympathetic, but he wasn't earning enough to keep them both. They were afraid to lose her regular wage from Dixon's— the same sweatshop where Mary worked. Then her husband was killed in a dreadful accident, and Dorothy's life fell apart. She lost her husband, she lost her home, she lost her hopes of a stage career; and less than a year later, she lost her job. Dixon's went under.'

'That was when you took her on as a wardrobe mistress?' Crook asked.

'No, no, that wasn't until at least ten years later. The first time I met Dorothy Want was in . . .' She hesitated. 'Better check the facts. Let's go into the office, shall we?' Moving creakily but with conscious grace, she got up and led the way from the room.

The office was immediately next door: a large, coldly functional room smelling strongly of perfumed wax polish. High steel shelving partitioned the room into bays; and every inch of shelf space was crammed with books, files, diaries, playscripts and untidy packages fastened with coloured tape. There were desks, filing cabinets, tables, manual typewriters, photocopiers and a rocking-chair. In a dominating position at the far end of the room was a massive Victorian roll-top desk. No one had worked in this place for ages; it had a sad, graveyard atmosphere.

'That,' said Bonnie, indicating the roll-top desk, 'was the control centre of the Lachlan empire for three generations. I sat at that desk myself for nearly a decade, and grew to hate it with a deadly loathing.' She stalked to the very centre of the room and looked all round her. 'I have been offered a fortune to write the Lachlan history,' she said wistfully, 'but that desk and this room lower my spirits to freezing point. I simply cannot face grubbing through all this paper.'

'Surely you could hire someone to do that for you?' Crook suggested.

'Ha!' This time, it was a scornful, unamused sound. 'Can you not visualize the kind of creature who would seek such boring, dry-as-dust work? I will not devote any of my precious time collaborating with some withered, inky-fingered old fuddy-duddy.'

'I know someone who might suit. She's young and bright, and loves poking about in old archives.'

'Is she pretty?'

'She's not in your class,' Crook conceded, 'but she has a certain style.'

'Ha. Good enough for farm work, as they used to say. Send her to me. Now let us collect some material and quit this depressing museum.' She put on half-moon spectacles and made a slow circuit of the room, plucking files, books and papers from the shelves and piling them in Crook's arms. 'There! That will do for a start. Back to civilization.' In spite of her professed dislike of the place, Crook noticed that she had a perfect knowledge of where everything was kept.

Back in the drawing-room, she instructed Crook to lay

out the material on an occasional table close to her chair. 'Now—' she opened a cardboard folder and pulled a theatre programme from an untidy mass of paper—'here we are. We first employed Dorothy Want as a wardrobe assistant in 'seventy-nine. Just after she came out of Sunbury gaol.'

Crook gaped. 'You knew she'd been in prison?'

'Of course. I knew her whole history before we took her on. Mary Kafko recommended her and went surety for her good behaviour. It was obvious to me that Mary desperately needed a friend near her. Kafko was being particularly beastly to her at that time.'

'So it was Mary who got Dorothy the job?'

'Yes. She did us a favour. Dorothy Want became an excellent wardrobe mistress and stayed with us until the very end. She never once stole while she was with us.' She handed the programme to Crook. 'This was the first show Dorothy ever did for us.'

Crook saw that the Kafkos opened the second half, not a favoured or prestigious place on the bill. On their publicity photograph they looked like circus performers, Mary in tights and spangled leotard, tiny beside her brooding, thickset husband. Dorothy Want's name was on the last page; and also buried in the small print was a big surprise. 'Ian Trimmer!' Crook exclaimed.

'Another no-hoper,' Bonnie commented calmly. 'And a perfect swine. I do hope he's not a friend of yours?'

'He and Dorothy Want work for the same outfit in Sydney—the Arrigo Choral Society. Mary also worked there, part time.' For the first time since he had left Sydney, Crook felt a stirring of genuine interest in the case. 'Trimmer told me he hardly knew her: yet according to this he was in the theatre band when she was a featured artist. Surely he couldn't have forgotten that?'

'I expect he tried to. He wouldn't want you to know that he had once been a lowly pit pianist. It doesn't go with his self-image.'

'Why did you say he's a no-hoper?'

'Because his ambition is bigger than his talent. He's a second-rate musician, a conceited snob and a poor communicator.'

'Yet you employed him for *The Golden Governess*.'

'He was cheap,' she said drily. 'Anyway, the score of *Governess* was a load of rubbish: he was good enough for that.' Some memory had depressed her. 'I suppose I acted meanly,' she said after a pause. 'I let it be known—to the theatre folk who matter—that he was inadequate and unsatisfactory. He has never worked in the theatre since.'

'Was that mean? If he really was second-rate?'

'It was meant as revenge. He angered me,' she said coldly. 'He seduced the daughter of a friend of mine. The girl was a pretty, empty-headed little thing, barely out of school. I gave her a job in the chorus, to please her mother. Everyone knew the situation: knew that Amy was my protégée. That, in a Lachlan show, should have been protection enough. Trimmer betrayed my trust, made the child pregnant and then abandoned her in the most callous and humiliating way.'

Crook remembered Bobby Cooper's version of the story. 'This was Amy Truelove?'

'Ah, so you know all about it.' Bonnie shook her head sombrely. 'Her mother and I are still friends, but there is a shadow over our friendship. I feel it.' With an effort she became businesslike again. 'But about Dorothy and Mary: I employed them both full-time until our little empire collapsed. They worked well together; in my opinion, they *needed* each other. There was a very strong bond between them: a feeling that I would call love, if you can accept that word in an innocent and non-sexual sense. It is no surprise to me that they eventually got together again.'

Crook said awkwardly, 'I know this is a virtually impossible question to answer, but I would be grateful for your opinion: can you imagine any circumstance which might have caused Dorothy to murder her friend?'

Bonnie shrugged eloquently and elegantly. 'Of course. Either of them could have killed the other. Conversely, either of them could have sacrificed herself for the other. They were both passionate, severely repressed women, subject to inner pressures we can only guess at. Any emotional crisis could have pushed either of them over the edge. One thing I *am* certain of, however: Dorothy could not have committed any murder in secret. She is a lady who dotes on an audience: any audience. An act of such drama would have culminated in a positive orgy of histrionics.'

So much for the Cassandra Tasse theory, Crook thought. 'What happened to them after . . .' He realized too late that it was a tactless question.

'After Lachlan's went bust?' Bonnie was unperturbed. 'I did my best to place all our long-serving staff. I fixed Dorothy up with a re-training course in Business Management. Laura Farrant took Mary on as a personal maid.'

'Are you sure?'

'Of course. Laura took a shine to her during the run of *Governess*, and offered her the job without any prompting from me.'

'That's strange.' Crook told Bonnie about his meeting with Mickey Swan. 'The upshot was that Laura wouldn't see me in person, but would answer questions through Swan. But when he asked her about Mary Kafko, she said she had no recollection of her at all. That seems odd, if she had employed Mary as her maid.'

'Yes, but—' Bonnie was philosophical—' she's a television person, now. Television people *are* odd. I—or, I should say, the Lachlan Organization—gave Laura her first big chance, you know. In a little piece called *The Moonflower*, back in 'eighty-three. Right here in the old Sullivan. She was incredibly beautiful in those days. Would you like to see a picture of her?'

Without waiting for a reply, she picked up another file and thumbed through the papers inside. 'Here we are.' She unfolded a sheet of newsprint and handed it to Crook.

In truth, Laura Farrant had not changed much over the years: the photograph showed the same dark hair, the same high cheekbones, the same lustrous eyes. What the camera had caught, though, was a quality that Crook had not been able to observe in the restaurant: Laura's intense and formidable sex-appeal. There was a hint of slyness in those dark eyes: something in her half-smile and the tilt of her head that was both an invitation and a challenge. She was powerfully attractive: and she looked to be fully aware of her power.

The photograph and the review of the play shared the page, rather incongruously, with a report on a medical conference at a Melbourne hospital. Crook read:

> *The Moonflower*, now playing at the Sullivan Theatre, is an old-fashioned weepie: a three-Kleenex job. Not, frankly, my cup of sweet, sweet tea; but the evening was made tolerable by the radiant presence of a young newcomer, Miss Laura Farrant. Older theatregoers will appreciate my enthusiasm when I assure them that I have seen no lovelier stage actress than Miss Farrant since Bonnie Clare (now Mrs Bonnie Lachlan) retired, nearly two decades ago.

Crook smiled a little at the old lady's vanity. She had wanted him to see the review for her own sake, not Laura Farrant's. She acknowledged as much with a faint blush. 'They all remembered me, all the critics. I got the best notices of my career for that show, and I wasn't even in it!'

Crook looked again at the photograph and then at the Meldrum portrait. 'I suppose those newspaper blokes meant well,' he said doubtfully, 'but honestly, she wasn't a patch on you.'

She grinned like a schoolgirl. 'You are a terrible flirt, Paul Crook. You are toying shamelessly with my foolish heart.' She offered her hand coquettishly, and he surprised himself by kissing it without a trace of embarrassment. 'Come again soon,' she whispered. 'Come back very soon.'

Cassandra Tasse waylaid him in the motel foyer as soon as he got back. 'News!' she said excitedly. 'News! News!'
'Me too,' Crook said. 'I think I fixed you up with a job.'
But Cassandra didn't want to listen, she wanted to talk. 'Dimitri Kafko died in his bath!' she cried. 'Asphyxiated by the fumes from a faulty water-heater. Exactly like Dorothy Want's husband, thirteen years earlier!'

CHAPTER 14

Crook returned to Sydney with no clear idea of what to do next. His trip to Melbourne had yielded a lot of information, but none of it shed any real light on Mary Dean's murder. He hadn't shared Cassandra's excitement over her latest discovery: when they discussed it in detail, it threw up more questions than answers. The fact that Kafko had died in a similar accident to Thomas Want's, years earlier, *might* have sinister implications, but on the other hand, it could have been mere coincidence. If it had been foul play—murder disguised as accident—then Mary was the obvious suspect; but in that case it was hard to imagine that Dorothy had not been involved, too. The women had been very close: Bonnie Lachlan had described the bond between them as akin to love. Whatever name one gave it, the relationship had endured for more than 30 years; could it, after all that time, have turned rancid and ended in acrimony, hatred—and murder? That, at any rate, was Cassandra's latest conjecture: she had jettisoned her black-mail idea in the face of this new development. Crook couldn't bring himself to believe any of it, but he hadn't been able to come up with any better theory. In fact, he hadn't come up with any theory at all. It seemed to him that every new development merely added another layer of perplexity to the problem.

In the end, after long and fruitless cogitation, Crook opted for the obvious and sensible course of action: he shared the problem with Mrs Parsons and asked her advice.

She did her best to be patient, but this was ground they had covered before. 'As I understand it, Mr Paul, we do not necessarily have to solve the Dean murder case. All we were instructed to do was to prove that Stanley Dean is innocent: and our Mr Basil has assured me that he has such proof. If that is so, our contract is fulfilled.'

'I suppose so.' Crook saw the logic of the proposition, but felt no enthusiasm for it. 'So your advice is to do nothing until we hear from Bam-bam?'

'It seems the most logical course of action, Mr Paul. Or inaction, I suppose I should say.'

Crook couldn't fault the advice, but the prospect of waiting around, just twiddling his thumbs was appalling. 'But you've no idea where Bam-bam is?'

'He's out in the field,' Mrs Parsons said comfortably, 'making assurance double sure, I have no doubt.' She was interrupted by the ringing of the phone in the outer office. 'That could be him now!' She made her exit on the run.

But in fact it was a call from Elspeth Cade. 'Paul, I've just heard from a friend that Robyn Paget is being transferred from the Perth hospital to a clinic in the States. Is that true? Has she had a relapse or something?'

'No, she's OK,' Crook said, thinking how pleasant it was to hear Elspeth's voice. It was strange: he could go for weeks without thinking of her at all, and yet whenever she popped back into his life, she raised his spirits. She was a lot of fun, and nothing like as hard-boiled as she pretended to be. If Crook had had a sister, he would have wanted her to be just like Elspeth. 'Robyn's fine,' he repeated. 'Didn't Mrs P. tell you?'

'Tell me what? I've been so busy with rehearsals I haven't been in touch lately.'

Briefly, Crook gave her the latest bulletin on Robyn's condition, touched by her concern. He couldn't remember why, but he had somehow formed the impression that the two women hadn't hit it off. It just showed that you simply can't fathom what's going on in a sheila's mind.

A thought suddenly struck him. 'Hey,' he said, 'you're a muso. Can I ask you something?'

'Like what?'

'Like, how do I find out all about the Arrigo Choral Society?'

'What sort of things do you want to know?'

Crook wasn't sure: he had asked the question on the spur of the moment. 'Well—for instance, who actually runs the place, pays the staff salaries? Where could I get a list of the membership? Things like that.'

'Why do you want to know? Is this connected with the murder of the woman who worked as a cleaner at Arrigo?'

'Yeah. I dunno whether the information will be useful, but it just might be. I'm clutching at straws, if you must know.'

Her response surprised him. 'Aw hell,' she said resignedly, and clicked her tongue several times. 'I suppose I *could* help.' She was clearly reluctant, however. 'Wait there, will you? I'll give you a bell as soon as I've fixed it up.'

It didn't take her long, but she still sounded unhappy. 'Are you busy right now?'

'Not at all.'

'OK. Get over to my place pronto. We might as well get this over with. Grab the first parking place you see: we can walk from here.'

When he arrived at her apartment in Woollahra, she was looking as worried as she had sounded. 'Look, I'd better warn you: this isn't going to be easy,' she said. 'Just try not to be fooled, OK? She acts fey as all get-out, but underneath she's sharp as a tack. Try to remember that, will you?'

'Can she tell me about Arrigo?'

'She should be able to. She's been a member for twenty years. She's on the Committee.'

'Then where's the problem? I'll just ask her a few questions, and we'll leave.'

'I pray it's that simple.' It was not like Elspeth to be so apprehensive: Crook had always pictured her as the tough, extrovert type, afraid of nothing.

'What's her name, Hecate? You make her sound like some kind of witch.'

'You're pretty close. I guess you can call her Catherine. I call her Ma. She's my mother.'

Mrs Cade's house was only a few doors down from her daughter's apartment. She received them with a slightly bewildered air, as if she had been expecting someone else. 'Come in, come in,' she said vaguely. 'You know where to go, I expect.'

'Yes, Ma.' Elspeth sounded resigned. 'Take your time.' She led Crook into a large sitting-room with a narrow view over Rose Bay. Mrs Cade, still looking rather bemused, backed slowly into a room on the other side of the hall.

'I'm sorry,' Elspeth said, her apology tinged with a certain pride, 'she doesn't usually practise until late afternoon. Just pray she's not on the first page of the Goldberg.'

Music sounded busily from another part of the house: tinny-sounding music, with a lot of notes. 'What's that?' Crook asked.

Elspeth smiled with relief. 'Bach. "The Well-Tempered Clavier."'

Musos were amazing, Crook thought. How the hell did she know what kind of mood the thingummy was in? 'I've never heard a clavier before,' he admitted. 'Doesn't sound too good-tempered to me. Sounds like a bottle full of bees.'

'It's a harpsichord,' Elspeth said, with no real expectation of being understood. 'Don't worry: she never plays the whole forty-eight straight through. She'll take a break after the next prelude and fugue.'

'Good-oh,' Crook said heartily. He knew what taking a break was, even if the rest of it was gibberish. Actually, now he had tuned in to it, the music was quite stimulating: a bit like having your ears sandpapered from the inside.

The music stopped, and Catherine Cade put her head round the door. 'Ah yes,' she said. 'There you are. I thought I heard someone come in. Are you staying to lunch?'

Elspeth sighed. 'No, Ma. I told you that when I phoned you.'

'So you did.' Mrs Cade decided to come into the room. 'That's the reason I didn't buy anything special for lunch. And *that's* the reason I haven't got anything special for lunch. There's salad, of course.' She beamed. 'There's always salad.' She sat on the sofa next to Crook and favoured him with a sweet smile. She was a small, plump, pretty woman, quite unlike her daughter except for a certain liveliness around the eyes and mouth. 'What I love best about Bach,' she told him, 'are the modulations. They're so—so crisp. Don't you think so?'

'I dare say I would agree with you,' Crook said gravely, 'if I knew what a modulation was.'

She looked at him anxiously. 'You're joking. Even a fiddler knows what a modulation is.'

'He's not the fiddler, Ma,' Elspeth said, exasperated. 'That was yesterday. This is Paul Crook. He runs that business I bought.'

Mrs Cade nodded. 'Ah yes, out of the insurance money from your viola, I think you said, although in my opinion it was not a top-class instrument. Paul Crook, yes. What was the name of that fiddler, dear?'

'Jan Travoli.'

'That's right. He was nice, too. Is this the one you're living with?'

'No, Ma.' Elspeth went rather pink. 'You know damn well I'm not living with anyone. This is Paul Crook. I explained to you, he wants to ask you about the Arrigo Choir.'

Catherine laid her hand on Crook's wrist. 'I don't mind if you're living together, you know. It's what you young people do, nowadays. I don't mind if you're not taking precautions; in fact I'd much rather you didn't. I'd love a grandchild. Even a little bastard.'

'Ma, for God's sake!' Elspeth was almost choking with rage. 'You're just being a mischievous old bat. Paul and I are not, repeat *not*, living together.'

'Pity.' Catherine looked wistfully at Crook's profile. 'It seems such a waste. Well, young man, I can't get you into the choir, I'm afraid. There's a long waiting list. Unless you're a tenor, which I doubt. You don't look like a tenor.'

'I'm not trying to join the choir, Mrs Cade. I just want to know who runs the outfit: who hires and fires the staff, for instance?'

'We have a committee,' Catherine Cade said doubtfully. 'Actually, I'm on it, I think. Yes, I'm sure I am. Almost sure, anyway. The Executive Committee does all the real work. I know I'm not on that.'

'How can I find out who's on the Executive Committee?'

'Well—may I ask why you want to know?'

'I explained all this, Ma,' Elspeth said impatiently. 'Paul is a private detective. He's investigating the murder of that cleaning lady.'

'Poor Mrs Dean, yes. Oh dear.' Catherine looked more bewildered than ever. 'But we've all been investigated already. By real policemen, I mean. None of us did it. Actually—' her brow cleared a little—'I remember now. Her husband did it.'

'Possibly, Mrs Cade,' Crook said. 'I just want to be sure.'

'Good gracious. Well, I must help if I can. What did you say you wanted?'

'What I would like, is a membership list and some information on how the Society is run.'

'Then that is what you shall have.' She addressed Elspeth. 'Better take Mr Travoli into the music room, dear.

All the Arrigo stuff is in there somewhere. I'll fix us some lunch.'

Elspeth gritted her teeth. 'This is Paul Crook, Ma. And I told you, we're not staying for lunch.'

'Nonsense, darling, you're hungry, I can tell. You always get tetchy when you're hungry. You don't want to look tetchy in front of your Mr Whatsisname.' She wandered out of the room, looking pensive, then put her head round the door again. 'If you want him to move in with you, you ought at least to try to look your best.'

Mrs Cade's music room was large, high-ceilinged and incredibly untidy. Books, papers and sheet music were piled everywhere in crazy heaps—on the elegant, leather-topped desk, on chairs, on shelves, on cupboards and cabinets, on window-sills and on the floor. The only unencumbered piece of furniture in the room was the harpsichord, looking, on account of its lack of clutter, rather grand and austere. One wall was completely papered with old posters of Arrigo Choral Society concerts.

'It's not as bad as it looks,' Elspeth said reassuringly. 'All the recent Arrigo stuff will be in the filing cabinet. The trouble is that the filing cabinet is permanently full, so when new stuff goes in, old stuff comes out, and gets filed on the floor.' She rummaged among the files and abstracted a few sheets of paper. 'There—that didn't take long.' She noticed that he had wandered to the far end of the room. 'I'm sorry—what did you say?'

Crook wasn't aware that he had said anything. He was staring at the poster wall as if in a trance. 'Look at this!'

'Oh, they're all ancient,' Elspeth said. 'Ma stopped collecting those posters about eight years ago. What's taken your fancy? Brahms' Liebeslieder? The Monteverdi Madrigals?'

'No, this one.'

'The Fauré Requiem. I guess I misjudged you, Paul. I thought you were a proper oik as far as music was concerned. That's a very pretty work.'

Crook read the date on the poster. '16th July 1982.'

'It's a popular piece. They do it a lot. Is it one of your favourites?'

'I've never heard of it,' Crook confessed. 'This is what caught my eye.' He knew it would mean nothing to Elspeth, but he pointed it out anyway. Two soloists were billed at the bottom of the poster. One of them was Laura Farrant, Soprano.

'Of course I remember her,' Catherine Cade said. 'An incredibly beautiful woman. Dark hair, fine bones. Voice like a boy's, with hardly any vibrato. Like so many gifted people, she had a tragic private life.' She picked daintily at her salad.

'Tragic? In what way?' Elspeth asked.

Crook cut in harshly: 'Her child was born handicapped. She decided she couldn't cope, so she ditched the kid and went back to acting.'

'No, no, that's too cruel.' Catherine's manner was still abstracted, as if her mind dwelt constantly on other things; but Crook noticed that most of the time her words were directly to the point. 'Laura and Roy Farrant desperately wanted a baby. They tried for years: spent a fortune on medical treatment from the best and most prestigious specialists in the country. In the end, they despaired and gave up. I don't know if you can imagine, young man, how disheartening it is for a woman to admit to that particular defeat. Some women simply never recover from the heart-break.' Mrs Cade wiped her eyes absent-mindedly with the back of her hand, narrowly avoiding impaling her left ear on her fork. 'It was only after all that depressing effort that she took up a theatre career. Roy encouraged her to do it: to fill her life with a new interest.'

Elspeth anticipated the end of the story: 'It was only after she stopped trying that she finally became pregnant!'

Her mother nodded sadly. 'One of life's ironies. Of course, after so many false dawns, Laura simply refused to believe it at first; then, when she could ignore her condition no longer, she discovered that her gynæcologist—the man who had supervised her treatment for so many years—had gone to Europe on family business. Laura was distraught: she refused at first to see any other consultant, and by the time she did seek treatment, it was too late for the usual tests.'

'Amniocentesis,' Elspeth murmured.

'If you say so, dear. Anyway, in spite of the dangers, Laura insisted on having the baby.'

'And then deserted it,' Crook said.

'Yes.' Mrs Cade looked at him with some concern. 'You find that hard to forgive?'

'I find it hard to understand.' He looked miserably down at his plate.

Elspeth, too, was concerned. Although the news about Robyn Paget was good, Crook was still obviously under a lot of strain. 'You still haven't explained why you're so interested in Laura Farrant?' she said.

Crook finally abandoned all pretence of eating. 'She's linked to Mary Dean. Mary was Laura's personal maid less than five years ago; yet Laura denies any recollection of her. Mary was working for the Arrigo Society when she was killed; and now I find that Laura was also connected with Arrigo.'

'But they didn't overlap,' Catherine said. 'Not at Arrigo, I mean. Laura left us eight or nine years ago.'

Crook was still struggling to explain, trying to order his own thoughts. 'Two things keep cropping up in this case: the Arrigo Choral Society and a musical show called *The Golden Governess*. Four people connected with Arrigo worked on that show five years ago: Mary herself, Laura Farrant, Dorothy Want and Ian Trimmer.'

'Dorothy and Ian!' Mrs Cade dropped her preoccupied air. 'You can't suspect them, surely? Dorothy was devoted to Mary; and Ian—well, apart from the fact that he's a total wimp and incapable of violence, he was working at the time Mary was murdered.'

'Yes, he was at pains to tell me he had a solid alibi. "Distinguished" was the word he used.'

'He's a terrible snob. He has a regular appointment on Fridays to play two-piano music with our President, Sir Peter Waystone. Peter fancies himself as a composer, and they've been working at some of his stuff.'

Elspeth homed in relentlessly on Crook's central problem: 'This connection between Arrigo and that musical comedy—couldn't it just be happenstance? It might not have anything to do with the murder at all.'

Crook grimaced. 'I told you I was out of my depth with this one. Every new fact I come up with just muddies the water a bit more.'

'It sounds to me,' Mrs Cade said dreamily, reverting to her old manner, 'that you simply haven't got all the facts yet. Perhaps you're not asking the right questions. In all the books I've read, detectives ask the most searching and surprising questions.'

'Yes.' Crook considered her advice carefully. 'Do any of your members have wire-haired terriers?'

'Wire-haired terriers?' Catherine clapped her hands with pleasure. 'Now, that's what I call searching and surprising. Just the sort of question to inspire confidence. No, don't tell me why you want to know; don't spoil it. Let me see that membership list.' She took reading spectacles and a pencil from her handbag. 'Yes, we do have a number of doggy ladies here. Excuse me for a moment, will you?' Moving with remarkable sprightliness, she got up and left the room.

'God, she's an embarrassing woman.' Gloomily, Elspeth began to clear the table. 'I knew I should never have brought you here. Outside of music, she's a total dill.'

'I like her,' Crook said truthfully. 'She has a lot of charm.'

'Charm? You cannot be serious.' Elspeth looked relieved, nevertheless. 'I'll get you some coffee.'

They drank a lot of coffee: Catherine Cade was away for the best part of an hour. She came back very pleased with herself. 'Golden retrievers and mongrels are the Arrigo favourites,' she announced. 'Otherwise, the variety is remarkably catholic. I use the word in its secular sense: no offence intended.'

'None taken,' Crook assured her.

'Thank you. It struck me, the moment I said that, that the only Crooks I know are Catholics. Though not vice-versa, naturally. Mrs Vodrey is the woman you want.'

'Who?' Crook was having difficulty keeping track of the conversation.

'Sally Vodrey. She has a terrier. Contralto. The woman, not the dog. Lives out at Clareville. But she can't be the one.'

'I beg your pardon?'

'She didn't do it. The murder, I mean. She was in hospital at the time.'

'Ah. Is she the only Arrigo member who owns a terrier?'

'I've no idea. The point is—' She broke off and looked anxiously at Elspeth. 'Are you all right, dear? Your eyes are closed and your face is all scrunched up.'

'I'm perfectly all right, mother,' Elspeth said tightly.

'You're not constipated, are you?'

'Don't be ridiculous, Ma. I was just thinking.'

'What about?'

'Matricide.'

'Rubbish. I bet you were thinking about sex. You need a man, my girl. Celibacy doesn't suit you. The point is,' she said, turning back to Crook, 'dog-folk talk to each other. About dogs. Swapping doggy stories *ad nauseam*. If anyone else in the choir has a whatsit terrier, you can be sure that Sally Vodrey will know about it. Ask her.' She giggled until the tears came into her eyes. 'I believe that's what they call a lead, in your trade.'

'Oh, Ma!' Elspeth groaned. She glared at Crook as if she

blamed him for everything. 'Come on, you. Let's get out of here.'

Crook phoned Mrs Vodrey's home, but her maid told him that the lady was taking a nap and couldn't be disturbed. Crook said he'd call back later.

He moped around the office for a while, feeling bored and superfluous, and then made up his mind to go home early. Perhaps it was just paranoia on his part, but he felt everyone was relieved to see him go.

It was a luxury to drive home before the evening rush hour. Crook hadn't lived in North Ryde very long, but he had grown very fond of his apartment. It was the first place he had ever owned; and he felt slightly guilty at feeling so proud of it. He hadn't yet found the time or the money to furnish it properly, but modest though it was, it was his very own. He looked forward to seeing it again.

The lock on his front door had become strangely stiff in his absence: he had a lot of difficulty turning the key. As he humped his suitcase over the threshold, he was aware of another odd thing: the hall reeked of cigar smoke. Crook's reactions were far too slow: before he had collected his wits, someone grabbed him from behind, pinning his arms in a powerful bear-hug; and a fist like a rock clubbed the side of his jaw. Crook's world turned red and then black; he was unconscious before he hit the floor.

CHAPTER 15

Harry Sheiling was a disappointed man. He sat in Crook's armchair and flicked cigar ash over Crook's best rug. 'Kid,' he said disgustedly, 'you are a total fuckin' ning-nong. A prat. A prawnhead.'

'Yeah.' Crook didn't feel disposed to argue. Any guy who took up the private-eye business as a career had to be all those things, and worse. He still felt dizzy and his face ached abominably. Blood from his cut lip trickled over his chin and spattered his shirt front. He thought about getting up off the floor, then decided against it. It wasn't worth the effort: for one thing, he didn't trust his legs to hold him up, and for another, the two bruisers with Sheiling looked as if they were itching to get in some more punching practice. One of the men was in a kind of uniform: Crook had seen him before, but couldn't call his name to mind; the other was a barrel-chested tough with an expression of impregnable stupidity.

'You disappoint me,' Sheiling said. 'I trusted you. I gave you a *job*, for Chrissakes. What the hell d'you think you're playin' at?'

This was unreasonable, Crook thought. 'I'm doing the best I can,' he said with feeling. 'I told you at the start I couldn't promise results.'

'You didn't tell me you was a sneaky bastard.' Sheiling thumped the arm of the chair. 'You didn't tell me you was as cronky as a snake-oil salesman. You didn't tell me you was a top-grade, twenty-four-carat dickhead.'

'I was a mug to get involved with you, that's for sure,' Crook said bitterly.

'And you're a bigger mug to double-cross me, sport. What the hell made you think you could shaft me and get away with it?'

'You're not going to believe this—' Crook recognized a closed mind when he saw one—'but I haven't the faintest idea what you're talking about.' The dizziness kept hitting him in waves, and his speech was slow and slurred, like a drunkard's.

Harry Sheiling spat a shred of tobacco from his lower lip. 'You're makin' me mad, you know that? Actin' dumb. You know what I do to people who make me mad?'

Crook nodded, remembering. 'You send hard, unpleasant men round to break their fucking legs,' he mumbled.

'You think I'm joking? You think I wouldn't do it?'

'I'm sure you would, Harry. Only in this case you'd be making a big mistake. I haven't double-crossed you. Why should I?'

'Because you're a sneaky bastard. Show him that list, Piney.'

The man in the uniform unbuttoned a pocket and pulled out a crumpled scrap of paper. 'Here.' Crook remembered his name at last: Piney Woods, chauffeur, ex-wrestler.

'See that?' Sheiling said. 'See what that is?'

The letters danced and blurred under Crook's nose: he had to close one eye before he could see them properly. But what he read made no sense. 'It's a list,' he croaked. 'It's a list of the people who work in my office.'

'Not just the names, buster. The addresses, too. Get it? I know where they live.'

Crook felt a sudden rush of panic. The man was obviously crazy. 'What are you saying? Is this a threat?'

'Damn right it's a threat.'

'But why? I haven't double-crossed you: I don't know what you're talking about.'

'You must think I'm as stupid as you are,' Harry Sheiling growled. 'I'm not gonna waste words on you. Get this into your skull: lay off. Any more hassle from you, and everybody on that list gets it, just like your fat friend.'

'You mean Bam-bam?' The giddiness was making Crook feel sick. 'What's happened to him?'

Sheiling smiled thinly. 'We shut his mouth.'

'He asked for it,' Piney Woods smirked. 'He got what was coming.'

'Where is he?'

'You'll find him. Just follow your nose.' Sheiling stood up and walked to the door, flanked by Woods and the barrel-chested minder.

'Wait a minute,' Crook said wearily. 'I'm supposed to be working for you, remember?'

'Oh, that.' Sheiling dropped his cigar butt on the rug

and mashed it with his foot. 'Forget it. Frankly, I don't give a shit what happens to Stan Dean. Thanks to you, he don't count no more.'

Chief Inspector Ricordi escorted Crook to a comparatively uncrowded section of the hospital waiting-room. 'Are you going to tell me what happened?' he asked.

Crook carefully moved his head from side to side, wincing as the movement made his headache worse. 'Nothing to tell. A guy hit me, is all.'

'A guy wearing brass knuckles, judging by the state of your face. Who was he?'

'I don't know.' This was the literal truth, although Crook didn't expect to be believed.

Ricordi bit his lip, controlling his impatience. 'So why did he hit you?'

'Look, I can't talk about it, OK?' Crook's eyelids drooped and he yawned hugely.

'Oh God, don't give me that confidentiality crap,' Ricordi snarled. 'Start using your brains, man. You're piling up trouble for yourself, acting this way.' He could see that he was getting nowhere, but he made one more try: 'Did you and Bam-bam Butcher have some sort of blue?'

'Me fight Bam-bam? Don't be ridiculous. I told you—'

'Yeah, you told me you found him on the steps outside your apartment, with his head bashed in. Was this before or after you got yours?'

'After.'

'Are you saying the same guy—or guys—assaulted you both?'

'I don't want to say anything. Not yet.'

Ricordi didn't press him. He had a pretty shrewd idea what was going on. 'You're a fool, you know that? Is Butcher still in Casualty?'

'Yes. They said they'd bring me word how he is.'

'You look as if you could use a little attention yourself. You're a mess.'

Crook was struggling to keep his eyes open. 'I'm fine.' There was a question he had been meaning to ask, but it kept slipping out of his mind. Now he remembered it: 'What are you doing here?'

'The hospital has to notify the police when an assault victim is brought in,' Ricordi said.

'Yes, but—' Crook was irritated that he had to spell out his meaning—'surely that's a routine detail for a rank-and-file cop, not a lordly CI?'

'For you, I make an exception,' Ricordi said drily. His tone was neutral, but then it always was: he prided himself on his self-control. 'I've been working for months on what would have been the biggest collar of my career. I think— I'm not sure yet, but I *think*—you've just screwed it up.'

This was so preposterous that Crook didn't trouble to respond. It was obviously one of those days when he was going to be blamed for everything.

A young man in a short white coat approached them: 'Mr Crook? I've been asked to tell you that Mr Butcher is in no immediate danger. He has a cracked rib and a broken jaw; but although he has lost some blood, his injuries are not life-threatening. He is being prepared for emergency surgery on his jaw right now.' He bent down and looked into Crook's face. 'Are you all right, sir?'

'Sure,' Crook said. 'Thanks for the message. I'm just fine.'

'Wait there just a moment, sir.' The young man hurried briskly away and returned almost immediately with another fresh-faced youth. The newcomer, however, wore a longer white coat than the other boy, and carried a stethoscope with the nonchalant ease of the newly qualified. He examined the bruises on Crook's face, shone a torch into his eyes, and held up fingers for him to count. He seemed pleased with Crook's responses. 'You're quite right,' he told his young companion. 'This man's concussed. Find a bed for him immediately.

*

Crook was discharged from hospital late the next day. If anything, he felt worse than he had the night before: his face was sore, and his headache seemed to have taken up permanent residence, hammering away inside his skull like a demented boilermaker. But he was relieved to be allowed to go: the ward, with its determined cheerfulness and its antiseptic smells, depressed him unutterably. It reminded him too sharply of the hospital in Perth, and the long, disheartening weeks he had spent at Robyn's bedside. Moving gingerly, he cleaned his swollen face, got dressed, and went in search of Bam-bam.

He met Elspeth Cade at the reception desk, on the same errand. She regarded his battered appearance with a notable lack of sympathy: 'What the hell have you been up to this time? Do you realize how often I've made this mercy dash to one hospital or another, worrying about whether you're alive or dead? And now I find you've dragged poor Bam-bam into the wars with you.'

'Not true,' Crook said. 'It's the other way about. I got barrelled because of him. I don't know why: you'll have to ask him.'

But the nurse on Bam-bam's ward made it clear that there was no point in asking him anything. 'For one thing, he's heavily sedated; and for another, he can't talk. The surgeons did miracles mending his jaw, but his convalescence may take weeks.'

'May we see him?' Elspeth asked.

'If you wish. But please don't disturb him. If he's not actually asleep, he'll be very drowsy.'

The old pug was an impressive sight. Helpless as a stranded whale, he lay supine on the narrow cot, his belly a substantial hillock under the bedclothes. His chest was swathed in bandages; and round his head was a plastic contraption with metal rods protruding from it at different angles, like a monstrous pincushion. His eyes were closed; but slowly a small tear squeezed through the scrubby eyelashes and hung glistening on the unshaven cheek. Elspeth made a mewing sound and turned away. 'How can anyone so ugly be so bloody pathetic?' she muttered.

'He's a lot better than he looks,' the nurse said reassuringly. 'He won't be much of a chatterbox for a while, and he'll lose a few kilos, but he'll finish up as good as new.'

Crook tried to be cheered by this, but his spirits sagged to a new low. He seemed to bring misfortune to everyone close to him: it was his fault that Bam-bam was in this plight. There had been others, before Bam-bam: too many others. This latest casualty was just one in a long list.

Elspeth, as ever, was sensitive to his mood. 'You need a break from all this,' she said ambiguously. 'Let's get out of here.'

But in fact she wasn't sure what to do next. She had spoken impulsively, with no real plan in mind. It was true that Crook really did need a break. The poor guy's mind was so overloaded, he'd surely blow a fuse if he didn't lighten up soon. What she ought to do was to distract him for a while, take his mind off things for a few hours. If we were lovers, she thought wistfully, there would be no problem. But that simple solution was out of the question: she had about as much chance of luring Paul Crook into her bed as of sprouting wings and a halo.

All the same, it occurred to her as she drove out of the hospital grounds, that there could be no harm in persuading him to relax a little at her place. A few drinks; a meal cooked by her own fair hands; candlelight; soft music . . . 'Oh hell!' she said.

Crook brought all his deductive powers to bear: 'You've forgotten something.'

'Yes, damn it. I've got a rehearsal.'

'Now?'

'Yes. Well, in a few minutes. At my place. Look, I'm going to have to step on it: I don't want to leave the guys hanging around on the street.'

'No problem. Drop me off and I'll pick up a cab.'

'Why don't you come along? It's just four guys making music. You can listen if you like, or go into another room and read. There's beer in the fridge, other booze in the cupboard. Just relax, eh? Afterwards, I'll make us something to eat.'

The beer was tempting, but Crook wasn't sure about the music. 'Is it that bark stuff?' he asked cautiously.

'No, this is quite different. You'll like it.'

It would be a new experience, Crook thought: better than moping alone. 'Sure, why not?' he said graciously.

It was a strange evening. Crook found the music a bit heavy going at first, but the musos were fascinating. They set themselves up in a circle, facing each other as if they were going to play cards. Then they all took a deep breath and dived into the music with the reckless abandon of kids bombing a swimming pool. They had different mannerisms, he noticed: Jan, the first fiddle, kept looking at the ceiling and moving his head sideways, as if his nose was following some delicious aroma; Norma, the other fiddler, kept licking her lips and crossing her eyes: she had pulled her skirt well above her knees, and Crook couldn't help noticing that her ample thighs quivered during the twiddly bits. Elspeth played her viola with her eyes shut most of the time; while the oddly-named Welkin snarled constantly at his 'cello as if he wanted to wring its neck.

But the oddest thing of all was the way they would all suddenly stop playing and slag each other off like drunken wharfies. Then they would take it in turns to play bits of tunes at each other, defiantly, as if throwing down a challenge. Eventually, at a signal from Jan, they would all dive in again, with nods and smiles all round. It was really weird.

Some passages they would play over and over again, frowning with concentration and tut-tutting with annoyance. Crook liked those bits best: they gave him a chance to catch up. He realized that he was actually enjoying himself. He didn't get bored with the repetitions: in fact the more they played, the more interesting the music became. Once you got the hang of it, it wasn't heavy at all.

The next time they stopped playing, the musicians seemed to have lost their appetite for argument. They sat quietly, avoiding each other's eyes, apparently too depressed to speak. After a long silence Jan said, 'That was OK. Now let's try the Andante again.'

'Straight through?' Welkin demanded sharply. 'No discussion?'

Jan smiled at the ceiling. 'There'll be no need,' he said dreamily. 'Let's just do it.'

Crook was pleased. He settled comfortably in his seat, closed his eyes, and waited for the music to wash soothingly over him.

He realized his mistake only gradually. The sounds were slow and sweet, but not soothing. This music was merciless. It invaded the mind, plucked at the nerve-endings; and in spite of its polished urbanity, skewered the heart. It spoke of a universal sadness, a vast tide of melancholy that engulfed Crook's own wretchedness, dwarfing it into insignificance. He knew that there was no remedy for his inner pain; but in some inexplicable way, the music made the pain bearable. He discovered a courage he never knew he had: in the face of this humanity, this uncompromising integrity, there was no room for self-pity. He felt strangely comforted: and grateful.

Later that night, still mellowed by the music, and under the influence of good food and good company, he had an urge to confide in Elspeth, tell her exactly what had made him so miserable. But in the end, although he knew he could rely on her sympathy, knew her to be a real pal, he just couldn't do it.

CHAPTER 16

Bam-bam wrote:

Dear Boss please exscuse bad wrighting but I got no choise becose my jaw is broke as you no. Piny Woods and Guss Fisher done me over on Harry Sheilins say so. There days is numbud and no error. Any way so hense my writen report. I new there had to be something fishy when a droob like HS gets in a tither abt a No Hoper like Stan Dean so thats why I checkt it out. This is what I lernt. The reason why Harry wanted Stan of the hook is becose on acount a Stan not having kiled his wife becose he was nicking a car for Harry at the time so hense he cant a done it. Thats the point. See Harry runs this nickt car racket on the side strickly delux Mercs and Jags and such. Stan hapens to be the smartest car blagger in the NSW and he works for Harry. Stan nicks the motors which get a repaint in Harrys shop in pancras road by the old alex canal and then get shiped out in Harrys trucks. At the time of the merder of his old woman Stan was out blaggin a Porch so hense he has got an ~~Alley~~ Alibi which puts Harry in a fix becose if Stan blabs Harry goes in the poky.

I got most a this of Percy Saltmarsh the penman what does the Paper Work for the hot motors, but I steaked out the pancras road ~~garri~~ garadge as well. I saw a truck going in and out a there and I reckond its what thay shifted the cars in. Any way I tayled the truck to a wearhouse in balmain and I was just takin a look around when them 2 bastuds jumped me from behind. Guss fisher clobered me with a tire iron he better watch out when I get out a here.

So thats all for now. I here your OK Thank God.

Miself I cant eat proply and any way I reckon I got a stummick ulster but the doc says no.

Hoping this finds you as it leaves me at present.

Yrs Faithfully

B. Butcher

CHAPTER 17

Ricordi read through the letter with no great show of interest, and pushed it back over Crook's desk without comment.

Crook said, 'It was Bam-bam's own initiative. I knew nothing about it. He figured out straight away that Sheiling had an ulterior motive for trying to help Stan Dean.'

Ricordi nodded, still impassive. 'I came to pretty much the same conclusion. I wanted to warn you about Harry Sheiling—I dropped some fairly heavy hints, if you remember—but I had to be cagey. I didn't know how deep you were in Sheiling's pocket.'

'You were investigating him yourself?'

'Yeah.' Ricordi sighed and settled back in his chair. 'I guess there's no harm in telling you now. I've been on special assignment to the National Crime Authority for the past eight months. The Feds and the NCA are cooperating with Interpol and a number of national police forces to break up a world-wide racket in commercial vehicles.'

'Commercial vehicles? Not cars?'

'Not cars. Vans, trucks, lorries. HGVs. Hundreds of them are stolen every week in Europe and shipped overseas: to the Far East mainly; but the market for stolen trucks is worldwide. It's a billion-dollar trade; and the main trade route is through Australia. We don't yet know how the system works: we think that the goods arrive here in small shipments and are brought to one collection point to be sent on in big consignments. The organization is impressive, but at the moment we don't know who's behind it. All we know is that it's there, and it's big. We think—*I* think—that Harry Sheiling is a part of it.'

'But you're not sure?'

'Yeah, I'm sure.' Ricordi's expression lost a little of its composure; he looked for an instant as if he had just taken a mouthful of lemon juice. 'The point is that, compared with the size of the operation, Harry is strictly small-time. I knew about the stolen-car scam, but I wanted to give the guy some slack until we were ready to reel him in. I was convinced that if we were patient enough he would lead us to Mr Big.' He blew out his cheeks. 'But your guy Butcher put paid to that. He blew our whole operation out of the water.'

'How?'

'Look, Butcher is about as subtle and inconspicuous as a bulldozer. By the time he'd finished asking questions and following people around, he'd spooked most of Harry's push—they thought he was a cop, for God's sake! I reckon the panic must have spread upwards to Harry's bosses, because his whole business got scrubbed squeaky clean in a matter of days. Which left our surveillance team with nothing to survey.'

'But they know now that Bam-bam isn't a cop,' Crook said. 'They'll think it was all a false alarm. Harry's not going to stay honest for long.'

Ricordi was doubtful. 'Maybe. But I've got a sinking feeling that eight months' work has just gone down the gurgler.'

Crook tried to feel sympathetic, but he had his own priorities. 'What's going to happen to Stanley Dean now? Isn't Bam-bam's evidence enough to get him released?'

'I wouldn't think so. All it amounts to is hearsay and conjecture, when you get down to it. And now Harry's cleaned up his act, it's going to be hard to corroborate Bam-bam's story.' Ricordi smiled, not without malice. 'You'll just have to find another suspect. Any luck with that, so far?'

'None. Everything that even looks like a lead doubles back on itself and winds up at the Arrigo Choral Society.'

'And that's a dead end,' Ricordi said smugly. 'Everyone there—members and staff—has a cast-iron alibi.'

'So everybody keeps telling me. Well, I'm more than ever convinced that Stanley Dean is innocent: I can't drop the goddam case now.'

'Rather you than me.' Ricordi yawned again and stood up to leave. 'Like I said, it's a dog's breakfast of a case.'

Crook jumped as if he had been stung. 'Dog!' he said. 'I knew there was something I'd forgotten!'

Ricordi gave him a strange look, but asked no questions. Enough was enough. As soon as he had gone, Crook found Sally Vodrey's number and picked up the phone.

The house was on Clareville Beach, with a screen of euca-lypts in front and an uncluttered view across Pitt Water at the back. It had weatherboard cladding to give it a rustic look, and a carefully artistic arrangement of pot plants and cane furniture on its wide verandah. The young woman who answered the door was broad-shouldered, deeply tanned and almost as tall as Crook himself. 'No, I'm not Mrs Vodrey,' she said, answering his question before he had chance to ask it. 'And I'm not Mr Vodrey either, or young Master Vodrey. But I *am* everything else. I'm Mona. That's my name, not my disposition.' She stood aside to let him enter. 'You're early. She's still doing her meditation bit.'

'Do you want me to wait in my car?'

'Nah, come in and watch. She'll enjoy that.' She conduc-ted Crook into a wide, low-ceilinged sitting-room with French windows overlooking Pitt Water and the wooded parkland beyond. Some of the furniture had been pushed back to clear a space in the centre of the room, and here a red-haired woman in pink pyjamas lay face upwards on the floor with her eyes closed.

Mona put a finger to her lips and mutely indicated that

Crook could sit down anywhere he chose. Before she tiptoed out, she winked broadly at him and silently mouthed something. Crook was no lip-reader, but he was fairly certain that what she had said was 'Bullshit.'

The figure in pink pyjamas lay quite motionless for another few minutes, then sighed and sat up. 'Yes,' she said dreamily. 'Ah yes. Close.' She regarded Crook with a kind of unsurprised familiarity, as if he was an old friend. 'Very close. Now I must go outside. I need to breathe air, touch earth.'

She rose clumsily and threw open the French windows with unnecessary force, like an impulsive child. She was a short, pear-shaped woman: her face and shoulders were fashionably thin, but there was a sturdy plumpness about her hips that would forever defy the most rigorous diet. What Crook had taken to be pyjamas turned out to be a smartly-tailored track suit with a chic logo over the left breast.

She trotted briskly down the back verandah steps and, choosing her spot with some care, sat cross-legged on the sloping lawn. With equal deliberation, she indicated where Crook should sit: in her eyeline, but not obscuring her view of the water. 'Ah yes,' she said again, 'I am close. I am almost there.' She pressed her lips tightly together and emitted a high, monotonous humming sound for about thirty seconds. 'That's good.' She shook her head slightly. 'I love it when you can hear the beat. You feel in touch with the pulse of the Cosmos.'

'Yeah.' Crook could tell some comment was called for. 'I guess you do, Mrs Vodrey.'

'Would you mind calling me Yvette?' She looked beseechingly into his eyes. 'It isn't my name—yet—but I am testing its vibrations. What shall I call you?'

'Paul Crook.'

'Oh no!' She shuddered and crossed her thin arms, hugging her breasts. 'Not Paul. Paul is so *mauve*, somehow. Pall-bearer . . . Pall of night . . . No, no: your aura is much brighter. Buttercup yellow, perhaps.' She peered short-sightedly at Crook's face, cocking her head from side to side, like a bird. 'I shall call you Philippe. My Philippe.'

'OK.' Crook shifted uncomfortably. He was pretty sure the grass was damp: at any rate his backside was getting colder by the minute. 'Whatever.'

'What a glorious day!' Mrs Vodrey lifted both her hands to the sky. 'I am in touch,' she confided to Crook. 'This is one of those rare days when I am really in touch with my inner self, my best self. My *soma* is in tune with the living earth.'

Bully for you, Crook thought; but some instinct warned him not to intrude on the lady's private joy.

Silently, copiously, Mrs Vodrey began to weep. She didn't seem to be in any particular distress: her smile was still in place and she caught her tears expertly on the tip of her tongue. 'If only one could share,' she said with sweet resignation. 'If only there were someone in one's life with whom one could really bond.' Her face shone with excitement. 'Someone who would take that inward journey with one, know the ecstasy of oneness with the Cosmos.'

'Yeah, that sounds great.' But it suddenly occurred to Crook that this drivel could go on for hours. 'Not that I'm much of a bonder, myself. My soma just ain't up to it.'

'You can't even visualize it?'

'Nope. Leastways—' Crook opted for honesty—'not right now. My bum's wet through.'

'What!'

'The grass is damp,' Crook explained. 'Do you mind if I squat on my hunkers for a bit?'

The tears dried up and the corners of the thin mouth turned down. 'You're making fun of me.'

'No, truly. I need your help.'

'Help?'

'Just a few questions. For instance, does anyone else in the Arrigo Choir own a dog like yours?'

'I don't have a dog.'

'But—'

'I did have one. My analyst explained to me that Moto was a child-substitute. So once I had a child, I obviously didn't need Moto.' Her eyes clouded with doubt. 'But I do miss him from time to time.'

Crook decided not to ask what had happened to Moto. 'Do you happen to know if anyone else in the Choir had a wire-haired terrier?'

'No. That is to say, I don't know.' She stood up just as awkwardly as before, and strolled away from him towards the water's edge. There was a dark patch on the seat of her trousers, Crook noticed. 'I wish you to go now,' she said, not looking at him. 'I was wrong about your aura. It is like a dense, dark fog.' Absent-mindedly, she tugged at the damp fabric clinging to her buttocks. 'Oh, where is the harmony now?' she murmured. It was a rhetorical question; but she was irritated that Crook hadn't waited to hear it.

Crook found Mona in the drawing-room. She pretended to be re-arranging the furniture, but it was obvious she had been watching from the window. Something in Crook's expression made her smile. 'How'd you make out?' she asked.

'Not good,' Crook said sourly. 'I think her soma's just come a gutser.'

'You're a mug. You just didn't handle her right. If you'd of fed her some bullshit about her inner radiance, she'd be eating out of your hand right now. I'm Mona, did I tell you?'

'Yeah. I'm Paul Crook.'

'I know who you are. Come and have some coffee?'

On the way to the kitchen, she stopped to peer round the door of a small bedroom. 'That kid's a great little sleeper,' she said approvingly. 'He's the sanest one of the family.' She grinned and slapped herself on the wrist. 'Don't mind me, I'm a cat. Sal ain't so bad, she's just a pea-brain. She believes in magic: you know, the modern kind. This month she's discovering the inner child, whatever that means; soon she'll go back to Royal Jelly and the mystical Tibetan formula for reducing the size of her ass. How are you making out with the Mary Dean investigation?'

Crook was startled. 'How did you know about that?'

'I overheard that creep Ian Trimmer gossiping about it.' She busied herself putting the coffee on the stove and setting out mugs. 'I go with Sal to the Arrigo rehearsals,' she explained. 'I don't sing: it's just that Sal doesn't like to go anywhere without her personal slave. I used to give Mary a hand with the catering—sandwiches, drinks and stuff.'

'So you knew her?'

'As well as anybody, I reckon. She talked to me a lot.' Mona gave him a challenging look. 'I liked her. She had guts. She'd earned a bit of happiness after the shitty life she'd had. I want to help you to nobble the creep who did her in.'

'You don't think it was her husband?'

'I'm bloody certain it wasn't. Look, I tried to explain all this to the cops, but they didn't want to listen. Mary and Stan loved each other. More than that, they *needed* each other.'

'How do you know?'

'Because Mary told me.' Mona's voice was calm, but her hand trembled a little as she poured the coffee. 'Look, it ain't hard to figure. They were both misfits, right? They both had problems. But where they couldn't solve their own problems, they could solve each other's. Let me tell you what Mary told me. She was a masochist—yes, she knew the word, knew what it meant. For her, sex meant pain, it meant violence. So you can imagine the kind of creep she tended to take up with. She was married for years to a stage conjuror, a real sadistic bastard; and after he died, her sex-life went from bad to worse. Until she met Stan.' She had been walking to and fro with her mug of coffee in her hand; now she made as if to sit down, then paused. 'Hey, you want sugar?'

'No, thanks.'

'OK.' She sat opposite him and stretched her legs, making contact with his ankle. 'Sorry. About Stan—he had his hang-ups, too.'

'He killed his wife and unborn child in a car accident when he was drunk,' Crook said.

'Oh, you know about that? Well, you can imagine the load of guilt that lumbered him with. His drink problem got worse: and when he got drunk, he got violent. His courtship of Mary consisted of beating her to a pulp. Two no-hopers, you would say. But they managed to work it out.'

'How?'

'Just a minute.' She got up and looked out of the window. 'Oh, it's OK, she's chatting to an old guy down by the jetty. How did Stan and Mary work it out? Well, I only have half the story, but what it came down to was that they played games.'

'Games?'

'Yeah. See, Stan was actually a gentle guy except when he was drunk. He was no sadist, but for Mary's sake, he pretended to be. He acted out her fantasies for her. His violence was all make-believe, like a stage-fight. What amazed her, was that it worked: the pretending was just as stimulating as the real thing. The sex was fabulous—her word—because the play-acting was an expression of love; and like most people, love was what she really wanted. She loved him in return. She was really happy for the first time in her life.

Crook did his best to assimilate yet another picture of Mary Dean. After a moment he said, 'So he helped her. How did she help him? Are you saying she tackled his guilt problem?'

'Yes, that's exactly what I'm saying! She told me she was working on it: that she'd had a brilliant idea, but she wouldn't tell me what it was. Look, Paul, they loved each other. There's no way it was a domestic murder.' She leaned forward, elbows on the table. 'OK, now it's your turn. Just what the hell did you expect to learn from our Sal? I suppose you know she was in the Lady Primrose Clinic, giving birth to young Master Lionel on the day Mary was murdered?'

'Yes, I know that. Mrs Vodrey isn't a suspect, in anybody's book. I guess I was just grabbing at straws—or dog-hairs, to be strictly accurate.'

'Dog hairs? You mean that scruffy mutt she used to have? Moto?' She half-rose to look out of the window. 'Oh shit, Sal's coming back. Look, I'll have to boot you out. She'll crucify me if she finds you still here.' Expertly, she cleared the mugs away and propelled him out of the door. 'Better go through the garage yard,' she said. She led him through a small laundry-room and opened a door. 'Just make sure you shut the gate after you.' She pushed him out into the sunlight. 'And keep in touch, why don'tcha?'

Crook loitered in the garage yard for a few minutes and then went round to the front door and rang the bell. Mona laughed aloud when she saw him there. 'Boy, when you stay in touch you stay in touch,' she said, grinning. 'Or did you forget something?'

'There's a car in the yard,' Crook said crisply. 'A white Merc with a small graze on the nearside rear wing. Whose is it?'

'It's Sal's. I keep meaning to get that wing fixed.'

'Look, this is important. How did that graze happen?'

She shrugged. 'No idea. Sal did it, I guess. She drives like a Valium junkie.'

'Well, can you tell me who had that car while Mrs Vodrey was in hospital?'

'Nobody.' She stared at him, bewildered by his air of excitement. 'Nobody else, that is. Sal had it.'

'But—'

'She had it with her at the hospital,' Mona explained impatiently. 'Her gynie wanted her in the clinic a full week early, right? In case of complications: Sal has a weird blood group, wouldn't you know? She was feeling OK, so she drove herself in.'

'You didn't go with her?'

'What, and leave Lionel Senior to get his own supper? You can't be serious. No, she went in alone; but I fetched her and the baby home about ten days later.'

'In the Merc?'

'Of course. What else?'

'So the car was in the hospital parking-lot all that time?'

'Yes. What are you getting at? What's all the excitement about?'

'I think,' Crook said, not really daring to believe it, 'I *think* it's a real, honest-to-God clue. At last.'

CHAPTER 18

Judging by the gleaming rows of Porsches, Lamborghinis, Bentleys and other non-indigenous transport in its parking-lot, the Lady Primrose Maternity Clinic was not your basic Medicare outfit. The place had the smell and the atmosphere of a luxury hotel. Its foyer was deeply carpeted and bright with chintzy furniture and massive floral arrangements. Bland, banal music tinkled discreetly from hidden loudspeakers.

The girl behind the Reception desk had a politician's smile and a complexion as flawless as wax fruit. Her smile stayed in place as she examined Crook's business card, but her baby-blue eyes lost their warmth.

'Detective Agency?' Her voice was plummy with distaste. 'May one ask what is your business here?'

'One certainly may,' Crook said genially. 'I'd like a quiet word with the manager.'

'The what?'

'Or whatever his title is. The bloke who runs the joint.'

'The Administrator?'

'He'll do.'

'No way.' The girl flicked the card back across the desk. 'That's quite impossible. You'll have to write in for an appointment.' The smile turned malicious. 'And even then, I wouldn't elevate your hopes if I were you.'

'OK, Miss—' Crook read the name badge on her lapel— 'Ms Rapper.' He took out his notebook and scribbled in it. 'Just sign here, please.

'Sign?' She bridled with suspicion. 'Sign what?'

'Nothing much. Just the date and the time. Please sign it, Ms Rapper.'

'Why?'

'It's just so's I can prove I really did speak to you.'

'Oh, I get it. You're padding out your expense account, right?' She scrawled her signature contemptuously across the page.

'Not exactly.' Crook half-turned from her desk and raised his voice. 'It's just that in a murder investigation we always take note of the people who refuse to cooperate.'

'Murder?' The blue eyes widened. 'You didn't say anything about murder. You didn't say anything about co-operation.'

'Look, it's OK.' Crook grinned and shut his notebook with a snap. 'Don't worry about it. My back's covered.'

His words made Ms Rapper distinctly uneasy. She couldn't help feeling that signing Crook's notebook made her vaguely responsible for something: and the way the devious bastard was smiling, it looked as if it could be something nasty. 'Wait,' she said tersely. She opened a drawer and plucked out a telephone handset. 'Lady Prim-rose, please.' She filled in the waiting time by glaring at Crook and drumming her perfectly-lacquered fingernails on the desktop. After a moment, she swung around in her chair and muttered inaudibly into the phone with her back to him.

The conversation did nothing to restore her poise. When it was over she clattered the phone back into its drawer and stood up. 'Come.' She led him to a first-floor office marked ADMINISTRATOR and ushered him into the presence of a large, plain woman sitting behind a large, businesslike desk. 'This is the man, Lady Primrose. I wouldn't have bothered you, but—'

'You did the right thing, Joyce.' The woman's lumpy, long-jawed face was considerably softened by a slow, sweet smile. 'I commend your initiative.' She glanced at the card Ms Rapper handed to her. 'Please have someone on hand to conduct Mr Crook out as soon as our business is finished.' She waited until the girl had gone before continuing: 'I suspect that you have bullied that child in order to see me, Mr Crook. Unless you convince me that you have good and sufficient reason for such conduct, I shall have you thrown out. Now please be brief: my time is valuable.'

'This won't take long, ma'am. I just want to know about the security arrangements in your parking-lot out there.'

She frowned. 'I thought you told Joyce you were investigating a murder?'

'That's right. Last March, the body of a woman was found on a street in Holroyd. The body had been dumped from a car. I believe that that car was taken from your car park.'

'Then your belief is misplaced,' the woman said decisively. 'We have never had a car stolen from these premises. Since we opened the Clinic, six years ago, a few cars have been broken into; but no car has ever been stolen.'

'I didn't say stolen. I think it was taken, used by the murderer, and then returned.'

The woman considered this for several moments, her long face expressionless. 'That is the most preposterous thing I've ever heard,' she said finally.

'That's as may be, ma'am. Persuade me that the idea is utterly impossible—that it could never have happened— and I'll have to agree with you.'

She was silent again, biting her lower lip. 'I suppose it's *possible*, just,' she admitted reluctantly, 'but it's so *unlikely*.'

'Can you tell me—'

'No, *wait*!' She had a voice that was used to command. 'You had better tell me what this is all about. In detail.'

'You asked me to be brief.'

'I changed my mind.' She smiled her slow, gentle smile again. '*You* changed my mind. Somehow, I feel there is more to you than meets the eye, young man.'

Crook cast around for a place to start. 'Let me tell you what I believe happened. A patient—Mrs Vodrey—came to the Clinic in March to have her baby. She came in about a week before the baby was due, on the advice of her gynæcologist.'

'I remember Sally Vodrey. She was one of my husband's patients. Bringing her in early was just a precaution. In the end, it was an easy delivery: a fine baby boy.'

'The thing is, that Mrs Vodrey drove herself here and left her car in your parking-lot for about ten days. Could anyone have borrowed it unnoticed during that time? In particular, on March 22nd?'

She had started doodling on her notepad as he talked: large geometric patterns, with the spaces between them carefully shaded in. 'I just don't know,' she said frankly. 'I suppose we had better find out.' She picked up the phone. 'Joyce? Is Oscar on duty right now? Ask him to see me right away, please.' She replaced the receiver and explained: 'Oscar is one of our porters. A very bright young fellow. If anyone can answer your questions, he can.'

Oscar turned out to be a brawny, blue-chinned young man in a short white coat. He entered the room briskly and stood near the door as if expecting to be sent away again immediately.

'Oscar, this is Mr Crook,' the woman said. 'I'd like you to tell him about the security arrangements in our car park.'

Oscar looked wary, but made no comment. He stared unblinkingly at Crook. 'Sir?'

Crook made haste to reassure him: 'I want to make it clear that this isn't a complaint, just a fact-finding exercise.

Do you have any special security arrangements for cars
that are parked here for several days?'

'Cars aren't parked here for several days, sir. Not unless
they've broken down. This is a maternity hospital: our
patients are usually brought here by relatives or friends.
The mothers stay here: the relatives take the cars away.
Otherwise, our car park couldn't accommodate the large
numbers of visitors we get.'

'You're saying that overnight parking just doesn't
happen?'

Oscar's face stayed impassive, but there was a hint of
impatience in his tone. 'Some of our night staff have cars.
But it's rare for a patient's car to be here overnight.'

'Rare enough for you to have remembered it, if it had
happened?'

'Maybe. Give me a f'rinstance.'

'Last March a woman came here alone in a big white
Mercedes. Do you happen to remember her?'

Oscar grinned unexpectedly. 'Oh sure, I remember *her*.
Red-haired lady with a sort of wispy voice. I took her bags
up to her suite. She told me I had an aura and she planned
to call me Hercule; but she never actually spoke to me
again, so it didn't signify.'

The woman behind the desk nodded but didn't look up.
'That sounds like Sally Vodrey, all right.'

'What happened to her car?' Crook asked.

'I parked it for her. Since it was going to be there for a
while, I put it in the north area, which is mainly reserved
for the hospital staff.'

'And the car keys?'

'I handed them in to Joyce at the Welcome Desk. She
said she'd send them up to the suite with one of the nurses.'

Lady Primrose took a clean sheet of paper and carefully
drew a large circle in the middle of it. 'Mrs Vodrey's car
was parked there for over a week, I believe?'

'If you say so, ma'am. I couldn't swear to that, myself.'

She sketched away, seemingly more intent on her

drawing than her questions. 'So you wouldn't have noticed if the car had gone missing?'

'Missing? We've never had a car go missing, Lady Primrose. Not since I've been here, anyway.'

'No. I don't mean stolen. But suppose the car had been—well, *borrowed* for a day and then returned. Could that have happened without anyone noticing?'

'Ma'am, none of the porters would do a thing like that!'

'No, of course not. No one's on trial here, Oscar. Mr Crook is just airing an hypothesis for my benefit. Just humour us, will you?'

Oscar did his best, but he was clearly unhappy about it. 'Well, anything's *possible*. I mean, we keep an eye open for vagrants and vandals—or in fact anyone acting suspiciously—but . . . well, say a guy in a business suit walks boldly up to a motor, opens it with a key and drives off—not looking furtive or anything—we probably wouldn't even notice. Cars are in and out of the place all the time.'

'I see.' Lady Primrose had drawn what appeared to be a giant cogwheel. She regarded it sombrely. 'Have you any more questions, Mr Crook?'

'No, ma'am.'

'Then we needn't detain you any longer, Oscar. Thank you for your help.' She rewarded the young man with one of her rare smiles, which stayed in place after he had gone. 'Not very conclusive, I'm afraid, Mr Crook,' she said mildly. 'How stands your theory now?'

'It still stands, I reckon. Oscar didn't say it was out of the question.'

'All the same, I still cling to the opinion that it is wildly improbable. Have you shared your hypothesis with the police?'

'Not yet. I wanted to be sure that it was at least possible.'

'Hm.' Idly, she began drawing geometric figures again. 'The logic of your theory is that this murder was planned; and that it must have been committed either by one of my staff or one of Sally Vodrey's relatives or close friends.'

'Not necessarily a *close* friend, ma'am. I would cast the net wider than that. A lot of other people knew about Mrs Vodrey's pregnancy.'

'A lot of people?' The woman looked up, startled. Her long face slowly became pink with animation. 'Wait a minute! I'm beginning to catch on. The last week in March, you said? That was when that woman got killed—the cleaning woman from the Arrigo Choral Society. Is that the murder you're talking about?'

'Yes.'

'But her husband was arrested for that, wasn't he?'

'He was.'

'But you don't believe he did it?'

'I'm sure he didn't.'

'Golly!' The way she said it, coupled with her expression of innocent bewilderment, gave her for an instant the air of an adolescent schoolgirl. 'Wait a minute!' she said again. 'Sally Vodrey was in the Arrigo Choir! And literally dozens of the choir members came to visit her here—a group of them actually serenaded her in her room! Are you suggesting that one of them stole her car keys and—and then . . . ?' She was suddenly as excited as a child.

'I'm not suggesting anything,' Crook said. 'But the Arrigo Society crops up again and again in this case—and always when I'm least expecting it.'

The woman pushed back her chair and stood up. The flush of excitement began to fade from her cheeks. 'You must forgive my manners,' she said calmly. 'I neglected to introduce myself. I'm Primrose Waystone. My husband, Peter Waystone, founded this Clinic. He is also, as I'm sure you are aware, President of the Arrigo Choral Society.'

CHAPTER 19

Chief Superintendent Graham Mintlaw put down the receiver and sat for several minutes with his elbows on his desk and his head bowed, rubbing irritably at his scalp. He had a problem he could do without. This Dean thing wasn't just a fiasco; it was showing all the signs of turning into a dangerous, career-threatening quagmire. Bert Rocco was already chin-deep in it and sinking fast: as Rocco's immediate superior, it was Mintlaw's clear duty to wade in and stand shoulder to shoulder with his junior officer. Loyalty was an essential quality of leadership.

However, another essential quality of leadership was protecting one's own ass. Mintlaw passed the buck smartly up the line.

The Commander heard Mintlaw out with the wary attention of the accomplished buck-dodger. 'Is there a reason why you didn't simply pass this information to Superintendent Rocco?' he asked coldly.

There were several reasons, as the Commander well knew; but he had his own position to protect. Mintlaw said: 'It's a manpower problem, sir. When Dean was arrested, the investigating team under Bert Rocco was split up and moved to other cases. There's no way I can pull 'em all together again.'

'Ah. Give Rocco a new team, is that what you're suggesting?'

Mintlaw smiled thinly. The Commander knew damn well that wasn't what he was suggesting. 'That's for you to decide, sir. But—'

'Yes?'

'Two things. One: Rocco still thinks Stan Dean is guilty. It's going to be hard for him to start again with an open mind. Two: there's this TV thing. Bert is being interviewed tonight on *The Copper File* about Dean's release.'

'I know. The programme director asked for him specially. We could hardly refuse.'

'No, sir. But I reckon Mollie Muffin intends to crucify him. Bert briefed her on the case, and she went on camera and practically accused Stan Dean of murder. She's going to feel pretty silly about that right now; and she'll be out for revenge.'

'I take your point,' the Commander said, as if he hadn't thought it all out for himself. 'Loss of face equals loss of authority with the men. Replace him, then. Any suggestions?'

'Ricordi's a good man, sir.'

'Ricordi it is, then. New broom, what? Put all this in a memo, will you? So's I can keep it clear in my mind.' Which was Department-speak for: *So that I can blame you if it's the wrong decision.* 'This PI feller with the stupid name—you say you know him personally?' His tone made it an accusation.

'I've had dealings with him,' Mintlaw said cautiously. 'He has a knack of being where trouble is. He's also a hell of a lot smarter than he looks.'

'So you think his tip-off is kosher?'

'The lab boys can easily prove it one way or the other, sir. If they can find dog-hairs in the car that match those on the woman's coat—'

'Yes, yes. But you know as well as I do that Forensics is stretched to the limit right now. They've got a case backlog as long as your arm.'

'Surely they can spare someone to collect the evidence? All it needs is a couple of guys with those little vacuum-cleaners.'

'But once the evidence is in, God knows when Forensics will get around to assessing it.'

'I understand that, sir. And as we know, any further delay is going to make it very difficult to get a result in this case.' Now that they had worked it out between them,

Mintlaw could at last say the magic words: 'But that isn't our fault, is it?'

'Exactly. One can only do one's best.' The Commander relaxed enough to make a small joke: 'Your friend Crook seems to be doing rather better than we are. It'd be damned funny if he nobbled our villain for us, eh?'

'Funny, sir?' Mintlaw stifled the notion that his superior officer was going off his chump. 'Funny? It'd be fucking farcical.'

'He insisted on waiting for you,' Mrs Parsons said. 'I told him I didn't know when you'ld be back, but he just shrugged and said he'd nothing better to do. I put him in the Interview Room.'

'I'll talk to him in my office,' Crook said. There was something he wanted to ask before it slipped his mind: 'Wasn't that Elvis I saw just outside?' Elvis was the young Vietnamese genius who had installed the Agency's computer system.

'Yes, Mr Paul.'

'What did he want?'

'Oh—' Mrs Parsons frowned, as if the question was particularly searching—'I asked him to call. It was about that anti-virus program he wrote for us last year.'

'The what program?'

'Anti-virus. You remember, we discussed it at the time.'

'Oh yes.' Crook didn't remember any such discussion, but he was happy to drop the subject: computer jargon brought him out in a cold sweat. 'Everything is OK, I trust?'

Mrs Parsons smiled a little grimly. 'Indeed yes, Mr Paul. Mr Elvis is expensive, but he's the best in town.' Still smiling, she made haste to usher in Crook's visitor.

Stanley Dean seemed to have shrunk since their last meeting. His brown suit looked too large for him; and his neck poked scrawnily from his buttoned-up collar. Even his old broad-brimmed hat looked bigger than Crook remembered it, dwarfing the gaunt, grey face beneath.

'That wasn't the way you was meant to do it, son,' Dean said, mildly reproving. 'If I'd wanted to dob Harry Sheiling in it, I could've done it myself.'

'Then you should've levelled with me right at the start.' Crook pointed to his bruised face. 'I got this because of you. And Bam-bam is still in hospital.'

'Yeah, I heard about that. I'm sorry. But you gotta say it was his own fault. He should'a known better than to try an' cross Harry Sheiling. Well—' he nervously fingered the strap under his chin—'they let me go, so I guess they know I didn't do it. I just wanted to say thanks.'

'What do you want me to do now?'

'Do?' Dean looked anxious, as if Crook had uttered some sort of threat.

'Mary's killer is still out there somewhere. Do you want me to go on with the investigation?'

Dean wasn't even listening: he seemed to be lost in a world of his own. He squeezed his eyes shut, and pressed his fingers against his forehead as if he was trying to locate the source of his pain. Finally he blurted out: 'Mary made a will!'

'Yes?' Crook nodded sympathetically. His instinct told him not to press too hard. Dean was clearly under as much pressure as he could take.

'She left everything to me!' He glared at Crook as if he was trying to provoke a quarrel.

'Did she have much to leave?'

Dean ignored the question. 'It was the cops that told me. They wouldn't believe that I didn't know about the will. They wanted to say I killed her for her money. "What money?" I said; and that shut 'em up.' He showed his teeth in a humourless grin.

'Look, sit down if you're planning to stay,' Crook said. 'You fidget me, jittering around like that.'

'Yeah, OK.' Dean settled himself in a chair and breathed deeply, just as he had that first morning at the beach. He was still tense: but his breathing routine seemed to calm him a little. 'There's a guy lives in the same apartment house as me,' he said after a while. 'A retired guy, name of Ashley Stuker.'

'I've heard of him,' Crook said levelly. 'He used to alibi you when you were stealing cars.'

'Yeah, well, it's hard for old guys like that to make ends meet,' Dean said combatively. 'Earning a bit on the side gave the old battler a bit of self-respect. The thing about Ashley, he behaves like he's lost his marbles, but that's just an act he puts on to squeeze a bit of extra attention out of Welfare. Actually, he's a cunning old sod. But he's the sort of bloke who would never let his mate down.' He took a bulky envelope from his pocket. 'He gave me this, after the cops let me go. He said Mary asked him to keep it for her. She told him it had to be kept a secret from me, because it was goin' to be a surprise.' His hands shook as he fumbled a paper out of the envelope and pushed it across the desk. 'I tell you honestly, son, it damn near broke my heart.'

The letter was headed *The Locksley Foundation Forest Appeal*, and it was addressed to Mrs M. Dean, c/o the Arrigo Choral Society, Vaucluse. It read:

Dear Madam,

    Thank you for your interest in our Memorial Scheme. As you may know, Locksley is a registered charity whose aim is the reclamation and re-afforestation of land which has been degraded either by neglect or ruthless over-exploitation. Grants and voluntary contributions have enabled us to plant and maintain over 2000 hectares of woodlands so far, to the immediate, lasting and increasing benefit of present and future generations.

    Our Memorial Scheme offers the opportunity to dedicate a woodland site as a Perpetual Memorial to a named individual or group. For administrative convenience, we have named these sites (in ascending order of acreage) SPINNEY, COPSE, GROVE AND GLADE: the enclosed schematic map illustrates the comparative sizes of the sites. Many caring people prefer to celebrate the memory of their loved ones with a living tribute, rather than a sad memorial in cold stone.

Our scale of fees for the dedication of Memorial Sites is set out in the accompanying literature. These sites will eventually be accessible to the public at large; but it is not our intention to allow picnics and barbecues in any part of the Locksley Forests.

Please contact me if you need further information.

Yours sincerely,
Paula Cotton, Marketing Director

As soon as Crook had finished the letter, Dean pushed another one across the desk. This one had the same heading and the same signature. It said:

Dear Mrs Dean,

With reference to our recent telephone conversation, I confirm that a woodland area of the size you require can be made available; and we can accede to your request that the area may be called a VALE.

On the enclosed large-scale map, the shaded area of approximately .42 hectares, shows the position of the site, which would be called The Janet Dean Vale of Remembrance. Besides native gums, exotic hardwood trees would be planted, along with wattle, bottle-brush and wild orange. An engraved plaque, with the name of the loved one and a tribute of not more than ten words, will be provided and placed on the site.

The donation required to dedicate a site of this size would be $30,000.

'Thirty thousand dollars!' Crook's voice was strident with disbelief.

'You see what she was planning to do?' Dean said emotionally. 'She was going to raise a memorial to my wife

Janet. She knew how bad I felt about the—the accident. She thought this would make me feel better.'

'Would it have made you feel better?'

'I dunno.' Dean's face was stricken. 'It all came out of something I said. I used to say I could mebbe cope a bit better if I could one day build something permanent to Janet's memory. I didn't know what: just *something*. It was just talk: we both knew I'd never be able to afford nothin'. But Mary was actually goin' to *do* it. Build something. She was doing it for me.'

'Yes, but—thirty thousand dollars! Where would she get that sort of money.'

'She was doin' it because she loved me.' Dean was talking to himself, working something out. 'We never talked about love, never. We talked about pain and cruelty. She couldn't—' he shook his head, embarrassed—'she needed me to act violent before she could, you know, make it . . . I had to hurt her a bit before she could . . . It didn't look like love, I know; but that's what it was.' He stared at the floor and swallowed hard. 'Mary loved me. She got herself killed because she loved me.'

'How did she get herself killed?'

Dean raided the brown envelope again and took out a Building Society passbook. 'Mary opened this only eight weeks ago.'

'Hogan's ghost!' Crook said. The passbook showed a credit balance of over $20,000.

'So you see she had some money after all,' Dean said.

Crook was still shaking his head. 'You say you knew nothing about this?'

'Not a thing.' Dean took yet another piece of paper from the envelope. 'Here.'

This letter was handwritten, in a hasty, barely decipherable scrawl:

Wed. 2nd March

Dearest darling—in case I miss speaking to you before

Fri: (your theatre phone is always engaged: by the time
I got through this eve, you were long gone) of course I'm
looking forward to this w/e—God, you don't know how
much! Three whole nights together! & courtesy of True
Love, too! How appropriate.

Darling, you must know by now how much I want—
no, need you. I'm already counting the minutes till you're
in my arms again . . .

No problems this end. Blanche is staying another
month, so H. is completely tied up here; and if R. is
really having to stay on in Brisbane, things couldn't be
more perfect.

Officially, I shall be staying at the S. Cross—they'll
field all my messages. Naturally, I must visit you at the
Sullivan!—it would look odd if I didn't. I want to see
the play, too—it's a tremendous turn-on for me, to see
you on stage. *Con amore*, my darling; *con molto
amore* . . .

The note was unsigned.

'Do you recognize the writing?' Crook asked.

Dean glanced up at his face, then looked quickly away.
'No.'

Crook felt a sharp pang of sympathy for the man. 'It's
not a recent letter,' he said. 'The Sullivan Theatre was
pulled down over eight years ago. I guess Mary just
hoarded this note out of sentiment. Women do things like
that. It doesn't mean she didn't love you.'

Dean sighed heavily. 'Son, I like you. I took to you right
at the start. But as a detective, I've gotta say you're a
king-sized wallie. That letter wasn't addressed to Mary.
She must have nicked it from one of them tall poppies she
worked for.' He picked up the passbook and held it close
to Crook's face. 'You asked me how she came by this
money. Are you catching on yet?'

Crook was offended. 'Are you trying to tell me it's blackmail?' He read through the letter again. 'I can't see

anything incriminating in this. Anyway, it's years old.'

'How else could she come by this sort of loot?' Dean's eyes were full of misery. 'She put the squeeze on some bastard, and the bastard killed her. And the sodding awful thing is—she did it for love.'

CHAPTER 20

'No,' Cassandra Tasse said positively. 'Laura Farrant was filming at the TV studios here in Melbourne throughout March and April. Even if one could visualize her as a murderer—and frankly, I can't—she has a cast-iron alibi.'

Crook had been hoping for a more encouraging response. 'She might have had it done,' he argued. 'That guy she was with—Wheeler—he looked like the violent type. You said as much yourself. And Mickey Swan called him "a closet psycho", whatever that means.'

Cassandra's long blonde mane swung heavily from side to side. 'I suppose it's possible. It's utterly bizarre, and I can't bring myself to believe it, but I suppose it's just possible.' She picked up the photocopied letter and read it yet again.

It was late at night and they had been talking for some time. They sat on opposite sides of the table in Crook's room at the Aquarius Motel, looking, in spite of their earnestness, remarkably relaxed with each other. At length Cassandra put the letter aside and peered at him over the top of her glasses. 'Questions?'

'Fire away.'

'First, do you think that Stanley Dean is right about Mary using this letter for blackmail?'

'I think it's possible. It's hard to see how Mary could have accumulated all that money unless she was blackmailing somebody.'

'OK. And you think that person was Laura Farrant?'

'I'm sure the letter was sent to Laura. The evidence is in the fact that it's addressed to someone who was in a play at the Sullivan Theatre on Wednesday, March 2nd.' Crook looked at his notes. 'March 2nd fell on a Wednesday in only three of the last fifteen years: 1977; '83 and '88. The Sullivan Theatre was closed for renovation in March '77; and by '88 it had been pulled down. That leaves March 2nd 1983; and on that date the play at the Sullivan was *The Moonflower*, featuring Laura Farrant.'

'She wasn't the only woman in the play,' Cassandra objected.

'She was the youngest by a good many years.' Crook was slightly miffed that Cassandra didn't seem impressed by his deductive powers. 'Also, there are two other details in the letter that point to her.'

'Two?' She had noticed only one.

'One of the people mentioned is identified by the initial "R". Laura's husband was called Roy.'

'Yes. And the other thing?'

'This is reaching a bit,' Crook admitted. 'I noticed the rather forced reference to "True Love". There was a girl called Amy Truelove in the cast of *The Golden Governess*, which Laura also starred in.'

'But that was years later, in another play, another theatre!'

'But the same town.'

'It's just a silly coincidence.' Cassandra shook her head, setting her hair swinging again. 'On the other hand,' she added irritably, 'it's one of those dratted coincidences that get under your skin. One thing you haven't mentioned, but I'm sure you were about to, is that Mary was Laura's dresser, and later her maid: so she had ample opportunity to steal this letter. Next question: why didn't Mary resort to blackmail earlier? Why wait nearly a decade?'

'We don't know for certain that she did wait. But it's possible that Laura wasn't worth blackmailing until she'd landed this big TV contract. Also, there's the matter of incentive: Mary didn't want the money for herself, but for Stan.'

Cassandra was still unimpressed. 'It's all so vague and inconclusive. There *may* be blackmail involved; this letter *may* have been sent to Laura Farrant. The only thing we know for sure is that Laura couldn't have murdered Mary Dean. And the idea that she hired someone to do it for her is frankly preposterous. All the same . . .' She took off her spectacles and massaged the bridge of her nose between finger and thumb.

Crook waited for her to continue. 'All the same?' he prompted.

She shivered. 'I'm not quite sure what I was about to say,' she confessed. 'I was suddenly hit by a feeling of blind panic—as if I'd reached into a bag and pulled out a rattle-snake. I realized that this isn't an academic discussion; we're talking about a real person, here: a murderer, no less. He's dangerous.'

'He?'

'Oh yes. It must be a man.'

'Must it?'

'It seems obvious to me,' she said infuriatingly. 'I just pray he doesn't yet suspect how close we are to unmasking him.'

Crook wasted the whole of the next morning trying to contact Laura Farrant. It was a frustrating and disheartening experience: her agent flatly refused to talk to him; the TV production company wouldn't pass on messages: her phone number was unlisted; and her house in Toorak, with its high walls and padlocked gates, looked like a miniature fortress. He returned to his motel room feeling ill-tempered and out of sorts; and his mood was not improved by the suspicion that Cassandra had made better use of her time than he had. She had left a typically chirpy and smart-ass message for him: *Contact CT chez BL PDQ.* He would have been more impressed if she'd had the wit to include Bonnie Lachlan's phone number.

The phone buzzed at him as he was hunting for the directory. He snatched up the receiver. 'Cassandra?'

'No.'

The voice was chillingly familiar, but surprise made Crook slow to respond. 'Elizabeth!'

'I made that old witch at your office tell me where you were,' Elizabeth said grimly. 'I have a bone to pick with you.'

'Elizabeth—' Crook just managed to stop himself apologizing as a matter of habit—'what's wrong?'

'You are, you cheat. You owe me an apology. An abject, grovelling apology. And don't imagine for a moment that I'm going to keep your beastly behaviour a secret. Everyone shall know what a swine you are.'

'Elizabeth, if you'd just tell me what I'm supposed to have done—'

'You tricked me, you beast. You broke off our engagement by a trick.'

'*You* broke off our engagement, Elizabeth.'

'You tricked me into it. You didn't tell me the truth.'

'I didn't actually lie to you.' It was a feeble excuse: he had manipulated her pride and wilfulness to his own advantage, and he knew it. 'Anyway, all's well that ends well: you've found someone far superior to me in every way.'

'Everyone is superior to you, you worm. You ought to have known that your lies would come home to roost in the end.'

'I suppose so,' he said wearily. 'I just thought that once you'd found someone else, it wouldn't matter so much.'

'You fool! How do you suppose I can face my friends in Albany now? They all know: gossip flies like lightning round our set.'

Crook suddenly felt coldly apprehensive. 'What are you talking about, Elizabeth? What is it they all know?'

'I got it from Angela, who got it from a friend who shares

a flat with a nurse from the hospital. Everybody knows by now. It's horrible to have people laughing at you behind your back; and it's worse to have them pitying you. I don't know that I can ever go back west now.'

'Please, Elizabeth—'

'The nurse didn't actually mention names, she didn't have to. It was obvious who she meant. So now everybody knows that you were going the whole hog with the Paget slut while you were still engaged to me.'

Crook dreaded what she was going to say next. He tried ineffectually to dam the torrent of her anger: 'It's old history now, my dear. You're really better off without me. Can't you just forgive and forget?'

'How can I, with people sniggering behind my back? They all know you were carrying on with that rich bitch. They all know the real reason she went doolally. And you ask me to forgive and forget! I've got to carry that humiliation until the day I die.'

Cassandra Tasse was waiting for him in the foyer of Bonnie Lachlan's apartment. 'I was worried you wouldn't get here in time,' she said. 'This is a real break-through, believe me.' Her excitement abated a little as she looked up into his face. 'Are you all right? You look terrible. Are you sick?'

Crook shrugged. 'I'm OK. Tell me what the fuss is about? What have you turned up this time?'

'I take it you haven't read the papers today?'

'No.'

'Then you won't have seen this in the *Daily Monitor*. This is what triggered today's development.'

Most of the page was taken up with a full-length photograph of a nun embracing a small boy. The headline, in a strange pseudo-Gothic type, said SISTER FELICITY'S SECRET LOVE. Crook read:

Laura Farrant (Sister Felicity in TV's *Grail Abbey*) today revealed that there is a secret love in her life—her severely handicapped son, Danny. Danny suffers from Down's Syndrome, a birth disorder affecting the development of the brain; and today Laura told the *Monitor*: 'I haven't talked about Danny before, because I didn't want him exposed to public curiosity on account of my fame. I am only speaking out now, because it has been suggested in some quarters that I am ashamed of Danny. What nonsense! I am proud of him: proud of the way he has risen to the challenge of his condition. I love him very dearly.'

Bizarrely, the rest of the article was devoted to a preview of the next episode of *Grail Abbey*.

'It's a PR exercise,' Cassandra said. 'The studio bosses have decided to grab the high moral ground before the real story leaks out. They're handling it like a story-line in a soap opera: you can bet "Sister Felicity" comes out of it with a bigger halo than ever.'

'You said this article had triggered something,' Crook reminded her.

'It provoked someone to speak out. Not generally, you understand: just to her good friend Bonnie Lachlan. I've persuaded her to talk to you, too.'

'Who?'

'If you notice, that article doesn't actually say that the child in the photograph is Danny; and it isn't. That photo is a fake: rigged up in the studio. The lady practically exploded with indignation when she saw it.'

'Quit being so maddening, woman,' Crook said tiredly. 'Who are you talking about?'

'I had to put you in the picture first,' Cassandra said blithely. 'Come and meet Mrs Truelove.'

But it was some time after meeting Mrs Truelove that Crook got to talk to her. This was, after all, Bonnie Lachlan's apartment; and on her own territory Bonnie did not yield centre-stage in a hurry. She greeted Crook fondly,

offered him cake and Madeira, told him affectionate anec-
dotes about his mother, and thanked him several times
for bringing Cassandra into her life. She introduced Mrs
Truelove as 'her old friend Hilda', which somehow suggested that they were contemporaries; although Crook
judged that Mrs Lachlan was at least twice as old as the
other woman.

Eventually Bonnie grew tired and allowed her friend
some of the limelight; but by that time Mrs Truelove had
begun to have second thoughts. 'I don't know that I ought
to broadcast this. I've never talked about it before. I got
all worked up on account of that newspaper report.'

'Paul won't divulge anything confidential,' Cassandra
said soothingly. 'He's a trained professional.'

This unlikely testimonial seemed to reassure Mrs Truelove. 'I've known Laura for over thirty years,' she said. 'We
were at school together—though she's a couple of years
older than I am.' She glanced shyly at Crook to see if he
believed her. 'We stayed in touch afterwards, even though
I moved to Melbourne after I got married. I knew all about
Laura's infertility problems, of course; and I was really
upset when she wrote to say that she and Roy had given
up trying for children.' Mrs Truelove was upset all over
again at the memory, and had to pause to dab at her eyes
with a handkerchief. 'Then Laura took up acting pro-
fessionally, and seemed to make a go of it—with Roy's
support, of course. It was in 'eighty-five that she wrote to
me that she was going to be in a play at the Sullivan
Theatre; and naturally I offered to put her up at my house.
My husband was away on a business trip, and my daughter
Amy was at boarding-school in Geelong, so I was glad of
the company.' She paused, pleased with her own exposition
and flattered by the rapt attention of the young people.

'Well, soon after Laura's play opened at the Sullivan, I
was invited by an old friend to visit her for a long weekend,
in Adelaide. Laura urged me to go: and she pointed out

that she was quite capable of looking after the house. So I accepted.

'It was just bad luck that on that very weekend there was a food-poisoning scare at Amy's school, and all the younger girls were sent home. I'm sure you've already guessed what happened. The poor child arrived home late at night, let herself in with her key—and surprised Laura in bed with a strange man.'

'Amy knew it wasn't Laura's husband?' Cassandra asked.

'Of course. She'd known Roy for years. The child was hideously embarrassed and fled to her own room. Laura followed her and tried to make light of things—talked a lot of guff about the bohemian life and so on. Amy guessed she was just keeping her occupied while the man packed his things and sneaked off.'

Crook said, 'Amy must have seen the man's face quite clearly?'

'She did. She told me she did.'

'But she didn't know who he was—either then or later?'

'He was a total stranger, as I said. If she found out who he was later, she didn't tell me.'

'Would it be possible for me to talk to Amy, Mrs Truelove?'

'I doubt she would be very forthcoming, young man. She had a sort of breakdown some years ago, and since then she has been very shy: nervous with strangers. But I'll give you a note of introduction if you like. She lives in Sydney: Didcot Street, near Bondi Junction. Her number's in the book.'

Crook thanked her and made a note of the address. 'You've been more helpful than you know.'

'Have I?' Hilda Truelove's plump face sagged with anxiety. 'I'm not really one to tittle-tattle, but—well, Roy Farrant's cared for Danny like a saint all these years, while Laura's done her best to forget him. And now she's talking about motherly love when she can't even bring

herself to cuddle the child for a photograph—well, I just
saw red, I'm afraid.'

Cassandra escorted Crook out and stood with him as he
waited for the elevator. 'Poor old Hilda,' she said. 'In the
end she just couldn't bring herself to say it.'

'What?'

'The thought that's been bugging her all these years. A
thought so ugly she still doesn't want to face it. The thought
that Roy Farrant may not be Danny's father.'

CHAPTER 21

The attacker wore gloves. Rubber gloves. It was the only
thing the girl was sure of. The attack had been so swift, so
unexpected, that even now it had the confused, unreal quality of a dream. This couldn't be happening to her—tied
up, gagged, blindfolded; lying helpless on the floor in her
own home. She struggled futilely against her bonds, moan-
ing with panic.

'Lie still.' The voice was quiet, barely above a whisper.
'I am going to ask you some questions, which you will
answer by either nodding or shaking your head. I must
warn you that I already know most of the answers, so please
do not attempt to lie to me. First, I shall remind you of
something.' The quiet voice spoke unemphatically at some
length. 'Do you remember that episode?'

The girl nodded.

'And later, you learned the man's name?'

The girl hesitated, then nodded again.

'Through your own investigations?'

The girl shook her head violently.

'Ah. You mean you found out by accident?'

Nod.

'And—please remember that if I catch you out in a lie,

I shall be forced to hurt you—you shared that knowledge with someone?'

Nod.

'With more than one person?'

Shake.

'I wonder if I believe you? Did you know about the letters?'

The girl moaned and rolled her head from side to side. She felt something sting her neck, briefly.

'Good. That's very good,' the voice said soothingly. 'No more questions. Here, that blindfold is distressing you. Let me take it off.'

The last thing the girl saw was the grotesque, huge-brimmed hat and the grey, melancholy face beneath it. It was a stranger's face, but she thought she perceived kindness in it. Hope made her dizzy, filled her with a warm, sweet, unexpected happiness. Her eyes were closed, and she hardly flinched as the rubber-clad fingers touched her throat.

The William Street Branch of the HS car Rental Company (*Not the Cheapest—just the Best*) was having a slack afternoon. Only one girl was on duty at the Reception desk, and she was listlessly turning the pages of a paperback novel. She had learned to be philosophical about the job: to take things as they came. You could be rushed off your feet one day, and kicking your heels with boredom the next. It wasn't a very demanding job at the best of times, but you occasionally met a few interesting people in among the thickos and the mug Alecs. That Vietnamese kid, for instance . . . She smiled, remembering the way he'd grinned at her all the time, never once stopped grinning. How anyone could talk so smart and be so stupid! He just didn't seem to understand that you need a licence to drive a car in this country. If the truth be known, the kid probably wasn't old enough to have a licence . . .

She pushed the book aside and looked up alertly as

someone came into the office. It wasn't a customer, though, but the assistant under-manager. It always amused her that all the men in the Company—except the mechanics—got titles, like *Manager*, *Supervisor*, *Controller*, and so on; while the women, who did all the work, got called by their first names. Jack was OK, though. He was a nice-looking, easy-going guy with a sense of humour: the sort of guy a girl could get romantic about if only he didn't wear nylon shirts all the time. Nylon shirts could get awfully niffy, if a fellow wasn't careful.

'Hi, doll,' Jack said. 'Where'd the other girls go?'

That was another thing: Jack always called her 'doll'. Dahleen hated that. 'They're out back in the yard, grabbing a few rays,' she said. 'There's nothin' for 'em to do in here.'

'Too right. This place is like a friggin' graveyard, today. That young Nippo's gone, then?' He looked round as if he thought there could be someone hiding behind a chair.

'He's not a Jap, he's from Vietnam. Yeah, he's gone. I told him over and over, he couldn't have a car without he's got a licence. He said he'd driven a jeep, and that ought to be good enough for anybody. "You gimme a car an' I'll show you," he said. 'What a dill!'

Jack held up a plastic bag. 'Did he visit the toilet?'

Dahleen eyed the bag nervously. 'He asked if he could, yeah.'

'This is prolly his, then. I 'spect he'll come back for it.'

'Maybe it's rubbish. He won't come back for no rubbish.'

Jack sniggered. 'No, it ain't rubbish. Well, some people might say it is, I guess, but it's real hi-tech, state-of-the-art rubbish.'

'What is it?'

He took a brightly-coloured box out of the bag. '*Xeneus and the Chians*,' he said. 'It's the latest in the *Ergo* series.'

'Is it a book?'

'No, doll, it's an adventure.' Jack read from the back of the box: ' "Deep in the subterranean caves of Mount Chiton lies the fabulous Amethyst of Psapho, guarded by the mighty Chians, whose devilish cunning—"''

'It's a game!' Dahleen said, enlightened. 'It's a kid's computer game!'

'Don't sneer,' Jack said. 'These things need a lot of skill, believe me. And they're fun. Move over, I'll show you.'

'What are you going to do?'

'This'll work on your machine.' He seated himself in front of her workstation. 'Just pop this disk in here, type in the magic formula, and—' he consulted a manual the size of a child's picture-book—'yes, I thought so. It works better with a joystick. I've got one in my desk drawer: I'll go get it.' He leered at her and looked waggish. 'Everything works better with a joystick.'

She smiled wistfully at his retreating back. He was a lot of fun, really. He'd be quite fanciable if it weren't for those nylon shirts.

But he was right about the computer game. It was a great giggle, and very exciting. She was amazed at how quickly the time passed. By the end of the afternoon, the whole staff had gathered round to watch, and to take turns zapping the deadly Chians.

Of course, the Vietnamese kid came back to claim his property, but he didn't seem at all put out to find that they had borrowed it. In fact he seemed pleased, and spent some time explaining the finer points of the game in his quaint pidgin English. As Dahleen told her friend later, that kid really brightened up a dull day.

Afterwards, although they all remembered the game very well, no one could describe the kid, except to say that he was Asian-looking and smiled a lot. And no one had thought to ask his name.

Dorothy Want entered her apartment very cautiously, and stood just inside the door, ready to run at the slightest sound. Hearing nothing, she dropped the latch, took the kitchen knife from its hook behind the coat stand, and made a rapid search through all the rooms. Satisfied at last that her home was safe, she bolted and chained the door and put the knife back on its hook.

Then, as she had done every day since Mary died, she searched the apartment from top to bottom for the missing letters.

She didn't find them, of course. Everything else she had stolen during the past year could be accounted for—although the secret caches were now crammed full, and many of her latest acquisitions lay around the place in full view—but the letters were definitely gone. It was silly to cling to the hope that she would one day find them: she had all but taken the place apart, night after night.

She wished now, that she had never stolen them. It wasn't like her to steal things out of simple malice; but the temptation to put the wind up that little creep had been too strong to resist. Also, she had been curious to know what he kept locked away in that oh-so-clever hiding-place of his? Why not keep whatever it was safe at his home?

Finding just a few old love-letters was something of a let-down, but she stole them anyway. She left the envelopes behind, thinking he might not notice the theft immediately. It had seemed a clever notion at the time.

Slowly, she wandered from room to room once again, switching off the lights. She knew by the growing tension in her neck and the hollow feeling in the pit of her stomach, that one of her migraines was coming on. Mechanically, miserably, she made her preparations, swallowing aspirin and then laying out more tablets in rows on her bedside table. Her other props were already there: eye-mask, ear-plugs, cotton-wool, eau-de-Cologne. With a pang of irritation, she remembered the other tablets she had been given by a fellow-sufferer only yesterday: really powerful ones, apparently. It was too late to take them now, on top of the aspirin; but she could try them later. She took the small bottle from her handbag and put it in the pocket of her skirt.

She left just one lamp on, in the hall: its glow filtered into the other rooms, giving her as much light as she needed or could endure. She took a glass and a bottle of vodka from a cupboard—someone had told her that alcohol speeded-up the action of painkillers—and sat in the darkest corner of her shadowy drawing-room to think things out before the pain got too bad.

There was no point in avoiding the truth any longer. Mary had stolen those letters from her. Nobody else could have.

Mary.

In the whole of Dorothy's life, only two people had ever mattered: her husband, Tom; and Mary Barrett. They were the only two people who had given her what she craved: a real respect for her acting talents and an undemanding, uncritical love.

She remembered the day Mary came to work at Dixon's—a sharp, bright-eyed kid of sixteen, as wary and inquisitive as a kitten. They took to each other from the start in spite of their different ages and temperaments: Dorothy, recently widowed, needed someone to care for; and Mary was genuinely moved and flattered by the friend-ship of the older woman.

And later, when Mary found out about Dorothy's pil-fering, she didn't go in for lectures or high moral attitudes. She met the problem head-on, with a child's directness: 'What do you do it for?'

'I don't know.' Dorothy had been going to say, 'To teach people a lesson,' but she realized that Mary would despise such a lie.

'Is it for money? Do you sell the stuff?'

'Oh no.' The very idea was shocking.

'You know you'll be in deep trouble if you get caught?'

'Yes.'

'OK, then.'

And Mary had collected together all the things Dorothy had stolen, stuffed them into plastic shopping-bags, and taken them away. Dorothy never discovered what she did with them: dumped them into rubbish bins, probably. It was a pretty high-handed action, particularly from a mere child; but Dorothy couldn't bring herself to resent it. In its strange way, it was a gesture of love.

On the other hand, Mary herself was far from perfect. Her partiality for violent men had worried Dorothy a lot, and she warned her friend over and over about the dangers; but she just laughed. The danger was the point, she said. 'You and I,' Mary used to say, 'are a couple of outsiders. That's why we get on so well with each other, and not so well with normal people.'

Outsiders.

It was such a bleak word; but the child was probably right. When you're an outsider, you mustn't look to the world for any favours. You're on your own. Even the people closest to you let you down eventually. Even Tom, that sensitive, unambitious soul, had shown himself to be utterly selfish in the end. Maybe other people could believe that an intelligent, well-educated man could be fool enough to drape a damp towel over a gas water-heater while he took a bath; but not Dorothy. She knew he had taken the easy way out; and she knew why. He had been afraid of her: afraid of her strength, afraid of her tongue. She was more of a man than he was, and they both knew it.

Her mind was wandering: probably because the migraine was creeping up on her, the sickness fluttering in her stomach, the discomfort beginning to squeeze the back of her skull. How had Tom forced his way into her mind? Tom was long dead, best forgotten. She had been thinking about Mary, remembering the good times.

And the bad.

She and Mary had been separated after the clothing factory went out of business. That was a bad time: ten years of sheer hell. Soon after she learned that Mary had married that swine Kafko, Dorothy went on a prolonged binge of thieving that finally put her in gaol.

She'd had some psychiatric treatment while she was inside; but only for a short while. The treatment just stopped, without warning. Lack of funds, they said. Government cut-backs, they said.

Then, in 'seventy-eight, a miracle. Mary came back into her life, wangled her a job with Lachlan Theatres. It was great to have work; but far more wonderful to know that Mary still loved her after all those years.

That was when Dorothy met Dimitri Kafko for the first time. The man was the most disgusting and poisonous creature she had ever encountered: not merely a bully, but a subtle and calculating sadist. Neither at the time nor subsequently had Dorothy felt a shred of remorse at killing him. Her only regret was that it took her two years to work out how to do it.

No one ever suspected her. Who would suspect a stately, middle-aged matron of crawling over a roof under cover of darkness and pushing a dead bird into a metal chimney? The death was judged an accident.

Dorothy discovered that her glass was empty. She reached for the vodka bottle, and pain sliced through her skull like a knife. She willed herself not to fight it: any attempt at resistance would be punished by an even worse attack, wave after wave of agony and those terrible coloured lights dancing in front of her eyes. But it was just that one stab: a warning of misery to come. The nausea faded slowly, and she sipped her vodka, the glass rattling against her teeth. The aspirin hadn't done any good; the time had come to try her new tablets. They were very small: but somehow that inspired confidence, Dorothy thought. She felt better the moment she had taken them: fighting her old enemy with a new weapon gave her a feeling of wild optimism. She closed her eyes and sipped her vodka, savouring its warmth in her throat.

It was a pity that Mary had never learned the truth about Kafko's death; if she had, she would have known what a huge debt of loyalty and love she owed to her friend.

But in fact, their friendship had never been the same after *The Golden Governess* incident. Mary was never totally convinced that Dorothy hadn't stolen things from the cast; and that was particularly hurtful since Dorothy never once thieved while she was in Bonnie Lachlan's employ. Never. When she really needed Mary's trust, it wasn't there.

The memory squeezed Dorothy's heart: she gasped, and tears started to her eyes. On a sudden impulse, she shouted aloud: foul, ugly words, words that her employers would have been amazed to hear from her lips. The effort made her dizzy and a little confused: she couldn't remember why she had been shouting. But it felt good: she shouted some more. Her voice made fine, resounding echoes in her head.

There was a small bottle in her hand. It looked familiar, but she couldn't recall where she had seen it before. It had pills in it. Little pills. Silly little pills. They made her laugh. She ate some pills and drank some vodka, spilling both down her dress, which made her laugh even more.

'Why don't I go to the cops?' She was talking aloud: it seemed only natural, since she was about to argue with herself. 'Because I got a record, that's why. I'd have to tell them I'd been nicking things again, and they'd shove me back inside.' She was using vulgar words, but that seemed natural, too: she'd always been good in character roles. 'Anyway, who says those letters've got anything to do with—with what happened? Could be nothing at all to do with it. She was a slut and she died like a slut.'

All the same, she owed something to the memory of her old friend. An idea that had been bobbing around in her mind for some time happily resurfaced. She would talk—in strictest confidence, of course—to that young man, that private detective with the funny name. He had a nice face, and he had been very—she had to concentrate hard to think of the word—*respectful*. She could trust him to be—well, something or other she didn't need to worry about at this moment.

Now that that was settled, she could relax. Everything

was going to be all right. Her head was spinning, but not throbbing, now: not aching at all. She felt fine. Better not drink any more vodka, though: her lips were quite numb. But no headache: no pain at all. She closed her eyes. She had never felt happier in her life.

CHAPTER 22

Mickey Swan gave his bald head an invigorating massage with both hands. It did nothing to relieve his irritation. 'I thought I liked you, kid, you know that?' he told Crook. 'I thought you were OK. Boy, was I wrong! You're a jumbo-sized pain in the bum.'

'It goes with the job,' Crook said. 'Just make the call, Mr Swan. I have to talk to her.'

'Or what?'

'Or she'll have to talk to the police. And probably a jumbo-sized posse of reporters.'

'That sounds like a threat.'

'Of course it's a threat, Mr Swan. How else am I going to get you to cooperate?'

Swan rapped himself on the head and nodded several times, as if this answer gave him a perverse kind of pleasure. 'Are you going to tell me what this is all about?'

'No, sir.'

'You've dug up some dirt, right? Something about her kid?'

'No comment.'

Reluctantly, Swan reached for the phone. 'This is a waste of time. She won't talk to you.'

'Ask her anyway. Give her a message from me.'

'What message?'

'I'll write it down for you.' Crook tore a page from his notebook and wrote on it in block capitals.

Mickey Swan had to use a lot of patience and persuasion

to get through to Laura Farrant. 'Look, I'm her goddam agent, for Chrissakes,' he kept saying, slapping his head lustily as if to identify himself by the sound. At last he made contact with his client. 'Laura? Look, I'm sorry to . . . Yeah, of course it's an emergency, darling: would I interrupt you otherwise? It's that private detective, honey, the one I told you about: he says he's got to talk to you . . . I don't know what about . . . Yeah, I told him that . . . Wait, don't hang up, he's asked me to give you a message. It's . . .' He glanced down at the paper Crook pushed across the desk . . . 'Amy Truelove . . . Yeah, that's it. Amy Truelove. Nothing else.' He listened for a few seconds longer, eyeing Crook with some bewilderment. 'Yeah. Sure. I'll—' He winced and slowly replaced the receiver. 'Magic password,' he said, examining the piece of paper. 'She'll see you right away, at the studio. Matter of fact, I'll take you there myself. If she's in serious schtuck, I wanna ditch her before she ditches me.'

Laura Farrant took off her wimple and handed it to her dresser. She acknowledged her agent with a dismissive flick of the fingers. 'Piss off, Mickey,' she said inelegantly. 'I want to talk to this young jerk alone.' She stretched out in a reclining chair, and let the back down as far as it would go. 'Tell them to hold all my calls, Trace,' she instructed her dresser. 'And wait outside, see we're not disturbed.' She watched the girl go, then closed her eyes. 'You wanted to talk to me, snooper,' she said crisply. 'So talk.'

'I want to show you a letter first, Miss Farrant.'

'Oh God. OK. Hold it up where I can see it.'

But after one glance, she sat up abruptly and snatched it from his hand. She turned her back on him and read it with intense concentration, head bowed. When she turned round again, her face was grey and hard. 'Mary Kafko, right? She *did* steal them after all. She swore to me that she hadn't, and I was fool enough to believe her. I even gave her a job, would you believe? OK, what do you want?'

'I want to know who wrote that letter.'

She wasn't listening. 'You'd better not threaten me, slimeball. If this is any kind of a shakedown, you're in deep shit, believe me. I've got friends in this town who'd rip your head off if I gave them the word.'

'I don't doubt it,' Crook said drily. 'I'm not threatening you. Your ex-maid, Mary Kafko—or Dean, as she called herself recently—was murdered a few weeks ago. Among her effects were that letter and a lot of money. Too much money. I'm looking into the possibility that she was blackmailing somebody and got killed because of it.'

Her face darkened. 'Are you saying you suspect *me*?'

'That letter was addressed to you, wasn't it?'

'I'm not admitting anything. Are you seriously accusing me of murder?'

'No, Miss Farrant. I know you didn't do it; and now I've met you, I can't imagine you submitting to blackmail. All the same, I know from Amy Truelove that you were having an affair with someone here in Melbourne in March 1983— probably the man who wrote that letter. Since Mary Dean wasn't blackmailing you, it's possible that she was blackmailing him.'

'No.' Laura Farrant smiled thinly. 'Let me put your mind at rest about one thing, laddie. This man—' she held up the letter—'didn't murder little Mary Kafko. Take my word for it. Anyway, the idea's crazy. This harmless little fling happened yonks ago: it would be embarrassing if it all came out now, sure; but a rational guy doesn't pay out a fortune—or commit a murder—just to avoid embarrassment.'

Crook said reluctantly, 'There could be more to it than simple embarrassment. Tell me his name, Miss Farrant.'

'No.' She had begun to relax, seeing herself in charge of the situation; now she stiffened with suspicion and suppressed anger. 'What do you mean, there could be more to it?'

'You know what I mean, ma'am. We're not talking minor peccadilloes, here. This man—whoever he is—could have been threatened with a major scandal.'

Her mouth twisted contemptuously. 'Scandal? Not even the most determined muck-raker could make a major scandal out of a little foolishness, so many years ago.'

'Miss Farrant, you know what I'm talking about,' Crook repeated. 'Your "harmless little fling" happened in March 1983; your son Danny was born at the end of that year.'

'You bastard!' Laura got to her feet, clumsy in her haste, and struck at Crook with her fists. 'You unspeakable, slimy, despicable bastard! What kind of a sick-minded creep are you? Don't you think I've suffered enough, giving birth to a Mongol kid?'

'Whom you've never cared for,' Crook said coldly. 'I don't like you, Miss Farrant, any better than you like me. But I'm not hounding you about your past: I'm trying to find the truth about Mary Dean's murder. Tell me who wrote that letter.'

She tore the letter up and threw the fragments in his face. 'Get out! You disgust me.'

'It's mutual, Miss Farrant. Just tell me what I want to know, and I'll be more than happy to leave.'

'No! Get out!' But before he reached the door, she said, 'The name won't mean anything to you, anyway. Promise me you won't pester his wife and family?'

'I'll be as discreet as it's possible to be, Miss Farrant: that's all I can promise. But if the guy is a murderer, there's no way it can be hushed up.'

She smiled: she had recovered her poise again. 'He's no murderer. He was a tenor in the amateur choir I used to sing with.'

'Name?'

'Claude Lasalle. I told you it wouldn't mean anything to you.'

'Does he live in Sydney?'

'Actually—' her smile broadened maliciously—'he doesn't live anywhere. He died two years ago.'

*

'She's lying, of course,' Cassandra said breathlessly. 'Look, could we stop for a minute? Or at least walk at a reasonable pace? Your legs are a lot longer than mine.'

'I'm sorry.' Crook came to a halt and glanced down at her with genuine concern. He raised his head and looked round at the trees, the grass and the brown river as if seeing them for the first time. 'Sometimes,' he said lamely, 'I feel the need to walk, to be on the move. It—' he invented an explanation, to deflect her questions—'it clears my mind.'

'Does it?' She wasn't convinced. She walked a few paces from the path and up the gentle slope of the bank. 'Actually, I believe that talking is better therapy than walking, Paul Crook. Come sit on the grass and talk to me.'

But he remained standing. 'What makes you so sure that Laura Farrant was lying?'

She shrugged. 'Laura was determined not to talk to you; but she changed her mind when you mentioned Amy True-love. Why? If her lover was really dead, what had she to fear from Amy's revelations? There is no one to corroborate the child's story: Laura could simply deny it.' Cassandra wasn't sure that Crook was even listening to her: his face had that tightly closed-in look he had worn all afternoon. But she ploughed on: 'Laura thought that you had talked to Amy face to face. When she learned that you hadn't, she tried to send you on a wild goose chase.'

Crook frowned and paused, as if she had spoken to him in some foreign tongue which he was having trouble under-standing. 'Are you saying this Claude Lasalle character didn't exist?'

'Oh, I'm sure he existed. But I don't think he was Laura's lover. He's a diversionary tactic, a red herring. Laura wants you to waste time investigating him while she and the real paramour cover their tracks.'

'Paramour?' Crook was distracted by the word.

Cassandra sighed heavily and lowered her gaze, moving her head slightly to ease the stiffness in her neck. After a moment, she took off her spectacles and pinched the bridge of her nose between finger and thumb. 'You really don't care, do you?' she said quietly. 'You're just going through the motions.' She replaced her glasses and half-turned away from him, letting the breeze push her hair back from her face. 'You give the impression—' she faltered, and seemed to change her mind, then went on bravely—'you give the impression that you're not really interested in Mary Dean or Laura Farrant, or indeed anybody. You're doing this job just to pass the time. You're floating around in some emotional limbo, wondering what the hell you really want to do with your life.'

'Is that what you think?' Crook sounded only mildly interested. At last he decided to sit down: at a cautious distance, as if he was afraid of some accidental physical contact. 'Emotional limbo? Maybe. But at the beginning, I *was* interested. I really wanted to help Stan Dean. I needed him to be innocent.'

'That's a strange thing to say. Do you mean you were sorry for him?'

Crook fidgeted: the conversation had taken an uncomfortable turn. 'I suppose I identified with him. In a way.'

'Why?' She was deliberately sharp, trying to bounce him into an unguarded answer. It was the wrong approach, and she regretted it immediately. 'Sorry, sorry: none of my business.'

Crook smiled in spite of himself. 'Does that mean you're going to drop the subject?'

She tilted her chin aggressively. 'Look, I've apologized, OK? I know you think I'm incurably nosey, but the truth is I'm concerned about you. The first time I met you I saw that you were a lonely, troubled man. There's something eating you up; and the sooner you get it out of your system, the sooner you'll get your head on straight, and the sooner we'll get this goddam case solved.'

Crook noted the 'we'. You really care about the case,

don't you?' he said mildly. 'It's not just an intellectual game, is it?'

'I've put in a lot of work and a lot of thought,' Cassandra said hotly. 'I just hate to think I've been wasting my time.' It wasn't the truth; but if the idiot couldn't read her real motives, why should she spell them out? He was a typical male oaf; but when his eyes went all dark with misery, she had this foolish urge to hold him and mother him. Well, hold him, anyway.

Crook lay on his back and looked at the sky. She was an oddball, this Cassandra Tasse, and no error. Bumptious, opinionated, insatiably inquisitive, she was just the kind of sheila he'd normally avoid like a swarm of blowies. But the weird thing was, he liked her a lot. He felt comfortable in her company. Maybe it was because he'd seen her face unprotected by those monstrous specs. It wasn't hard to have a soft spot for a kid who looks as vulnerable as a blind puppy.

The sky was cloudless, fathomless. Without really meaning to, he began to talk: awkwardly at first, and then with increasing confidence, as to an old friend. He talked about Robyn: about their whirlwind love-affair and about the mis-adventure that had put her into hospital. 'It was my fault,' he insisted. 'All my fault.' He told her about the hours he had spent, day after day, at Robyn's bedside; how he had talked endlessly, making himself believe that she could hear him in her sleep. He tried, inadequately, to describe the miracle of her awakening.

Crook closed his eyes and fell silent for a long time. Cassandra sat perfectly still, fearing that any sound, any move-ment might scare him back into his shell.

'To me, she seemed unchanged,' he said eventually. 'I saw what I wanted to see, I suppose. There were a few holes in her memory, which made her a bit depressed; and some of her muscles didn't work so well, but I was sure that now she was out of the coma, she would mend, and mend quickly.' Once again, he paused. Cassandra forced herself to keep her head averted, afraid of breaking the spell. Then he spoke in a rush, wanting it over with: 'She was having treatment for her depression. One day the psychiatrist sent for me and asked me to stop visiting her for a while. He said I was hindering her recovery. He said she had dangerously ambivalent feelings about me which were making her confused and unhappy. In the end he had to tell me the real reason for her state of mind. While she was still in a coma, the doctors had discovered that she was pregnant; and for all the right reasons, they had aborted—had terminated her pregnancy.'

'What!' Cassandra could keep quiet no longer.

'For the sake of her health, and because the fœtus was seriously . . . malformed.'

'But they did that without consulting you? Without even telling you?' Cassandra was appalled.

'I'm not actually a relative. I don't have any rights. Her father had to make the decision.'

'But how could you not know about it? You were there all the time. You just said so.'

'No.' Crook still stared at the sky, wooden-faced. 'I was away from her for a couple of weeks. I was called to give evidence at an inquest in Dubbo.'

'Are you sure—' She bit her tongue, but it was too late.

'Am I sure it was my child? Yes.'

'I'm so sorry.' She took off her spectacles.

Crook said dully: 'Much of the time, I just don't know how to deal with it. It's like I've swallowed a great lump of misery, and I can neither digest it nor vomit it up. It just sits there in my guts, hurting.' He sat up and regarded her impassively. 'Satisfied now?'

She blew her nose on a massive handkerchief. You needed to tell someone.'

'Did I?'

'Yes.' She blinked at him short-sightedly through her curtain of hair. 'And you need a woman to tell you this: if the fœtus was seriously damaged, then the doctors did the

right thing—for her sake and for yours. Think what happened to Laura, for heaven's sake! Call me heartless, but
I think you're over-reacting to a situation which you didn't
know about at the time, and which was all for the best
anyway.'

'But I'm responsible, don't you see? Responsible for her
pregnancy; responsible for leading her into danger—'

'Rubbish!' She hid behind her spectacles again. 'If you're
determined to clobber yourself with guilt, nobody can stop
you. Do you want to hear the truth?'

Crook almost smiled. 'You're going to tell me, anyway.'

'Too right. You're being silly and self-indulgent.' She
lifted her head challengingly. 'I'll bet you a zillion dollars
to a bent penny that Robyn gets over this before you do.'
That's enough, Cassandra, she told herself sharply. *Calm down.*
But although she could get her exasperation under control,
she could never rein in her curiosity. 'You said you took
this case because you identified with Stanley Dean. Was
that because he had lost an unborn child, too? And felt
guilty about it—like you?'

'Yes. But there was something else he said that struck a
chord with me.' Crook leaned forward earnestly. 'He talked
about life being laid out in advance, like a railway track.
You might think you can influence where you're going, he
said, but you can't. You're just a helpless passenger. No
matter how much you struggle and holler, you can't stop
the train or move the track.'

'So your whingeing about your life being laid out in
advance is preordained, is it?' Cassandra said scornfully.
'That's not a philosophy, it's an excuse for just rolling over
on your back and waiting for somebody to scratch your
belly. I don't believe that's your style. Tell me what you
plan to do next?'

'To see her when she gets back from America. I can't
realistically make any plans beyond that. I'll write to her
in the meantime, of course.'

'No, I don't mean about Ms—about Robyn.' Cassandra

sucked air irritably between her teeth. 'I don't believe your situation is as hopeless as you think. If you love each other, you'll work it out. If you don't love each other, there's nothing *to* work out. Anyway, you can't just loll around feeling sorry for yourself. What are you going to do about the Mary Dean case?'

Crook yawned. 'I suppose I should talk to Amy Truelove. I reckon she has the key to it all. She knows who Laura's lover was.'

'Who Laura's lover *is*,' Cassandra insisted. 'I mean, I'm sure he's still alive; and I'll lay odds he was the one Mary was blackmailing. We know a few things about him already. He's rich; he's sexy; he's—' She froze, her mouth hanging stupidly open.

'What's wrong?' Crook looked round apprehensively, but saw nothing untoward.

'Something just went through my mind; I'm trying to . . .' She was uncharacteristically incoherent. 'It was something you said, I think, or maybe I read it somewhere . . . Hell!' She scrambled excitedly to her feet. 'I'll contact you at your motel, OK? I think—no, I'll tell you later!' She galloped away towards the city with a slightly knock-kneed gait, her hair streaming in the wind.

Crook stayed where he was and watched her go. All that soul-searching had left him strangely lethargic; and yet— he had to admit it—feeling more optimistic than he had in weeks. He still couldn't understand the impulse that had made him confide in Cassandra Tasse. She was some oddball, and no error. A good kid, though. Nice legs, too.

'Paul!'

The familiar voice froze him in mid-stride, half way across the motel lobby. His new-found optimism dissolved on the instant. That voice—that tone—could only mean trouble. 'Elizabeth?' He couldn't see her at first; and he had a wild, desperate hope that he was mistaken. Then he became aware that someone was waving impatiently to him from a seat near the window.

If he hadn't known the voice, he would never have recognized her. She was wearing dark glasses and a dowdy head-scarf; and she looked, to Crook's incredulous eyes, slightly dishevelled. He hurried to her side. 'What's happened? What are you doing here?'

'God, I thought you were never going to turn up!' she snapped. 'I've been waiting here for hours. You've got to help me.'

'Help you? Of course, Elizabeth. But what—'

'Come with me.' She stalked ahead of him to the Reception counter. 'I've come to reclaim my property,' she announced to the desk clerk. 'This gentleman will pay what I owe.'

The clerk flushed, not sure whether to be offended or amused. 'I didn't ask you for any pledge of security, madam: you insisted on giving it.' He took a wristwatch from his pocket and put it on the counter.

'I did it to ease your mind,' Elizabeth said grandly. 'I didn't want you worrying about your money.'

With an effort, the man kept his smile in place. 'The lady came out without her purse,' he explained to Crook. 'She borrowed fifteen dollars to pay her taxi-fare. That's all there was to it.'

'Pay the man twenty dollars, Paul,' Elizabeth commanded. 'He deserves a *pourboire* for his courtesy.' She picked up the watch and marched back to her seat by the window.

Crook's expression of bewilderment and dismay afforded the desk clerk some satisfaction. 'The lady's a bit put out,' he said. 'She's been sat there for nearly an hour.' He accepted the money with a nod of thanks. 'I wasn't really worried about this, you know.'

'Of course not. Thanks for helping out.'

'Don't mench.' The man looked past Crook at Elizabeth's unbending profile. 'Good luck, mate.'

Now that the first shock was wearing off, Crook began to feel more irritated than apprehensive. It was unfair of Elizabeth to do this to him. It was obvious what had happened: Elizabeth had quarrelled with her new boyfriend, had flounced out in a tantrum and didn't want to ruin the effect of her exit by going back for her purse. He drew up a chair and sat opposite her.

Elizabeth sensed his lack of sympathy. 'I wouldn't have bothered you if I had anyone else to turn to.'

'There's no need to apologize, my dear. Just tell me how I can help you?'

She scowled ferociously and gave him a hard glance. 'The beast tried to rape me,' she said grimly.

'Good God! Are you—' Crook had been about to say 'Are you sure?' but collected his wits in time. 'Who? Not your friend Barry?'

'Gary.' Elizabeth gritted her teeth. 'Gary Fordson. He hit me.' She pulled back a fold of the scarf to reveal a swollen bruise above her cheekbone. 'He was drunk.' She bit her lip and turned her head away.

'Don't cry, Elizabeth,' Crook pleaded desperately. Elizabeth's tears always reduced him to blind panic. 'Try to keep calm and just tell me what happened.'

'He took me to lunch at that new Italian place,' she said in a low voice. 'We both drank a little too much, and— anyway, he proposed to me. I was amazed: his mother loathes me, and I thought . . . Anyway, he did. Oh, damn, damn, damn!' She clenched her jaw and turned towards the window, trying vainly to check her tears.

Embarrassed, Crook gave her his handkerchief. 'Did you accept him?'

'Of course I did, you fool! He's amusing, he's handsome, and . . .'

'And he's rich,' Crook said thoughtlessly.

She glared at him. 'You're one to talk. You couldn't wait to chuck me for that millionaire's daughter.'

'I'm sorry,' Crook said ambiguously. 'Let's not rake over old quarrels. So, you accepted him. And—?'

'We went back to his parents' house. I began to suspect something right there: everyone had gone out—not just the parents, but the servants, too. We were alone. That's when he suggested . . . We were as good as married already, he said. When I refused, he got violent and tried to take me by force. He struck me.'

'So you ran away?'

She hesitated, as if the question was a complicated one. Then she said simply, 'Yes.'

Crook studied her anxiously as she dabbed the tears away. Her face was still tight with anger but she was in control of herself. 'Shouldn't you complain to the police?'

'And make a thoroughgoing spectacle of myself? Don't be such an idiot. I've been going out with the fellow, and living at his parents' house for weeks. Think how that would sound in court. Anyway, I couldn't face the publicity.'

'So what's to be done?'

She twisted the handkerchief in both hands, as if she was wringing it out. 'God, I must look a fright!'

'You look just fine, Elizabeth. You've never had to worry about the way you look.'

She smiled, a little shakily. 'You used to say I was beautiful.'

'You still are, my dear. You don't need me to tell you.'

'I know you think I'm a tiresome prude. Most men do.' She bowed her head and spoke so quietly that he had to bend close to hear her. 'Men tell me I've got a "hang-up" about sex, which is a roundabout way of saying I'm mad not to give them what they want. But I can't help the way I feel. Am I such a freak?'

'No, Elizabeth. It's—' Crook was well out of his depth, but he struggled on—'it's just that the right man hasn't come your way. Yet.'

'No.' She looked meaningfully at him and gave him back his handkerchief. 'Of the two men I've fallen for, one was a spineless wimp and the other a shameless cad. What does that make me, I wonder? A fool, I suppose.' She straightened her back and lifted her head with a belligerent air that reminded Crook disconcertingly of her mother. 'We must make a plan,' she announced.'

'Yes.' Crook had no difficulty in decoding this remark: it meant that Elizabeth was about to issue commands.

'You may as well know that I have no money,' she said with a touch of defiance, 'and no credit either. The little I had, I spent on providing myself with an adequate wardrobe. So I shall have to borrow from you.'

Crook assented with as much enthusiasm as he could muster. 'Of course,' he said manfully. 'How much, er . . . ?'

She brushed the question aside. 'Oh, I don't know. You'll just have to sponsor me until I can get a job. I'll pay you back when I can. Is this place full?'

'The motel? I don't think so.'

'Then I'll take a room here. It can go on your bill. I expect your firm's paying, anyway. When do you go back to Sydney?'

'Tomorrow, probably. Soon, anyway.'

'I'll travel with you. I'll ring Angela, and see if she can put me up.'

'I thought you'd be going back to Albany.' Crook couldn't quite keep the dismay out of his voice.

'I'm not welcome there,' Elizabeth said coldly. 'I've had serious words with Mother, and Daddy's lost his job. He's so wretched, I can't bear to look at him right now. No use looking for help from that quarter. Right—' Elizabeth was completely back on form—'we'll book my room here and then go and collect my things from the beastly Fordson house.'

Collecting Elizabeth's luggage turned out to be less embarrassing than Crook had feared. They found her cases packed and assembled by the front door; and one of the servants helped Crook carry them out to the car. The whole proceedings were carried out with an icy formality and the minimum of words, Mrs Fordson watching haughtily from the drawing-room window while her son slouched moodily on the front step. It was difficult to be completely sure, but Gary Fordson appeared to have his right arm in a sling. Crook commented on this as he was driving Elizabeth back to the city.

'A girl has a right to defend herself,' Elizabeth said stiffly. 'You told me that, years ago, when we were at University. You showed me a few simple ju-jutsu holds, don't you remember?'

'Yes.' What Crook remembered was that in those days he had used any and every stratagem to get his arms around Elizabeth's supple body.

'I have never forgotten your advice, or your instruction,' Elizabeth said primly.

Crook was amused. 'What did you do, break his arm?'

'Don't be ridiculous. It was nothing. He was just being pathetic to impress his mama.'

'But you must have done something?'

'Well,' Elizabeth conceded with a gleam of satisfaction, 'I may have dislocated one of his fingers. Or possibly two.'

Elizabeth's room was on the same floor as Crook's, a few doors away. She instructed him to put all her suitcases on the bed, so that she could check their contents and pack them 'properly', as she put it. No, she didn't want to go out: she wasn't hungry and anyway she wasn't fit to be seen with this awful black eye. 'I would rather do this,' she said, looking affectionately at the bulging cases. 'It'll soothe me.' Which was the literal truth, Crook knew. Clothes were her real passion: buying them, caring for them, or just looking at them with the fierce joy of a miser with his gold. He left her to her therapy.

In his own room, the light on his telephone was blinking. He picked up the receiver. 'You have a message for me?'

'Yessir.' The operator was bored or tired, or both. 'From a Ms Cassandra Tasse. Message reads: "Get here soonest. I've cracked it! By George, I've cracked it!"'

CHAPTER 23

'Peter Waystone!' Crook wondered if Cassandra had been drinking. She certainly seemed to be high on something.

'*Sir* Peter,' Cassandra insisted. That's important. That's part of the story.'

'But he was—'

'Laura's gynæcologist, right. Laura's fellow member of the Arrigo Choral Society. Laura's lover. Probably the father of Laura's child.'

'No.' He dismissed the idea. 'It's just not credible.'

'Look, hear me out, OK? You remember you told me about the newspaper review of *The Moonflower* at the Sullivan Theatre in '83?'

'Yes. Bonnie showed it to me because she got a favourable mention in it.'

'I looked up that cutting in Bonnie's files. I've got a copy of it right here.' She had photocopied the whole page. 'Next to the theatre notice is an article about a medical conference at a local hospital. I don't remember reading it, but something must have caught my eye, because it's been nagging at my mind ever since.' On the copy she handed Crook, a few lines had been highlighted with a fluorescent marker. Crook read:

> On Friday morning, Mr P. Waystone, the eminent gynæcologist, read a paper on 'Keyhole' Surgery—New Techniques and Applications . . .

'So that proves that Waystone could have been Laura's lover,' Cassandra said. 'He was in Melbourne at the right time.'

'*Could* have been,' Crook echoed. 'But it doesn't prove that he was.'

'OK, let's go back to The Letter.' Cassandra's excitement provided the capitals. '*Somebody* was making an assignation with Laura Farrant for a dirty weekend at Hilda Truelove's house, right?'

'That's what I believe, yes.'

'Good. Now, the letter said—I quote—"Blanche is staying another month, so H. is completely tied up here." Who do you suppose H. is?'

'No idea.'

'I have. Waystone's wife.'

'No. Waystone's wife is called Primrose. I've met her. He named his hospital for her.'

'Primrose is his *second* wife. In '83 he was married to a woman called Hélène. French-born. Her aunt's name, incidentally, was Blanche.'

Crook looked as startled as he felt. 'How the hell did you find all that out?'

'Inspired guesswork.' Cassandra was still mightily pleased with herself. 'I tracked down a personal friend of the Waystones and persuaded her to chat to me.'

'Who?'

Cassandra dimpled at him and played peekaboo over her spectacles. 'Claude Lasalle's widow.'

'What!'

'I went through the Lasalles in the Sydney phone book until I hit the jackpot. Told Mrs L. I was doing an article on Waystone for a woman's magazine. Said I'd got her name from Laura Farrant.'

'And she believed all that?'

'She's an old dear,' Cassandra said sentimentally. 'Loves a gossip. She's in the Arrigo Choir too, incidentally. This is what she told me: Hélène Waystone, a pretty, vivacious woman, became suddenly and seriously ill in '83. When she learned, in the May of that year, that she had an inoperable tumour, she insisted on travelling to France for one last visit. *La nostalgie*, as Mrs Lasalle said. Waystone accompanied her, of course. However, the trip aggravated her condition: she died in Paris a few days before Christmas that same year. Waystone stayed on in France for some time—Hélène owned property out there, and he had to wind up her affairs. In fact, he didn't get back to Oz until the end of '84; and by then he'd married again: a wealthy spinster, some years older than himself.'

'Jeeze, you're describing some kind of monster,' Crook said. 'You're telling me this guy was having an affair with his own patient while his wife was terminally sick? And then having got his mistress pregnant, he dumps her for another woman?'

'He may not have known that Laura was pregnant,' Cassandra pointed out. 'Also, he may not have realized how serious his wife's illness was, until that winter. Her condition deteriorated with horrifying speed, apparently. We can only guess at his state of mind at that time. But we know he suffered two serious shocks within the space of a few months: being caught *in flagrante* by Amy Truelove; and learning that Hélène was terminally ill. I suspect that those two events made him rethink his relationship with Laura Farrant very radically.'

'You mean, he did his best to forget her.'

'Something like that. *Her* emotional state at that time doesn't bear thinking about; particularly as she seems to have been truly in love with the fellow. She kept that letter, after all.'

'So your scenario is this,' Crook said, working it out for his own benefit: 'Laura kept that letter out of sentiment. Four years later, Mary stole the letter from her, and some years after that, used it to blackmail Waystone. So Waystone is a prime suspect for Mary's murder.'

'I suppose so.' Cassandra's tone was uncharacteristically cautious. 'But there are two awkward bits of the puzzle that don't fit anywhere, and I'm sure they're important. First: why did those three theatre people, connected with

The Golden Governess—Ian Trimmer, Dorothy Want and Mary Dean—all end up working for the Arrigo Choral Society?'

Crook was dismayed. 'You're not suggesting they were all in it together? You don't think they were all blackmailing Waystone?'

'It's hard to see it any other way, though I'm trying to keep an open mind. But the other puzzle is: where does Amy Truelove fit in? She was also in *The Golden Governess*, remember.'

Crook groaned. 'Not Amy, too? You're talking this thing up into a full-blown conspiracy.'

'No, that isn't quite what I mean. But Amy has to be part of the pattern, don't you see? Think about that letter for a moment. It's not in itself very shocking. It only becomes so when you know that it's evidence of an adulterous relationship between a gynæcologist and his patient. Who was in a position to know about that relationship? Not Mary Kafko or Dorothy Want. Who but Amy Truelove?'

'Amy had seen *someone* in Laura's bed,' Crook protested. 'How did she know it was Waystone?'

'Because—' Cassandra was proud of her reasoning— 'when Waystone got his knighthood as a reward for establishing his Clinic—which, incidentally, his new wife's money paid for—his photograph appeared in the papers. That's when Amy must have recognized him as Laura's lover.'

Crook was beginning to see what she was getting at, though he couldn't bring himself to buy a sherrick of it. 'Your idea is that Amy shared that secret with Mary and Dorothy—and with Ian Trimmer, her boyfriend at the time. Later, those three used that guilty knowledge to force Waystone to employ them at the Arrigo Choral Society.'

'It begs a lot of questions,' Cassandra said, 'but it sort of hangs together. Shall I go on?'

'No, I think I see where you're heading. Waystone had submitted to blackmail once—finding jobs for those three people, possibly also giving them money. But these later demands by Mary were too greedy, too persistent. He killed her.'

'There is a snag. Waystone has an alibi.'

'Provided by Trimmer.' Crook was rather enjoying the game now. 'A crucial point of your scenario is that Ian Trimmer is corrupt and thoroughly venal. And don't forget that providing a fake alibi would give him an even stronger hold over Waystone.'

'Yes, but—' Cassandra's patient tone indicated that she was still keeping an open mind—'suppose it turns out to be true?'

'In that case—' Crook concentrated on keeping a straight face—'your whole beautiful theory thuds to the ground.'

'My theory?' Cassandra was gently reproving. 'You don't know what my theory is.'

'Yes I do. You think Waystone dunnit.'

'I think he might have. But there's another strong possibility. If there was a conspiracy to blackmail Waystone, it must have persisted over a number of years. From the point of view of the blackmailers, it was a cosy, profitable arrangement. Mary's actions threatened that arrangement: possibly even threatened their very freedom. She was rocking the boat. Perhaps the other two decided it was time to pitch her over the side.'

They had made some definite progress, Crook thought, as he drove back to the motel, but Cassandra's boast that she had cracked the case was some way off the mark. The stuff about Waystone had been very interesting, and she had made a very strong case for him being Laura's lover; but it was a long step from there to naming the man as a murderer. Then that complicated yarn about conspiracies and blackmail—it just didn't ring true, in Crook's opinion. Moonshine. Guesses piled on more guesses. Some solid evidence was what was required. He must interview Amy Truelove. Question Ian Trimmer and Dorothy Want. And

Peter Waystone, if possible; though that could be tricky. But he was getting close to the answer: he could feel it. The case was unravelling in his hands.

It occurred to him that he ought soon to consult with Stanley Dean. Dean was now officially his client, but the investigation was becoming expensive. Dean ought to be warned about the cost.

Thinking about money led Crook inevitably to the problem of Elizabeth. In theory he could put Elizabeth's motel bill and airfare on his expense account; but in practice he knew he couldn't face trying to explain those items to Mrs Parsons. He'd have to find the money out of his own pocket, damn it. He told himself it was mean-spirited to resent it so much; but saying it didn't make the resentment go away.

His mood wasn't improved by finding his reserved slot occupied by someone else's car: he had to drive to the far end of the lot to find a space to park.

He heard the slither of rubber-soled shoes as he bent to lock up the car. He looked round sharply, but too late to protect himself. The man, bent almost double, shoulder-charged him at full tilt, sending him staggering across the asphalt. Arms flailing, Crook cannoned into one car, then another. He side-stepped in a reflex action as the man charged him again. Someone punched him in the small of the back; and as he lurched forward he was aware of yet another figure closing in on him from the left. He couldn't see how many of them there were; but there were too many to fight. He ran.

He made it half way to the side entrance of the motel, dodging and weaving between the parked cars. Then a car door swung open directly in his path. Winded, he backed away, looking for an escape route; but he saw that he had been herded into a trap. His three pursuers fanned out behind him, cutting off his retreat; ahead, an elegantly-dressed man ducked out of the car and faced Crook over the open door. 'School's open, dickhead,' Hogarth Wheeler said unpleasantly. 'We're going to teach you a lesson you won't forget.' He slammed the car door and pulled on a pair of black leather gloves, moving with deliberate menace, like a bad actor in a cheap movie. Crook took no comfort from the theatricality of the performance: he read in Wheeler's eyes that smug, impervious stupidity that is only a hair's-breadth away from utter madness.

The men on either side of Crook feinted to grab his arms. Crook stepped back instinctively, and the third man, rushing from behind, kicked his feet away from under him. In a moment he was pinned face down on the ground. Joshing each other and sniggering, the men clumsily twisted Crook's arms behind his back and hauled him to his feet. Beer-fumes enveloped the group like a thick fog.

Wheeler stood four-square in front of Crook and punched him on the jaw. Crook rode the blow, but it made his head ring. Wheeler stood closer. 'What you're going to learn, snooper, is that you don't harass Hog Wheeler's woman and get away with it.' He jabbed Crook in the midriff. 'You're going to learn to be a lot more careful in future. You're going to learn that if you blab about that lady—if you so much as mention her name—your life won't be worth living.' He hit Crook again, warming to the task. 'You're going to get it into your thick head that snooping is no kind of a job, even for a mug like you.'

Only a few metres away, pedestrians were strolling along a busy street. Crook tried to shout to them for help, but managed no more than a breathless croak. Some people heard him, however: and a few stopped and watched interestedly from the pavement. But no one was in a hurry to interfere.

One of the men holding Crook said, 'That's enough speechifying, Hog. The kid's got the message. Let's get it done.'

'Sure.' Wheeler stared unblinkingly into Crook's eyes. 'Stomp him good, fellers. Give him something to remember.'

'Stop that!'

At last someone had decided to intervene. A tall figure strode out of the shadows by the side of the motel and marched purposefully towards them. 'Stop that nonsense immediately!'

If Elizabeth sounded like a schoolmarm, she didn't look like one. She was still wearing her headscarf, but she had discarded the rather dowdy dress she had been wearing in favour of close-fitting black slacks and a frilly blouse that from a distance appeared virtually transparent. A raucous cheer went up from the onlookers in the street, and the men holding Crook bellowed with drunken mirth.

'This is a private matter, lady,' Wheeler said, grinning. 'Nothing to worry your pretty little head about.' Like all the other males present, he seemed mesmerized by the sight of Elizabeth's impressive and scantily-covered bust.

'Are you the ringleader?' Elizabeth demanded, straight-backed and imperious. 'Tell them to release that man at once!'

'But he's been a very naughty boy, Miss,' Wheeler whined, playing up to the shouts and the laughter. 'He deserves a good whipping, honest.'

'You're drunk!' Elizabeth sounded deeply shocked by the discovery. She raised her voice. 'You're all drunk, you beastly hooligans!'

'Listen, girlie—' Sensing the audience was turning against him, Wheeler turned nasty—'just mind your own business, right? Piss off before you get hurt.'

Elizabeth gaped, apparently lost for words. Some of the fire went from her eyes, and her shoulders relaxed. She hesitated, then made one last appeal: 'You have the outward appearance of a gentleman, at least. Please—' She extended a hand to Wheeler in a tentative gesture of entreaty.

Wheeler was embarrassed by her change of approach. 'It's, like, a question of honour,' he mumbled. He took the proffered hand and shook it. 'This guy insulted a lady, see? He—'

The rest of the sentence became a garbled shriek. Suddenly Wheeler found himself on his knees, his look of indestructible stupidity slowly turning into surprise followed by an expression of keen concentration. The thing that was occupying his mind to the exclusion of all else was an acute, unbearable pain in his right hand. Almost immediately, this was followed by a lesser but still excruciating pain in his right elbow.

'I had better explain—' Elizabeth's voice floated down from somewhere behind him—'that I am now in a position to dislocate your finger, your elbow or your shoulder. If I used all my weight, I might even break your arm. *Now* can I persuade you to call off your thugs?'

Wheeler kicked out blindly and tried to twist out of her grasp, but his struggles only served to increase his agony. 'Get this bitch off me, you bastards!' His voice tailed off into a whimper.

The next few minutes were chaotic. Wheeler's toughs, drunk and irresolute, relaxed their grip on Crook, who started throwing punches energetically, thirsting for revenge. Wheeler began roaring like a bull and thrashing about on the ground, ruining his expensive suit, while Elizabeth circled him, stepping delicately as a matador and manipulating his rigid right arm much as a boatman might wield a punt-pole. Inevitably, Wheeler's head connected with the fender of a car, and his struggles became less enthusiastic.

It was at this point that the bystanders decided to join in. They clambered over the low fence, shouting encouragement to Elizabeth and each other, and charged towards the fray. The car that Wheeler had head-butted started up, revved furiously and sped away, tyres squealing. Wheeler's thugs also fled, hotly pursued by a rowdy posse of young men. Most of the crowd, however, reverted to the spectator role. In no time, what had been an ugly scene began to look like a garden-party, with people happily congratulating themselves and each other while taking a particularly close interest in Elizabeth's well-being. Aware of their concern, Elizabeth released her victim and modestly folded her arms. There was suddenly a carnival atmosphere in the motel parking-lot. The only one not having a good time was Hog Wheeler. He remained face down on the ground, still as a corpse.

The photographer from the *Monitor* arrived on the scene first, beating the police to it by a good half-minute. As a result, he got the best pictures, particularly of Elizabeth standing Amazon-like over the prostrate Hog Wheeler. These, and the close-up of Crook looking dazed and apprehensive, were the pictures used by most of the daily newspapers and all the weeklies.

But the TV cameras were not far behind. They arrived in time to get dramatic pictures of Wheeler being stretchered into the waiting ambulance. He wasn't dead, but he was in considerable pain: the car that had left in such a hurry had run over his foot. Some people said that it had been Wheeler's own car, with Laura Farrant at the wheel; but that rumour was not reported by the media. The revelation that Elizabeth had been preparing for bed when the ruckus started, and had pulled on a pair of slacks over her frilly nightgown came in for much detailed and informative comment, however; as did the fact that the man she had rescued was formerly her fiancé. That this hapless fellow should happen to be a private detective called—would you believe?—*Crook*, filled the reporters with ineffable joy: their copy fairly bristled with infantile witticisms and puns.

The reaction of the police was less jocular. An eminent and influential local citizen had been seriously injured: that circumstance could not be taken lightly. What, they wanted to know, had Crook done to provoke Mr Wheeler? Amateur lawmen might be allowed to run amok in *Sydney*; but Sydney's ways were not Melbourne's ways. This whole incident was going to be investigated very thoroughly, he could bank on that. They advised him not to leave town until they had given permission.

Next morning, Crook cancelled the flight bookings and phoned Mrs Parsons to tell her about the delay.

'Oh, how unfortunate, Mr Paul.' Mrs Parsons sounded uncommonly agitated. 'Please try to get here at the earliest opportunity. A situation has developed. It concerns Mr Dean. He is still our client, I take it?'

'Yes.' Crook thought he detected an implied reproach. 'I'm sorry, Mrs P. I didn't get him to sign a contract. I forgot.'

'That may be a blessing, Mr Paul. I have just learned that the police have taken him in for questioning in connection with the murder of a girl at Bondi Junction.'

'A girl?' Foreboding thickened Crook's speech. 'What girl? What was her name?'

'One moment.' Mrs Parsons tut-tutted as she rustled through papers: it was unlike her not to have the information to hand. 'Truelove,' she said finally, 'a Miss Amy Truelove.'

CHAPTER 24

The hoped-for letter was waiting for him at the flat in North Ryde. It looked as if Robyn had written it in stages over several days. The first part was in an awkward, wish-you-were-here style, full of banal comments about air-travel, the American countryside, and the kindnesses of nurses and doctors. Then, as if overnight, the handwriting became firmer and more legible.

Robyn wrote:

Your long, careful letter arrived today. How wary you are, either of presuming too much or saying too little! I think I see the cautious hand of John Garland in this.

Lots of reassurance, but no pressure, right? He's a sad old battler, but his heart's in the right place. Actually, I reckon his pathetic look is just a professional ploy. His patients work hard to get better just to cheer him up . . .

And getting better is just what I've been at—so fast, you wouldn't believe. Yes, I am all but cured—practically as good as new!—and I shall be coming home very soon.

Thank you for writing. Thank you for everything: for saving my life, for being so loving, for being so *solid*. (That's not the right word, but it's the nearest I can get. Durable? Dependable?)

I have a mental picture of you sitting by my bedside with that sad, sweet look on your face, wondering what the hell was going on in my head. Do you know that for ages I didn't know who you were? And when I finally remembered, I *didn't* remember that we had been lovers? And through it all you showed not a flicker of doubt, uttered not a syllable of complaint. Saint Crook.

The future? You don't talk about it: nor will I. We shall meet, soon. And talk. And try to understand.

I'm sorry about the baby. Do you know—perhaps you won't believe this—I regret it more for your sake than my own? Don't ask me to explain that. I still get confused, sometimes; but I am sure of one thing: I need—I hunger—to see you again. Soon, soon. Love, R.

PS. That is probably me knocking at your door right now . . .

With impeccable timing, the doorbell rang, scaring him out of his wits.

The works manager at HS Auto Repair Pty gripped the telephone receiver as if he wanted to pull its head off and eat it. 'What the frig do you think you're playing at?' In spite of his anger he moderated his language because the person at the other end of the line was female. 'I've got the friggin' things all over my friggin' yard. *Two* sets of brake calipers I ordered. How many friggin' cars d'you think I've got here?'

'I'm sorry, Mr Roddy,' the despatcher at HS Autoparts said, not sounding sorry at all, 'but I have your order on the screen right here in front of me. Forty-two caliper sets. We've despatched all we have—the rest are on order from the supplier.'

'Forty-two sets! You must be crazy, woman!'

'That's what you ordered. I've got the details on the screen right here.'

'Bloody system,' Roddy complained. 'Some bozo must've hit the wrong key. Look, I'm sending these parts back, OK? And you'd better cancel the order to the supplier. Now, what about the rest of the stuff?'

'Ah, the seven Audi fuel pumps—'

'*One* fuel pump!'

'We don't seem to have any in stock at the moment.'

'What! The Audi fleet is our biggest contract. You've gotta have Audi parts. We use them all the time.'

'I'm looking at the stock control list right now, sir. No pumps in stock. Also no carburettors, no valves, no gaskets, no—sir?'

'What?'

'I think, sir—it's only my opinion, mind—I think we've got a computer crash.' She rang off before Roddy had got properly into his stride. She wasn't paid to listen to language like that.

The stranger on Crook's doorstep was middle-aged, but carried himself with the sprightly confidence of a young man. Broad-shouldered, trim-waisted and deeply tanned, he was obviously a man who took a pride in his physical well-being. Long, sensitive face, dark hair winged with grey. 'Paul Crook?' he said, smiling. 'I'm Peter Waystone. May I come in?'

Dumbly, Crook stood aside. The bloke might very well be

a murderer, but one had to observe the common courtesies.

'You're younger than I expected,' Waystone remarked pleasantly. 'From the way my wife described you, I had pictured someone altogether more . . . *case hardened*.' He seemed pleased with his choice of words. 'Mr Crook, I won't waste your time. A few days ago, you showed a copy of a certain letter to Miss Laura Farrant. I should like to buy the original of that letter from you. I am prepared to offer you ten thousand dollars. Cash. Yes or no?'

'You admit you wrote the letter?'

'Of course. Why else would I be here?' Waystone continued patiently: 'Let me make one thing clear: the only profit for either of us lies in cooperation. Suppose, for argument's sake, that you refuse my offer and publish the letter. Then, you might do me some harm—though that is by no means certain—but you would be not a penny richer. The only sensible course is to trade.'

'Sensible or not, I can't do it. I don't have the letter.'

'Of course not.' If Waystone was irritated by Crook's response, he didn't show it. 'Stanley Dean has it. I assumed you were acting on his behalf.'

'To investigate his wife's death. Not to blackmail you.' Now that the shock of surprise was wearing off, Crook felt a wave of dislike for this well-dressed, over-confident man.

'To investigate . . . ?' Waystone looked thoughtful, but not greatly put out. 'That's rather subtle of him, don't you think? Do you mind if I sit down?' He arranged himself gracefully on Crook's settee. 'Tell me honestly now, do you really think any good purpose is served by punishing me for an indiscretion committed a decade ago?'

'"Indiscretion"? Other words spring more readily to mind. "Betrayal of trust", for instance. Gynæcologists aren't supposed to sleep with their patients.'

'It happens, young man,' Waystone said blandly. 'Your idealistic soul would be shocked to learn just how often it happens. We are just as frail as the rest of humanity, believe me. However, I am not trying to justify my actions, nor do

STAGE FRIGHT

I relish a discussion on ethical values, illuminating though it might be. I am simply trying to clear up a messy situation. However, since I now know the contents of the letter, I also know that without its envelope it is not particularly incriminating. If Laura and I keep our nerve, we might well bluff it out.'

'Then why are you here?'

Waystone responded with a barely perceptible lift of the shoulders. 'I would rather not have to bluff it out, obviously. As I say, I wanted to bury this skeleton as discreetly as possible.'

Crook said, 'How do you know that Dean hasn't got the envelope?' It was an inconsequential detail, but it niggled.

Waystone took his time answering. 'Now that is interesting,' he said slowly. It was obviously interesting enough for him to think about very deeply. 'You don't know as much as I thought you did. I wonder if you're being played for a mug?' He frowned heavily, like a chess player contemplating a difficult move. 'You say that Dean hired you to investigate his wife's murder?'

'Yes.'

'And he was the one who showed you the letter?'

'Yes. He said he found it in Mary's effects.'

'As I say, the letter seems harmless on its own. What made you think of blackmail?' Imperceptibly, Waystone was shedding his nonchalant manner.

'With the letter was a pass-book showing that Mary had recently deposited large sums of money.'

'So you jumped to the conclusion that it was hush-money, illegally obtained?'

'I didn't *jump* to the conclusion,' Crook said defensively.

'You were led to it?'

'I suppose so.'

'Who inherits the money in Mary's passbook?'

'Stanley Dean.'

'Tell me honestly, who first mentioned the word blackmail?'

'Stanley Dean.'

'Right.' Waystone nodded vigorously. 'So you got to work and cleverly deduced that I was the author of the letter, and the source of the payments into Mary's account. So: if those payments were hush-money, then it follows that Mary was blackmailing me, and therefore I had a motive for getting rid of her. In your book, I'm a prime murder suspect.'

'Are you saying it wasn't hush-money?' Crook couldn't like the man, but he was impressed by his pugnacious debating manner.

'At Dean's prompting, you have built up a case against me, bolstered with the physical evidence of a letter in my handwriting. You're trying to frame me for Mary Dean's murder.'

'But you have an alibi. You were having a piano lesson at the time of the murder.'

Waystone eyed him quizzically. 'Primrose warned me not to underestimate you. I'm beginning to understand what she meant.'

'How much does your wife know about all this?'

'She knows about my affair with Laura. She has known about that since before we were married. But it was only recently that I had the courage to tell her that I had been blackmailed for many years.'

'By Mary Dean?'

'No, no, Mr Crook. You've got it the wrong way round. I had no motive to get rid of Mary. Just the opposite, in fact. *I didn't kill her.*' He seemed embarrassed at sounding so emotional. In a calmer voice he said, 'Her husband did it. Stanley Dean.'

'He has an alibi, too.'

'He must have done it. Why else would he try so hard to get me framed?' Waystone spoke forcefully, jabbing holes in the air with his forefinger. 'You had better know all the facts before you rush to judgement. Yes, I was being blackmailed. I had written indiscreet letters to Laura

Farrant, which fell into the wrong hands. Mary Dean stole those letters from the blackmailer and returned them to me—all but the one Stanley Dean has kept as evidence against me.'

'She did that out of the kindness of her heart?' Crook was incredulous. 'And you handed over thirty grand out of gratitude, I suppose?'

Waystone controlled his exasperation with an effort. 'Cynicism doesn't suit you. Particularly since you're nearer the truth than you think. Let me tell you exactly what happened. It began last January, when Mary made an appointment for a consultation with me at the Clinic. I knew she was on the staff at the Arrigo Hall, and that she was a personal friend of Dorothy Want; but that was all I knew about her at that time. I examined her and had to confirm what she already suspected: that it was virtually impossible for her to have a child. She took the news stoically, though I could see it distressed her. When she got up to leave, she took something out of her handbag and gave it to me. "This is yours, I believe," she said. It was a letter I had written to Laura in the first flush of our affair—passionate, silly, hopelessly indiscreet. I looked up at Mary in horror. What did she want?

'"I'll tell you," she said. "Miss Farrant liked me once. But in the end she came to despise me: treated me like dirt. She thought that I stole those letters from her and sold them for profit. But I never did. She treated me unjustly. I should like her to know that."' Waystone had watched Crook's face intently throughout this recital, trying to judge the effect of his words. 'Then she turned on her heel and walked out of my rooms.'

Crook said bluntly: 'Yet you did give her money. A lot of money.'

'But not because she asked for it. I suppose—' The confidence ebbed momentarily from his voice and he sounded oddly tentative—'I suppose it was because she *didn't* ask for money, that I offered it. I came to respect Mary Dean very much. To admire her, even. She brought those letters back to me, one or two at a time, over the next few weeks, under the pretence of further consultations. We talked, during those visits, and I learned a lot about her. I learned a good deal about Stanley Dean, too, and about his psychological problems. She wanted to help him; and I wanted to help her. We devised a scheme to help him—it was my idea, in fact, and I insisted on paying for it. We were going—'

'You were going to buy trees,' Crook said.

'Ah, you know about that.' Waystone was slightly deflated by the interruption. 'Of course, you're a detective. Then, since you know that part of my story is true, perhaps you can believe the rest of it?'

'You still haven't told me about the envelope,' Crook said.

'The letters were hidden in different places. Mary took the letters but left the envelopes behind, to delay discovery. The blackmailer didn't know until too late, that the envelopes were empty.'

'Trimmer was the blackmailer?'

'Yes. He extorted money from me on a regular basis for five years. But he was careful not to bleed me dry. By the end we had formed a kind of ghastly conspiracy: he was dependent on my money, just as I was dependent on his silence. I even began to exploit him in subtle ways, to remind him that if he killed the golden goose, the golden egg supply would dry up. What I'm saying, is that if I was going to murder anyone, it would have been Trimmer. But I didn't. I'm not the murdering type. Sooner or later, you'll have to face the possibility that Dean killed his wife. For her money. The money that I gave her.'

'The police are questioning Dean about the murder of Amy Truelove,' Crook said. 'What possible motive could he have for killing her?'

Waystone flinched. 'Amy Truelove murdered? When?'

'A few nights ago. I don't know the details.'

'Oh God!' Waystone's vitality seemed to be draining

away by the minute. 'The clever bastard! He's always one step ahead.' He leaned forward urgently. 'Dean has a motive for killing Amy. But you won't want to hear it.'

'Tell me anyway.'

'It's part of his scheme to incriminate me, don't you see? If I'm supposed to be murdering people to protect my guilty secret, then I would have to silence Amy as well as Mary. I'll lay odds that Dean is at your office right now, waiting to urge you to take your evidence—including the letter—to the police.'

The man's confident veneer was definitely cracking. Crook pushed harder: 'For someone with a solid alibi, you seem uncommonly worried. What's the problem? Surely Trimmer will back you up? Particularly if he can see a profit in it?'

Waystone didn't get to answer. The phone rang, its clamour parting them like combatants in a boxing ring.

The voice on the line was vaguely familiar, but Crook couldn't place it at first. 'It's Oscar,' the voice said.

'Oscar?'

'The porter at the Clinic. Is Sir Peter with you?'

'Yes. Do you—'

'Put him on, please. It's very urgent.'

'For me?' Waystone looked puzzled, but his telephone manner was crisp and authoritative. 'Yes? Who? How did you ... Wait, wait, wait! Slow down, man, you're not making sense ... Where? Good God! Are you—stupid question, of course you're sure ... Did *she* say that? I mean, you actually heard her voice? Yes, as soon as I can ... No, not yet: we won't bring them in unless we have to ... Just stay there. Lock the doors, keep everybody out until I arrive ... Do what you can, but don't do anything silly. I'm on my way.' He slammed the phone down and looked grimly at Crook. 'Do you have a car?'

'Yes.'

'Thank God. This is an emergency. I'll have to borrow—no, better still, come with me. You'll handle your car better than I can. It'll be quicker.'

'What's happened?'

Waystone was already on the move. 'It's Ian Trimmer. He's gone completely off his head. He's holding my wife hostage at the Arrigo Hall. He's threatening to kill her.'

CHAPTER 25

They made good time as far as Darling Harbour, but from there the traffic slowed them to a crawl. Waystone talked virtually non-stop, his former composure shattered by this new development. 'The man must be completely mad,' he kept saying. 'I knew he was rattled at losing his meal-ticket: I meant him to be rattled. I swore I'd make his life as miserable as he'd made mine. But I never envisaged a reaction like this. He's a slimy piece of work, but I never thought he would turn violent.'

'When did you talk to him?' Crook asked.

'The night before last, soon after Laura phoned me. When I knew that the last letter was accounted for, I couldn't wait to let Trimmer know that his leverage was gone—and so was his livelihood, if I had anything to do with it. I intended to hound the fellow, and I let him know it.'

'How did he react?'

'He looked terrified—I think he expected me to beat him up then and there. But what really took him aback was when I told him that the letters had all been returned to me.'

'Did he know who had stolen them from him?'

'I think so. I don't know. We didn't talk about that. It wasn't in fact a long conversation. The thing is, the man looked sick with fear. Nothing in his manner suggested that he would do anything as drastic as this.'

'You haven't told me exactly what happened?'

'Primrose missed a staff meeting at the Clinic this morn-

ing. Her secretary tried to contact her at the Arrigo Hall,
but their phone was out of order. So she sent Oscar round
on his motorbike. Nobody was alarmed at this point: they
just assumed she had forgotten about the meeting.'

'What was your wife doing at the Arrigo Hall?'

'She's been going over there early every morning to sort
out the mail and do general office chores. The Secretary is
ill in hospital, and the place is short-staffed at the moment.
Primrose feels a sort of responsibility towards the Society
because I'm its President.' Waystone rocked back and forth
in his seat, impatient at their slow progress. 'When Oscar
got there he heard the sounds of a violent quarrel between
Primrose and Ian Trimmer: he couldn't make out the
words, but they were shouting angrily at each other. Oscar
knocked on the door, and the shouting stopped. He called
out, but nobody answered. He could hear sounds—shuf-
fling sounds, he called them. He tried the door, but it was
locked. Then Primrose began to cry, quite loudly, and
Oscar called out to her again. He was very worried by this
time. After a minute she said, "Get Peter." She said it over
and over, gabbling the words: "Get Peter, get Peter." That
really alarmed Oscar: Primrose is not an hysterical person.
He begged her to open the door, but she said she couldn't.
She said, "Tell him he must come. Tell him Ian Trimmer
is here with me." Oscar said, "Is that why you can't open
the door? Are you being threatened?" There was a long
silence, and then she said—sounding almost calm, according to Oscar—"Yes. He is hurting me. Tell Peter he is
hurting me." Then she began crying again.'

The traffic thinned a little, and Crook made faster progress, switching lanes recklessly. 'You're right, it's crazy,'
he said. 'What does Trimmer hope to achieve? What does
he want?'

'Money. He wants to pick up one last pot before he gets
kicked out of the game.' Waystone was no longer suave: he
looked as savage as any street fighter. 'If he really has hurt
her, I'll kill him.'

At last Crook pulled into the driveway of the Arrigo Hall and parked behind a white car and a black motorcycle. Oscar was alongside before the Holden's wheels stopped turning. 'I think we should get the police, sir,' he said anxiously. 'I'm sure I heard a shot in there a few minutes ago.'

'A shot?' Waystone got stiffly out of the car, panting slightly with the effort. 'You mean Trimmer's got a gun?'

'It seems like it, sir. But I think Lady Primrose is OK. I heard her say something after the shot was fired. I couldn't make out the words, though.'

'Where are they?'

'They're in the storeroom, sir: the cellar. The door's locked.'

'I didn't even know this place had a cellar.' Waystone sounded petulant, as if he thought he had been deliberately deceived.

'This way, sir.' Oscar led them through the shadowy lobby to a flight of shallow steps behind one of the cloakrooms. At the foot of the stairs was a short, box-like corridor with a row of wooden lockers along one wall. At the end of the corridor was a metal-banded door marked STOREROOM in faded gilt lettering. Waystone banged on the door with his fist. 'Trimmer?' he called. 'Trimmer, this is Peter Waystone. I want to know what is going on here? Just what the hell do you think you're doing? Come to your senses, man: you're just piling up trouble for yourself.'

There was no answer: no sound at all from behind the door. Waystone changed his tone: 'Look, just tell me what it is you want. Let's negotiate. I promise you I'll leave the police out of it as long as my wife is unharmed. I give you my word on that.' He listened again, becoming more and more unnerved by the silence. 'Let me talk to my wife, you bastard!' he yelled. 'Prim, can you hear me? Are you all right? What the hell is going on in there?' He banged on the door again. He was becoming frantic, dishevelled: not elegant at all.

There was still no response. Waystone listened tensely for a few minutes, then crouched to look through the key-hole. He straightened up, shaking his head, and walked back to the stairs, beckoning Oscar to follow. 'Is there another door to this place?' he asked in a low voice. 'Any other way to get in?'

'No, sir. This is the only entrance of any kind. I checked.'

'It looks as if we may have to break it down.' Waystone drew a bunch of keys from his pocket. 'Here's the spare key to Prim's car. Find the toolkit. See if there's anything there we can use as a jemmy.'

'Don't you think it's time we brought the police in, sir? They're used to hostage situations.'

'No!' Waystone was sweating. 'Not yet. Not till we know what's happening in there. Look, just go and find something to open that door with. I'll keep talking, see if I can raise any response at all.'

Crook raised a hand in warning. 'I can hear something,' he whispered. 'Someone's moving in there.'

They could all hear it now: a scraping sound, as if heavy furniture was being pulled across the floor. Under his breath, Waystone voiced the thought that occurred to all of them: 'He can't be barricading the door, surely?'

The noise stopped, and the cellar was deathly quiet again. Waystone urged Oscar up the stairs. 'Get going! Find something—anything—to break that door down!'

But no sooner had Oscar clattered out of sight than it became apparent that his errand was unnecessary. Slowly, noiselessly, the door began to open.

The strip lighting in the cellar was dazzling compared to the feeble illumination in the corridor: Crook screwed up his eyes against the sudden glare. The door swung wide, gradually revealing the scene, like a theatre curtain.

Facing them, two or three paces back from the doorway, a body was slumped grotesquely in a low-backed chair. Its arms dangled limply, and its legs were splayed puppet-like at freakish angles. The head was tilted back, and the face was almost completely covered in blood, with a thin, pink-ish froth of bubbles over the mouth and nose. Ian Trimmer had lost his look of languid elegance: his silk shirt was ripped from collar to waist, as if clawed by some huge animal. Blood smeared his expensive jacket and blotched his white Italian slacks.

'Jesus Christ!' Shock constricted Waystone's voice to an awed whisper. 'That's what the shot was. He's killed him-self!' He looked sick and barely able to stand. He clung to the door frame for support, his body trembling uncon-trollably. He called, hoarsely, 'Prim? Prim, where are you? Are you all right?' He stepped uncertainly into the cellar, blinking under the harsh light.

At last, after an interminable pause, he was answered: 'I did it for you. I did it all for you.'

The words echoed whisperingly round the bare room, drifting in the air like motes of dust. Crook's scalp prickled with alarm. There was a deadness in that voice, a desolation beyond the reach of any comfort.

Primrose Waystone stepped slowly into Crook's line of vision. She walked carefully, as if testing the ground for firmness. Her hair was unkempt, and her broad, lumpy face looked tight and stretched. Her eyes were as wide and vacant as a wondering child's. In her right hand, held almost casually by her side, was a squat, short-barrelled pistol. 'I believed you, Peter.' She sounded tired, listless. 'I believed every word you told me. My family said you were just after my money like all the rest, but I believed you. You said . . .' She frowned, as if trying to remember the exact words. 'You made me feel special. In your eyes, I was beautiful, that's what you said.' She touched her cheek with the muzzle of the gun. 'You said you loved me.'

'I do, Prim. I do love you.' Waystone was still trembling, and he looked as if his knees would buckle under him at any moment. 'Look, my dear, you're still in shock. Let me—'

She went on as if he hadn't spoken: 'I was so proud when you named the Clinic after me. "The Primrose Maternity Clinic"; and later, "The *Lady* Primrose Maternity Clinic". I was so proud. But more than that, more than that, I was so *honoured* to have your love. To have the love of a man like you. That's why I did it. I wanted to give you something in return for all the love you gave me.'

'Prim darling, you're not making sense. What is it that you've given me? What have you done?'

'I just wanted to clear up the mess,' Primrose said, tiredness slurring her words. 'I wanted everything to be perfect. If you had told me about the blackmail earlier, I would have done it years ago.'

'You would have done what, years ago? I don't understand you, Prim. What would you have done?'

'Killed them, of course,' Primrose said calmly. 'They were blighting our love.'

Crook edged into the room. Something had distracted him from the drama being played out between Waystone and his wife, and he wanted to verify what he thought he saw. Air was still bubbling from Ian Trimmer's mouth and nostrils. 'This man's alive!' Crook said. 'We must get him to hospital!'

'Leave him!' Primrose raised the gun threateningly. 'He's not worth saving.'

There was a noise on the stairs, and Oscar came headlong into the room. He was carrying a tyre lever in one hand a broad-brimmed brown hat in the other. 'I found this in a plastic bag in the back of her car,' he panted, holding out the hat to Waystone. 'It's just like the one . . .' He tailed off, staring open-mouthed first at Ian Trimmer and then at the gun in Primrose's hand.

'Go away, Oscar, please,' Primrose said wearily. 'There's nothing you can do now. You, or anyone else.'

Suddenly, Ian Trimmer began to cough. His head came

upright and his eyes gradually focused on Waystone. 'She knows,' he said thickly. 'She knows everything. She made me tell her. She . . .' He slowly toppled sideways on to the floor.

'That's right,' Primrose Waystone said. 'I know everything.' She made a raw sound deep in her throat, a compound of pain and anger. 'Speak their names.'

'What?' Waystone shook his head, puzzled.

'I want to hear you speak their names.'

'I don't understand you. What names? Who are you talking about?'

'*Their* names, *their* names.' She shook her head impatiently. 'Melanie-Ann Sorrell.'

'Who?' Waystone's face was grey.

'Pearl Colebrook. Melanie-Ann Sorrell and Pearl Colebrook. You remember their names.'

'Of course I do. But—'

'You should do, dear husband mine, because you've been fucking them regularly for months. My friends. My dear friends.'

'No.'

'It was all a lie, wasn't it? In your eyes I was beautiful, you said. Beautiful! So every Friday you screwed one of your beautiful wife's beautiful friends.'

'No!' Waystone pointed at Trimmer. 'Did he tell you that? He hates me!'

'Don't lie to me any more.' She sighed: a bitter, world-weary sound. 'Be honest. For your own sake.'

He shuffled towards her, his hands held out in entreaty. 'You're overwrought. I swear to you—'

'Careful!' Her tone was sharp.

'I have never been unfaithful to you.'

'Liar!'

'I swear it. I love you. In my eyes—'

'Liar!' she screamed again. She pushed the gun at his chest and shot him three times, the reports booming like thunder in the little room. Then, as he collapsed at her feet, she pressed the muzzle of the gun against his cheek and shot him again.

She straightened up and looked at Crook with yellow-rimmed eyes. 'You!' she shouted. She pointed the gun at his head and pulled the trigger.

CHAPTER 26

'Oscar saved me,' Crook said. 'He batted off the light-switch with that damned hat, threw the jemmy at Lady P., and floored me with a footie tackle. Primrose loosed off four more shots that went whanging round the room like mad hornets, and that was the end of it. She'd emptied the clip.'

'She's crazy, of course.' Ricordi switched off the tape-recorder and slipped it into his pocket. 'The trial's going to be a bloody circus.' He yawned and stretched, making the flimsy wooden chair creak. They were sitting in a corner of the rehearsal room at the Arrigo Hall. 'The hospital says that Trimmer's going to be all right, did I tell you?'

'No. I was sure he was a goner.'

'Looked worse than it was. The gun was his, by the way. He bought it, he says, because he thought Waystone was going to have him killed. He also said it was true, about Waystone screwing other women.'

'Yeah. I'll lay odds they were his patients, as well as being personal friends of his wife's. The guy got a kick out of cheating and philandering.'

'Don't we all?' Ricordi said bleakly. He thought of leaving, then changed his mind. Crook still looked badly shaken: he probably needed company a little longer. 'Lady Primrose is still talking, incidentally,' he said. 'I doubt we could stop her, even if we wanted to. She just goes on and on in a sort of dead voice, as if she was talking in her sleep.'

'She's admitted everything, then?'

'Yes, only she doesn't seem to realize that she's done

anything wrong. In her view, her victims were the wrong-doers, she was just the sword of justice. She's proud of the way she planned Mary Dean's murder—borrowing Mrs Vodrey's car, making a copy of Dean's hat, and all that. It was she who removed Mary's underwear, and anointed her as if for sex: she thought that would convince us that the killer was a man.' Ricordi had been observing Crook closely during this recital. 'Are you all right?'

Crook took a deep breath and sat up straighter in his chair. 'Got a fit of the shakes,' he admitted. 'I suddenly remembered her eyes and that gun pointing at me . . . I guess I'm going to have nightmares about that.'

'Do you want to hear the rest?'

'Tell me about Amy Truelove. Did Primrose kill her, too?'

'Yes. That was pretty cool. She ambushed Amy outside the girl's own flat, then simply opened the door and dragged her inside. She was wearing jeans and that wide-brimmed hat as disguise; but that was just a token gesture. She really didn't think she could be caught. One chilling little detail Primrose did let slip, before killing both women—Mary and Amy—she gave them a sedative jab—a sort of pre-med. So's they wouldn't suffer, she said.'

'Jeeze. What about Dorothy Want?'

'Primrose didn't fear Dorothy. She knew that the old girl had nicked those letters from Trimmer, but she also knew—because Mary told her—that Dorothy had no interest in them. She only pinched them to freak out Ian Trimmer: she'd been spying on him and knew he'd got some secret hidden away. Then Mary stole them from Dorothy, and sold them back to Waystone. Nice crowd.'

'But I heard that Dorothy had been taken to hospital. What happened to her?'

'Somebody at Arrigo gave her some herbal tablets for her migraine. What this helpful person didn't know was that Dorothy habitually dosed her headaches with vodka and aspirin. The mixture made a cocktail that was damn near lethal: her temperature shot up, and she hallucinated for hours. She's still in hospital, but she's recovering. And that's about it.' Ricordi stood up. 'I'll need a detailed statement from you pretty soon. Can you manage that on your own, or do you need help?'

'I've got to write a report anyway, for Stan Dean. I'll let you have a copy.'

'That'll have to do.' Ricordi walked to the door, then looked back, rubbing his chin. 'I guess old Mintlaw was right about you, at that. Death just seems to follow you around.'

'It isn't anything like they made it sound,' Crook said desperately. 'I can explain it all.'

'Go on, then.'

'Well—it's a bit complicated. I'd rather not do it over the phone.' He wished now that he'd shut his door: there was a tense, abnormal silence in the outer office that meant that four women were shamelessly listening to every word.

'When I said I wanted to see your face,' Robyn said coolly, 'I didn't expect to see it plastered over every cheap rag in the country alongside pictures of that over-developed blonde who used to be your mistress.'

'No, we were only engaged. Elizabeth was never my—'

'Why on earth was she cavorting around topless?'

'She wasn't exactly, um—' Crook lowered his voice—'*topless*. They made it look like that. The photographers, I mean.'

'She looks bloody topless to me. I'm looking at her picture right now. It's the one where she's trying to cram her nipple in your ear.

'It's a fake, a mock-up!'

'And the caption—*Damsel Delivers Dick in Distress*?'

'You know what journalists are like. You used to be one.'

'It says here that you were in adjoining rooms and you paid her hotel bill.'

'She hadn't any money. Look, I know how it sounds, but

it was just a chapter of accidents. I can explain it all.'

'It had better be good, ol' buddy.'

'Rob, I really need to see you. Are you at home? Where are you?'

She chuckled unexpectedly, her good humour rising irrepressibly to the surface. 'I'm on your trail, buster. That's where I am.' She rang off abruptly, leaving him mopping his brow. That was a helluva lot worse, he thought shakily, then facing a mad woman with a gun.

It wasn't just a sense of duty that made Crook decide to report to Stan Dean in person. It was partly that he couldn't settle to anything constructive in the office, and partly out of a sense of respect—affection, almost—that he felt for Mary Dean. Then too, there had been that first meeting with Dean at the beach: that had made an indelible impression on Crook's mind. He felt he had a personal debt to pay.

He got to Richmond after dark, and parked outside the dilapidated apartment house where Dean lived. There was a cold breeze blowing from the south, and the air was dry and gritty. He climbed the flight of stairs to Dean's apartment and rang the bell. Almost immediately, an old man shuffled out of a doorway further along the corridor. 'He ain't in,' the old man said. He wore a faded check shirt and his loose-fitting trousers were held up by canvas braces. 'He ain't gonna be in, neither.' He hobbled unsteadily towards Crook, peering through small, wire-framed spectacles. 'Go see for yourself. Door ain't locked.'

'Mr Stuker?' The name came unbidden to Crook's mind. 'Ashley Stuker?'

'Yeah.' If the old man was surprised that Crook knew his name, he didn't show it. 'You a cop?'

'No.'

'The bastards won't leave the poor sod alone. Go on in, why don'tcha? Door ain't locked.'

Crook pushed the door open and looked speechlessly at

the wreckage that had once been Dean's apartment. Everything breakable had been broken and scattered chaotically about the room. Chairs, tables, wooden drawers, lay in splintered heaps; upholstery had been ripped, curtains torn, pictures smashed. Shards of glass and china lay thickly over everything.

'He wrecked the lot,' Ashley Stuker observed sombrely. 'Took him all night and the best part of the next day. Nobody could stop him. In the end, they had to smash the lock to get him out of there.'

'Why?' Crook was still struggling to believe the evidence of his own senses. 'Why would he do this?'

'Why d'yer think? He'd shared all this with Mary. With her gone, he couldn't bear the sight of it. 'Sides, he was drunk. The cops 'rested him for the murder of a kid he'd never even heard of. When they let him go, he hit the grog.'

'And he just smashed the place up?'

'Thass right.'

'Where is he now?'

Stuker thrust his head forward aggressively. 'Whaddyer wanna know for? He hasn't got the money yet, see? Never will have, I reckon.'

'No, I'm—' Crook settled for an approximation of the truth—'I'm just a friend. I just want to talk to him.'

The old man snorted but made no other comment. 'OK. Come with me.'

They didn't have far to go, but it took some time since Ashley could only move at a painful shuffle. 'Me feet's bad and me knees is worse,' he said.

They came to a gap between the low buildings, a paved area not much bigger than a tennis court. 'Shoppin' plaza, thirty-odd years ago,' Ashley explained. 'Smart, then: Bootickses and that. Went downhill. Nobody's gonna smarten it up now, what with money so tight.'

Most of the shops were empty and boarded up: the few that remained were run by charities and voluntary aid organizations. In one derelict corner were six men and two women. All wore headgear of some sort or another, and all were muffled up in several layers of clothing. Although their top clothes were all different—greatcoats, duffels, cardigans, blankets—their dun shapelessness made them drably uniform. Five of the men sat in a row on the ground, their backs against a boarded-up shop front. The two women lay on their backs, holding hands, apparently asleep. Stan Dean, easily identifiable by his oddly-shaped hat, sat in a doorway a little apart from the rest. His was the only bottle not shrouded in brown paper. He drank with a flourish, tipping his head back and sucking extravagantly at the bottle. When it was empty, he skidded it away across the flagstones.

As Crook watched, three of the other men got to their feet and shambled unsteadily to Dean's doorway. One of them squatted down in front of Dean and began talking, waving his arms about. Dean leaned forward and pushed the man over. In a moment, all four of them were fighting, cursing, jostling each other, their violence as puny and ineffective as a child's tantrum. One of them fell to the ground: it signalled the end of the quarrel. Dean produced another bottle and handed it round: someone brought out half a cigarette and lit it at the third attempt. The two women lay on their backs, not stirring.

'Seen enough?' Ashley Stuker tugged at Crook's sleeve.

'I ought to talk to him,' Crook said wretchedly.

'He don't want to talk to you and thass a fact. Do him a favour, son. Walk away.'

'But he's an alcoholic. He shouldn't be drinking at all. He'll kill himself.'

'Thass the point,' Ashley Stuker said. 'Thass what he wants.'

On Friday afternoon, the Agre Detective Agency closed its doors early and the whole workforce went to visit Bam-bam Butcher in hospital. 'Work always tails away to nothing on

Fridays,' Mrs Parsons announced. 'There's hardly anything for us to do, anyway.'

Crook suspected that Mrs P. influenced the Friday workflow by judiciously unplugging her telephone, but he lacked the nerve to challenge that formidable lady. Anyway, he felt guilty that he hadn't visited Bam-bam more often.

The old pug was making progress. He was sitting up, and he looked leaner and fitter than Crook had ever seen him. He wore a high neck-brace, and his head was still cocooned in heavy bandages which held his jaw still and his mouth tightly shut. He could still make sounds through his clenched teeth, however, and Mrs Parsons translated these sounds into intelligible conversation with the skill and loving pride of a mother interpreting her baby's gummy babblings.

Bam-bam's moth-eaten eyebrows waggled with pleasure at Crook's appearance. 'High, hoss!' he mumbled indistinctly. 'Who hooky gate!'

'He's pleased to see you,' Mrs Parsons explained. 'He says you're looking great.'

There followed an exuberant and excessive display of sentimental affection from Mandy, Jane and Lilian, who all told Bam-bam in round terms what an old darling he was, and how badly he was missed in the office. Then in turn they planted damp kisses on his shapeless blob of a nose, which was the only part of his face available. Bam-bam accepted it all with lordly aplomb. When they had finished, he sat up, his little eyes glinting. 'Eh!' he said, addressing Mrs Parsons, 'helly agout Arry Ely.' His belly shook and his chest rumbled. He was laughing.

Mrs Parsons turned slightly pink, and the girls tittered. 'Yes, do tell about Harry Sheiling, Mrs P.,' Lilian said, interpreting Bam-bam for herself.

'I know little more than you,' Mrs Parsons said evasively. 'It appears that Mr Sheiling's business empire has suffered a commercial setback. The computer system on which his whole operation relies has suffered an unfortunate malfunction.'

The mere mention of computers sent Crook's brain running for cover. 'His system has crashed, do you mean?'

'I think it's more accurate to say it has been infected. It has caught a virus.'

'Mrs P., you know that jargon is so much gibberish to me. What's actually happened?' Crook was dismayed that he couldn't see the point of the joke everyone else was enjoying.

Lilian took pity on him. 'A computer virus is a program that fastens like a parasite on the computer's working system, and gradually corrupts it. Just like a real virus, it reproduces itself incredibly quickly, and when it reaches a crucial size, the whole system gets sick. A virus can gobble up databanks, reduce information files to garbage, change passwords so that confidential files are inaccessible. A computer virus is definitely bad news, sir.'

'And Harry Sheiling's caught this bug?' An ugly suspicion began to form in Crook's mind.

'The particular difficulty for Mr Sheiling,' said Mrs Parsons serenely, 'is that, like many dishonest businessmen, he prepares two sets of accounts: a false set, which he delivers to the tax man, and a genuine one, which enables him to keep track of his true financial position. The false accounts were in the computer, and being fictional, will not be easy to reconstruct. Mr Sheiling will be faced with the biggest tax bill he has paid for years.'

'Gurgle high!' Bam-bam said, obviously gratified.

'Indeed, Mr Basil, it does serve him right. He should not be allowed to mistreat Agency employees with impunity.'

At last Crook saw the light. 'Elvis!' He had seen the little Vietnamese computer wizard in the agency office only days ago. He had even questioned Mrs Parsons about him. 'You bribed Elvis to plant a thingummy in Harry Sheiling's computer! God, Mrs P., that's illegal! Isn't it?'

'Mr Elvis assured me he would not hack into the Sheiling computer. However, he did explain that there were several ways by which a system might be invaded by a virus. Accidentally, as it were. I am quite sure that Mr Elvis would not put his personal liberty in jeopardy.'

'That's a very Jesuitical answer, Mrs P.,' Crook said severely. 'Just how much Agency money has gone into this revenge plan of yours?'

It was Jane who answered. 'Not a lot. We had a whip-round, and everybody chipped in.' She winked broadly at the invalid. 'No thug's going to harm our Bam-bam and get away with it.'

Crook regarded his staff with a mixture of indignation and awe. 'Just remind me to stay on your side, will you?' he said.

At that moment, another visitor arrived: another woman. 'I just knew you'd all be here,' Elspeth Cade said, in mock disgust. 'Friday afternoon Bam-bam worship. This old fraud's never going to get better, if you make his convalescence so pleasant.' She kissed the old fraud lightly on the nose. 'And how's the gladiator?' she said, turning her attention to Crook. 'Rescued any damsels lately?'

'Very funny,' Crook said sourly. He was thoroughly sick of that particular joke.

Elspeth grinned. 'Well, perhaps I can put a smile on your face. I bumped into a friend of yours today.'

'Who?'

'She was hanging around the Agency office, looking for you. I guess she expected you to be working. I was smarter: I only half-expected you to be working. "Never mind," I said, "I know where he'll be." And here you are. She came with me, but was too bashful to come up. She's waiting downstairs.'

'Robyn?' Crook exclaimed.

'We never got on to a first-name basis,' Elspeth said

drily. 'I call her Ms Paget.' But Crook was already out of the room.

Mandy, Jane and Lilian sighed in unison; Mrs Parsons looked pleased; Elspeth smiled a little wanly. Bam-bam supplied the philosophical touch. 'Iss lovat aches der girl go ow, eh?' he said.

Mrs Parsons gazed at him fondly. 'How true, Mr Basil, how very true. It's love that makes the world go round indeed.'